ONE LITTLE YES

JAMEY MOODY

One LIttle Yes

©2021 by Jame Moody. All rights reserved

Edited: Kat Jackson

Cover: Lucy Bexley

This is a work of fiction. Names, characters, places, and incidents are the product of the author's imagination or are used fictitiously. Any resemblance to an actual person, living or dead, business establishments, events, or locales is entirely coincidental. This book, or part thereof, may not be reproduced in any form without permission.

Thank you for purchasing my book. I hope you enjoy the story.
If you'd like to stay updated on future releases, you can visit my website or sign up for my mailing list here: www.jameymoodyauthor.com.

I'd love to hear from you! Email me at jameymoodyauthor@gmail.com.
As an independent author, reviews are greatly appreciated.

❦ Created with Vellum

ALSO BY JAMEY MOODY

Live This Love

The Your Way Series:
Finding Home

Finding Family

Finding Forever

It Takes A Miracle

One Little Yes

CONTENTS

Chapter 1	1
Chapter 2	7
Chapter 3	15
Chapter 4	25
Chapter 5	33
Chapter 6	42
Chapter 7	49
Chapter 8	57
Chapter 9	65
Chapter 10	71
Chapter 11	78
Chapter 12	86
Chapter 13	93
Chapter 14	100
Chapter 15	106
Chapter 16	114
Chapter 17	120
Chapter 18	126
Chapter 19	134
Chapter 20	141
Chapter 21	149
Chapter 22	155
Chapter 23	160
Chapter 24	165
Chapter 25	171
Chapter 26	177
Chapter 27	187
Chapter 28	195
Chapter 29	201
Chapter 30	207
Chapter 31	213
Chapter 32	222
Chapter 33	228

Five Years Later	237
Acknowledgments	243
About the Author	245

1

"What are you waiting on?" Gina Gray questioned the universe loudly while spreading her arms out wide and looking upward. She sighed, put her phone on the table and walked to the window of her apartment.

Looking out on her little piece of New York City, she watched people hurrying down the street, living their lives. Christmas decorations dotted the street lights and entrances to the other buildings. There were lights that would twinkle behind various windows across the street as the sun went down.

If she opened the window she'd hear the sounds of life from below. The cold air would pillow around her face and if she was lucky the aroma of fresh bread from the bakery down the street might waft through her apartment.

She usually loved Christmas, but not so much this year. Her father was back in Texas in an assisted living center and she wasn't able to go home. These were the times when she missed her mother the most. She'd been gone five years now and sometimes it felt like yesterday, others it felt like decades. Her parents had tried to have kids for years and thought it wasn't going to happen and then surprise, there she was. Even though they were older she'd had a good childhood and they were at every sporting event, play, choir concert, and anything else she participated in.

A familiar sound came from her phone announcing a text message. She walked over and picked it up and read the message. Then she walked to the buzzer next to the front door and pushed the button that unlocked the door below to allow entrance to the building. A few minutes later there was a knock at the door.

Gina opened it to let her best friend, Shannon, in. "Why are you here?" asked Gina.

Shannon walked in and pulled a bottle of wine out of the sack she was carrying and set it on the cabinet in the kitchen. She took two glasses down and rifled around in a drawer for the wine opener. "You had a doctor's appointment today. Of course I'm going to be here." She opened the bottle and poured each of them a glass. After handing one to Gina, she walked over to the couch and sat down. "So? What did they say?" she asked, taking a sip from her glass.

Gina joined her on the couch and took a sip of the wine. "Mmm, this is good!" she exclaimed, looking at her glass.

"You don't drink very often so when you do it should be good," Shannon said matter-of-factly. She waited patiently.

"Just as I've always known would eventually happen, having been diagnosed with kidney disease at sixteen, I need a kidney transplant."

"And?"

"And it needs to be sooner rather than later."

"Okay. Let's find you a donor, then," Shannon said.

"I hope it's as easy as you make it sound. You do realize I don't have any siblings."

"I seem to remember growing up together that it was just you and me. Duh!" she teased, rolling her eyes.

"My good kidney, and I use that term loosely, is failing. Dialysis is in my future if I can't find a donor," she said, dropping her head to her chest. She sighed and looked back up with tears in her eyes. "I really hoped I'd never have to do that."

Shannon set her glass down and scooted closer to Gina, putting her arm around her shoulders and grabbing her free hand with her own. "Then we'll find you a donor before that happens."

Gina loved Shannon like she could only imagine a sister would. She sank into her comfort for a few moments before sitting up and taking another sip of her wine. "You know it's one thing to find a match, but it's a whole other thing to find someone willing to give up their kidney."

"I'd do it in a heartbeat," Shannon said quickly.

"I know you would, but you love me."

"I sure do and I'll tell you right now if Travis is a match, I'll make him give you one of his," Shannon said, sipping her wine. Travis was Shannon's boyfriend and when they'd started dating, he and Gina had become fast friends. "Actually, I wouldn't have to make him; you know he loves you too."

Gina chuckled. "Lucky for you, I love women or I think Travis might be my boyfriend."

Shannon laughed. "There's my girl! Look GG, it's okay to be upset today. You didn't get the best news from the doctor. Let's enjoy this wine and order some food. Besides, we have Christmas in a few days and I promise you it'll be merry even though we can't go home this year."

"I know, Shan. Thanks. I can always count on you."

"And after that, Travis's and my New Year's party will be the best! We will find you a donor there. I promise," Shannon stated.

"Careful with those promises," Gina warned.

"You let me worry about that. We're having our friends, but also people from my work and from Travis's. It's a done deal."

Gina loved Shannon's optimism, but she knew it was going to be a lot harder than that.

"Come on, Gina," Shannon said, snapping her out of her thoughts. "I'm in media. I'll design a campaign if I have to."

Gina chuckled. "I hadn't thought of that. I can see billboards in Times Square now." Gina put her arm up waving from left to right, looking at an imaginary billboard. "'Be kind, give this girl a kidney.'"

Shannon frowned. "Ugh no! That's why I'm the creative one."

"Well, this problem solver," Gina said, pointing to herself. "Has a ton of work to do before Christmas. This just happens to be the busiest time of the year. We've got to get those packages delivered."

"You know," Shannon said, an idea forming in her head. "You manage a very large team with a lot of people under them."

"I don't like that look on your face. I can tell what you're thinking. Give the boss a kidney, get a promotion."

Shannon laughed. "Not exactly. You have a huge network of people in your distribution chain. There's no reason not to use that resource if you have to. You may have to think out of the box, so to speak, even though your business is delivering boxes." Shannon laughed at her own play on words.

Gina chuckled and shook her head.

"Let's move on to more important things," Shannon said.

"What's more important than saving my life with a kidney?"

"Saving your love life. You haven't been on a date in forever."

"Are you kidding me! You know how busy I am this time of year. And let me tell you one more time that people don't like to date sick people."

"GG, you are an extremely beautiful, smart, and talented person. You don't have to tell someone your medical history to fool around and have a little fun."

"And here I thought you were continually setting me up so that I could find a partner. Which is it?"

"I want you to find the happiness I have with Travis. Is that such a bad thing?"

Gina sighed. "No, it's just hard, Shan. How can I not tell someone that I have a medical condition that could kill me or at least limit my quality of life."

"But you don't even give them a chance," Shannon said, pleading. "What about the woman I set you up with a few months ago from our legal department?"

"Her name is Kim and she was very busy, just like me. When she happened to see all the pill bottles in my cabinet, I had to explain so she wouldn't think I was some kind of drug supplier."

"Wait, what was she doing in your cabinet?"

"I told you all about it, remember?" Gina looked at her pointedly.

"You did not! Did she spend the night?" Shannon said, her voice rising.

"I told you she did and then when I explained the situation she listened and we went out one other time and that was that."

"But she seemed like a stand up person. Why didn't you tell me this, GG?"

Gina sighed. "I really thought I did. We talked about what I was expecting with my health and she was very honest. She really is busy and her career is very important to her; she wasn't in a place to start a relationship, much less take care of someone else."

"So she was open to meeting up and having sex, just not more than that?"

"Nope. She liked me and felt like it would become more. But my *more* has some added problems that come with it."

"I swear you didn't tell me this," Shannon said, her brow furrowed. "That must be why she asked about you a couple of weeks ago," she said to herself. She turned to Gina. "I ran into her and she asked how you were doing. I didn't think anything about it because I thought you didn't hit it off. Hmm, I guess you made an impression."

"Well, it's not often you spend the night with someone and find out the next morning they need a kidney."

"Do you want to tell me the real reason why you didn't say anything about this?" Shannon said, pressing Gina.

She hesitated for a moment. "It made me sad. It showed me that there's no way anyone is going to want to be with me when I have this going on. I knew you'd try to cheer me up and tell me I'm wrong, but this time I'm not, Shan. This is my life. Just me, no partner, no girlfriend—hell, not even a date."

Shannon put her glass down and grabbed Gina by her shoulders and looked her in the eye. "It's not always going to be that way. And please, don't do that again. Of course I'm going to try to make it better, but if you don't want to hear it then tell me. Just please don't think you're going through this alone, because you have me. We've always had each other. Always."

Gina smiled. "Okay, I won't do it again. And I know you're always with me. It's just that it feels like you're the one that's had to do all the heavy lifting."

"Oh darling. We don't keep score. Please remember back to middle school and then to high school. Who took care of me? You did! It's just the way it works sometimes. Okay?"

"Okay," Gina said, pulling Shannon into a hug. "I'm so glad I've got you."

"Me too."

Gina's phone beeped, pulling them apart. She read the text and groaned. "A delivery disaster just in time for Christmas." She turned to Shannon. "Will you order us food? I have to take care of this. Hopefully it won't take long."

"Go solve Santa's sleigh problems. I'll order." Shannon got up and opened the drawer with the take-out menus while Gina went to her desk and opened her laptop.

2

Gina woke up and with a small smile, remembering it was Christmas morning. Her thoughts drifted for a few minutes. She wondered what it would be like to wake up next to someone she loved on Christmas morning, full of promise and happiness. Of course she'd been in love before. There was the teenage love in high school that at the time felt like everything. This thought made her giggle. In college she and her girlfriend had lived together their last year before graduation. They went their own ways when job offers didn't match up.

And then there was Victoria. It had been four years since she and Victoria had broken up. They'd only made it two years, but Gina thought she was the one. Maybe she would have been if Gina had one healthy kidney. For several months Gina had been sick and it all became too much for Victoria. They were young and weren't supposed to have to deal with something like that.

Her doctor was finally able to find a treatment that worked and Gina slowly got better. And to Victoria's credit she didn't want to leave, but Gina all but made her. She didn't want someone to feel like they had to take care of her and she was afraid Victoria would end up resenting it all.

She sighed and closed her eyes. Why was she thinking about all this now? Her Christmas wish was obvious. She wished for a new kidney, so she could have a chance at a normal life. But maybe this was how her life was supposed to be. If that was true then perhaps her thinking needed to change. Why couldn't there be someone that not only wanted to love her, but take care of her if need be? Wouldn't she do the same for someone she loved?

"Stop!" she said out loud, putting her hands over her eyes. She sat up and reached for her laptop. It was Christmas morning and she had to check and make sure her team came through once again. Everything appeared to be delivered the way it should have been. She quickly fired off an email commending everyone on a job well done. She wished them a Merry Christmas with instructions to enjoy their day. Working for a global delivery company meant business didn't stop even for Christmas. They all knew this and accepted it when they began work there.

She closed her laptop and got out of bed knowing she could forget about work for now. A glance at the clock let her know she had time to shower before Shannon came to spend the day with her. When they'd both taken jobs in New York City, they knew that they might not always be able to go home for holidays. They'd made a promise to one another that when that happened they'd spend the holiday together.

Let's see, Gina thought. She and Shannon had been spending some part of Christmas together since the first year they'd met. They were ten then and now at thirty-four this would be their twenty-fifth Christmas together. How crazy was that! She jumped into the shower, humming "Jingle Bells."

* * *

Gina's phone pinged with a text from Shannon.
Ho Ho Ho, you ho! Let me up!
Gina laughed out loud.
Come on up, ho.

She hit the buzzer to unlock the door and minutes later Shannon threw open the door. Gina was waiting for her, holding a cup of hot chocolate.

Shannon had a Santa hat on and carried a bag along with her purse. She dropped everything and took the mug, inhaling the rich chocolate aroma and letting the warmth smoking from the liquid caress her face. Then she took a sip.

"You've out done yourself, GG. This is delicious," she said with a big smile. "Come here." She carefully hugged her best friend, not spilling a drop of the decadent treat. "Merry Christmas," she said, kissing Gina's cheek.

Gina responded with her best smile. "Merry Christmas to you." She winked and added, "Ho."

Shannon threw her head back and laughed.

"Come sit," Gina said, nodding toward the stool on the opposite side of the bar that separated her kitchen and living room. "The popovers are just about done." She walked over to the oven and peeked through the window.

"We may not be home, but our parents would be glad to know we are respecting our long held Christmas traditions," Shannon said. "Popovers and hot chocolate. It wouldn't be Christmas without them."

"I have my favorite, cherry, and yours, blueberry. And I even have apple just for Travis. He's still coming by, isn't he?"

"Of course. He's the sweetest. He said he was giving us time to do our thing and then he'd be over to watch movies and whatever else we wanted to do."

"You're still going to his folks this evening though, right?"

"Yeah, but we want to spend the day with you. It's tradition."

"Have you talked to your folks yet?" Gina asked.

"Nope. Have you talked to your dad?"

Gina looked at her watch. "I'm supposed to call in a bit. We have time to eat first. Dad's getting pretty good with FaceTime, but I feel better when I know one of the aides is going to be around to help out just in case."

"Your dad does great for an eighty-two year old. He wouldn't have to live there if it wasn't for that dang heart of his."

"I know, but he likes it. Can you imagine how lonely he'd be at home without Mom? At least he has friends there that he can beat at dominos and cards." Gina chuckled.

"I'm not surprised. The last time we were home he beat me three games straight in chess. That reminds me, I've got to practice before we go home again. I'll be ready next time." She laughed.

"I wish I could find someone that would go by and play chess with him occasionally. The woman he used to play with moved to the town her daughter lives in and no one else plays."

"Maybe someone new will move in that plays. Hey, we should see if there's a chess club at the high school. Maybe one of them would play with him. I'll check into that after the holidays."

"Thanks Shan, that's a really nice thing to do."

"He's like my second father, GG. I love him, just like you love my parents."

"That I do." Gina took the popovers out of the oven and iced them. She put them on a plate and set them between her and Shannon.

"Aw, Gina. You wrote my initials on them. Just like your mom used to do."

Gina smiled and remembered how her mom could make anything special. She loved to surprise her and write words or her name using icing on the popovers. One morning she had a big speech she had to give for a class and her mom knew she was nervous. On her popover she wrote 'be bold.' When Gina read it, she looked at her mom who winked and didn't say a word.

They ate and Gina checked the time, then grabbed her phone to call her dad.

She went around to sit next to Shannon so they both could see her dad. On the third ring the phone connected and she saw her dad's smiling face.

"Merry Christmas, Daddy!" she said, smiling.

"Merry Christmas! How are my girls?" He smiled.

"Hi Pops. We've just had popovers and Gina made the best hot chocolate this morning," Shannon said.

"She makes hot chocolate like her mother. They must have a secret," he said, grinning.

"Have you had a good morning, Daddy?" Gina asked.

"Yes honey. I'm wearing those fancy socks you sent me and I'm going out later for a walk and I'll be wearing the new cap. I love it."

"Oh, I'm glad, Dad. When I saw it, I thought of you."

"Listen honey, I need you to do something for me, and Shannon I'm glad you're there to help, too."

"What is it, Dad?"

"I've been thinking about your diagnosis since you told me last week."

"Daddy, don't worry about that. I told you, it will all work out."

"Hold on now. I know everything is going to be all right. You will find a donor; I believe that with all my heart. But what I need is for you to come see me before you have the transplant. I need you to promise me, and Shannon, I need you to make sure she does."

They looked at one another. "Okay, Dad. I promise."

"And I'll make sure she gets there," Shannon said.

"Okay, good. Sorry girls, that's been weighing on my mind since you told me. And Gina, thank you for not keeping that from me. I know you don't like upsetting me, but as you know it upsets me more if you don't tell me everything."

"I know, Daddy. A promise is a promise. You and Mom made me promise that I'd always be honest with you about my health a long time ago."

"Now, what are you girls going to do today?"

"I think we're going to watch Christmas movies all afternoon. Shannon and Travis are going to his folks this evening and I may lay on the couch and rest. As usual it was a very hectic week at work, but my team was great. What are you doing?"

"I'm going to your Aunt Jane's for Christmas dinner and I'll eat too much. I'll have a piece of pecan pie just for you."

Gina chuckled. "Thanks Dad, I appreciate that."

"Please eat an extra roll for me. You know how I love homemade rolls," Shannon requested.

"I'd be happy to," he said, laughing. "Okay girls, go have a wonderful day."

"We will, Daddy. I love you!" Gina said, choking up, tears in her eyes.

Shannon threw an arm around her. "Don't worry, I'll take care of her. Love you, Pops."

"I love you, too!" He disconnected the call and the screen went black, but not before Gina could see tears in his eyes too.

"I got you, GG," Shannon said, pulling her into a hug.

After a few moments Gina pulled back and blew a breath out. "Whew, I don't know where that came from. I guess making that promise got to me."

"You know I'm going to hold you to it."

"I do. Now, where's Travis? We have movies to watch."

As if on cue, Shannon's phone pinged. "There he is." She went to the door and buzzed him up.

Gina got another plate out and poured Travis a mug of hot chocolate.

Shannon opened the door and a few moments later a smiling Travis walked in. He kissed Shannon on the cheek and then walked over to Gina and wrapped her in a hug. Gina loved Travis like a brother. He had the most beautiful blue eyes that went along with his blond hair, giving him an All-American look. He was two years younger than them and loved to tease them about being older women.

"Merry Christmas to my favorite delivery person," he said, a big grin plastered on his face.

Gina laughed at his usual greeting. "You know, I don't actually deliver the packages, Travie," she said, knowing he only let her get away with calling him that.

He cocked his head and said, "But really, don't you? I mean, if it weren't for you, those drivers wouldn't get there on time. So, you kind of do." He winked at her and took the plate she held out to him.

"I even made apple popovers for you this year."

"Thank you. That brings up an interesting question. Are they popovers or turnovers?"

"I call them delicious," said Shannon, biting into another blueberry pastry. A little of the filling ran down from the corner of her mouth.

Gina grabbed a napkin and wiped her face. "If your group could see you now. The always put together, genius media mogul Shannon DeWitt with blueberry all over her face." She chuckled.

"She's adorable, as always," Travis said, biting into his own pastry.

"To answer your question, I think it's regional. We southern girls call them popovers," Gina said with a smile, exaggerating her accent.

"I will accept that answer," Travis said, always the analytical one.

"Whew." Gina dramatically wiped her brow in relief. "Glad he let us make it on that one, Shan."

They all laughed.

"Did you tell her yet?" Travis asked Shannon, who shook her head.

"Tell her what? I'm assuming I'm the *her*," said Gina.

"Analysis is my jam, as you know," Travis said. "And I've been looking into this plight. Your kidney disease is not yours alone. We share it with you because we love you and want to help. That being said, I'm putting my big brain to work on this. If I can make millions of dollars for my clients then surely I can figure out how to get you a donor."

"Travis," Gina said, her voice full of affection.

"Seriously, I'm formulating a plan and it starts at our New Year's party. You can't be bashful or embarrassed. Please, let me do this."

"What did you have in mind?"

"Well, you have to let people know. So we'll do that and explain what to expect. Most of the time if people have information, then taking a risk is less scary," he said.

Gina looked at him then at Shannon. She would normally protest and tell them to let her handle it, but she hadn't expected to need a kidney so soon. She was reminded of her thoughts this morning and realized she did need help. And here were her best friends offering. How could she say no?

"Okay. I don't know how to thank you, but I sure do love you guys," she said, holding her arms out and bringing them in for a group hug.

"Woo hoo!" Shannon said. "This year is going to be our year, GG!"

Gina smiled at them both and sure hoped she was right.

"Can we have Christmas now? Enough talk about kidneys." Gina walked over to her small Christmas tree and got presents for them both.

They exchanged gifts and settled in for a movie marathon until it was time for Shannon and Travis to go to his folks'.

Gina settled back on the couch and began to make a list of their friends, her cousins, and a few co-workers that might be willing to be tested. The quest for a kidney began.

3

Gina helped Shannon spread out the bowls of snacks on the table they'd pushed up against the wall to make more room for people to move around the apartment. Travis walked in from the balcony where he finished icing down beer, hard seltzers, soda, and sparkling water.

Shannon looked around the room. On the bar that separated the kitchen from the living room there were several different bottles of wine and liquor, cups, napkins, and koozies. She nodded, seemingly satisfied with their preparations, and started a playlist that began wafting through the room from the discreetly placed speakers.

Travis and Gina looked at one another and shrugged, waiting for their instructions as Shannon went to the bar, lined up three glasses and poured each of them a small amount of wine. She handed each of them a glass, picked up her own glass and turned to them with a smile.

"Good work getting everything ready. Thanks for helping, GG, and thanks for listening, Travis." She smiled and held up her glass for them to clink together and toast.

"We are ready to get this party started," Travis said, taking a sip of wine. He opened the front door and looked out into the hallway.

They weren't the only ones having a party on their floor. Music played from down the hall and three people walked by smiling at him.

When the elevator dinged, Travis turned and saw four people from his division walk into the hallway and smile excitedly. They made their way down the hall and into the apartment.

Shannon greeted the group and Gina remembered three of them from previous parties they had attended together.

Gina listened to them recounting their Christmas holidays, but couldn't help being a little nervous because Shannon and Travis had both assured her they would find people to at least get tested to determine if they were a match and maybe a donor.

She listened to Travis telling a story as she stood on one foot then the other when Shannon pulled her aside. "You're fidgeting. Relax."

"It's hard to relax when I don't know what you two are going to do."

"You promised to trust us and not be embarrassed. We're going to wait a while and make sure everyone is having a good time, and then we'll bring it up. It'll be okay."

Gina tilted her head, stared at Shannon and then sighed.

"We won't embarrass you, I promise. Now go have a good time. Travis has some new people in his department you haven't met yet. And I think Kim is planning to come by. Who knows, you two might connect again."

Gina shook her head and chuckled. "Stop worrying about me and host your party. I'm fine." She finished the wine in her cup and walked into the kitchen. She cleaned up around the sink and made sure there were plenty of cups for the wave of people that had just come in. She recognized a few people that worked with Shannon mixed in with a few she didn't know.

One of the new arrivals was a woman that caught Gina's eye. She had dark hair and light brownish green eyes that scanned the room continuously. Gina couldn't tell for sure, but she appeared to be Hispanic. Her light eyes and dark complexion gave her an aura of mystery. She was wearing black jeans that looked like they were made just for her. Paired with those jeans was a deep blue-green sweater with sleeves pushed halfway up her forearms. Her thick, slightly wavy hair cascaded around her shoulders and Gina wondered if it would feel as soft between her fingers as she imagined.

This thought made Gina smile. Good to know she could still appreciate a beautiful woman because she hadn't been interested in anyone since her one night with Kim months ago.

The woman walked into the kitchen and smiled at Gina as she looked around.

"Could I help you find something?" Gina asked kindly.

"Uh, I was looking around to see if there was anything to drink besides wine or liquor," she said, shrugging her shoulders unapologetically.

"I can help you. Follow me." Gina beckoned her with a nod. She led them out on the balcony and turned to the beautiful mystery woman while pointing to the ice chests. "There's beer, different flavors of hard seltzers, soda, and sparkling water. What can I get you?"

"I think I'll start with sparkling water. What flavor would you suggest?" she asked, her eyes twinkling in the glow of the fairy lights strung around the balcony.

Gina looked in the ice chest and reached for a grapefruit flavored water. "Would you like it over ice, in a glass? By the way, I'm Gina," she said, holding the water out to the woman.

The woman smiled and peered into Gina's eyes as if she was discovering hidden secrets. "I'm Angelica," she said with a hint of an accent. "You can call me Angel."

"Nice to meet you, Angel." She grinned, still holding the can of water.

"I can drink it out of the can," she said, taking the water from Gina.

"Here, let me get you a koozie." Gina reached for a can hugger that had her company's logo on it. There were a few stacked on the table next to the ice chests.

She handed it to Angel as Travis walked onto the balcony. "Hi

Angel, so glad you could make it," he said, smiling. "Have you met Gina?"

"I have. She kindly helped me find something to drink."

Travis turned to Gina. "Angel is the new IT Strategist for our department. She has already made my job easier and shown me new analytics that will make forecasting more accurate."

Angel smiled and dropped her head, appearing uncomfortable with the praise.

Travis looked at Gina and said, "Do you mind if I steal her away? I want her to meet Shannon."

"Of course," Gina said, nodding at Travis.

"I've told her how much you've added to the department in such a short amount of time. She wants to thank you for getting me home earlier at night." He chuckled.

"Thanks for the drink, Gina," Angel said before following Travis inside.

Gina nodded and watched her go. Maybe this party would be more fun than she thought. She walked back inside and talked to a couple of people she knew from Shannon's office. The noise level had definitely increased as more people came into the apartment. Gina walked out into the hall and could see several people lingering outside the apartment a few doors down. With a small smile she meandered down to the elevator then continued to walk down the hall to the window and looked out down to the street. She wondered if the people she saw were hurrying to New Year's parties.

She couldn't help but think about what was to come in the new year and vowed right then not to let this disease get the best of her. She had lived with it for over half her life and she planned to keep on living. It was time to have some fun. She walked back into the party with a smile and headed for the snack table.

Shannon curled her arm through Gina's and pulled her into a lively discussion about games that was just beginning. "Here's my partner," she said, plopping them both down on the couch.

"Come on," Travis said. "You two always win. You have to split up to give us a chance."

"We don't always win," Gina said. "You always lose. We can't help it if we're good."

Travis looked at her with shock on his face and then laughter barked from his chest as he fell back on the couch. "I can't believe you said that! You're never snarky!"

"You brought it out," Gina said, laughing with him.

"I'll be your partner," Angel said, sitting forward in her chair. She looked over at Gina with a challenging smirk on her face.

A smile grew on Gina's face that lit up her eyes. "Let's do it," she said firmly.

Two other people joined in for a lively trivia game. Angel turned out to be a very good player and as the game continued, she and Gina faced off several times. Gina could feel Angel watching her when it was other players' turns and it made her tingle inside. Maybe she'd get an opportunity to learn more about this mysterious woman.

When the game ended, once again Gina and Shannon were victorious.

"That was so close," Travis said, feigning bitterness, dropping his chin to his chest.

Gina couldn't keep from laughing. "I'll tell you what, Trav, how about I switch partners with you? Maybe you and Shannon against Angel and me?" She looked over at Angel who nodded slightly, a very sexy smile on her lips.

Travis looked at Shannon happily. "What do you say, babe? We've never been partners."

"There's a reason we haven't been partners." She looked over at Gina, her eyes narrowing. "You could be ending a beautiful relationship."

"What? You might win!" Gina exclaimed.

"I'm not talking about me and Travis. Of course we're going to win! I'm talking about you and me!"

Gina's mouth fell open and her eyes widened. "Bring it on! Let's go."

Angel looked between the three friends and then said, "Are you sure this is a good idea?"

Gina smirked at Shannon and then looked at Angel. "It'll be fine. If we lose it'll be your fault and if we win it'll prove who's the best player. Me," she said, pointing to herself.

"Who are you?" Shannon laughed. "And what have you done with my best friend? You're not a trash talker." Shannon grabbed Gina's glass and smelled.

Gina chuckled. "It's just sparkling water."

"As much as I want to play this game, give me a second to restock the snack table," Shannon said, getting up and walking to the kitchen.

"Let me help," Travis said, following her.

"I'm going to get another drink. Can I get you one?" asked Angel, nodding toward the balcony.

"I'll go with you. I could use the fresh air." Gina walked to the door and stepped into the cold night.

Angel looked around in the ice chests and pulled out a beer. She looked over at Gina and watched her gaze up into the night sky. The playful look that had been on her face was replaced with a pensive one.

"What's the new year going to bring you?" Angel said softly.

Gina's hands were on the railing of the balcony as she looked down and then over at Angel who was now standing beside her. There was something about this question and the look in Angel's eyes that made Gina feel like she could be honest and her answer wouldn't scare Angel away. "Actually, I hope it brings me a kidney."

Angel's brow raised, but she didn't seem fazed. "That is very specific and not the trendy response that question usually gets. Would you mind telling me more?" she said gently.

Gina wasn't sure what she saw in Angel's eyes. "Sorry, you seemed to want an honest answer and not a trendy one."

Angel waited, her eyes encouraging Gina to continue.

"I've had kidney disease since I was a kid. I found out a couple of weeks ago that it's progressed to the point that I need a kidney transplant. So, that's what I hope this year brings me." Gina was afraid to look at Angel because she knew she'd see pity in her eyes. She liked her and wanted to know her better, but she was sure she'd quickly messed that up with her honesty.

"You must be an incredible person to have lived with that and thrived," she said, bowing her head and trying to capture Gina's eyes with her own. "I mean, I just met you, but I can tell you love life."

When Gina looked up she saw Angel's eyes shining at her with kindness. She smiled shyly, but before she could say anything, Travis yanked open the door.

"Get in here! We have good news!" he yelled, his voice full of joy.

She looked at Angel and they both quickly walked inside.

"I was telling my team about our new project to find you a kidney," Travis said, turning to Gina.

She looked around and noticed all eyes in the room were on her. Shannon walked over to her and Gina could feel her cheeks flaming red.

"My co-workers heard Travis and they want to get involved."

"We're putting our big and creative brains together to work on this and several people have offered to be tested," Travis said, beaming a smile at Gina.

She'd promised to not be embarrassed because she knew they were going to do something, but with everyone looking on, she was a bit overwhelmed.

"I..." she mumbled. "Thank you."

Thankfully Shannon put an arm around her shoulders and thanked everyone and told them to get back to the party. Then she faced Gina and said, "I told you. It's all going to work out."

Gina blew out a breath. "Sorry, that was intense."

Shannon chuckled. "Have a drink with me, please. We have something to celebrate. One drink won't hurt you."

"Okay. We do." She hugged Shannon to her. "I couldn't do this without you."

"We've got each other." Shannon hugged her back and then led them to the kitchen.

Gina turned around to see what had happened to Angel, but she couldn't see her anywhere. Maybe she was back outside or had gone to the bathroom. She would be sure to find her later.

"Here you go," Shannon said, handing her a glass. "To a year of good health," she said, clinking their glasses.

They both drank and Gina's gaze wandered over Shannon's shoulder.

Shannon turned her head and looked behind her. "Who are we searching for?" Shannon asked, pretending to conspire with Gina.

Gina chuckled. "I was looking for Angel. We were on the balcony when Travis came and got me."

"Travis said she's been all over the world and is super smart. He said they're lucky to have her."

Gina nodded and couldn't help but wonder what Angel thought of Travis's announcement.

"Hey Kim!" Shannon suddenly exclaimed as a woman walked into the kitchen.

"Hi Shannon," she said and then turned to Gina. "Hey you," she said, giving her a quick hug.

"Hi Kim," Gina responded, surprised by the affection.

"I overheard Travis talking about the quest for a kidney. Sorry you're having to go through that."

"Thanks. I knew it could happen eventually," Gina said.

"Well, I'm signing up to be tested," Kim stated.

"Thanks Kim," Shannon said gratefully. "That's what we're hoping everyone will do."

"Yeah, thanks," Gina said, feeling awkward. All this attention, as grateful as she was, had become uncomfortable.

"Let me get a drink and let's catch up." Kim gave Gina a dazzling smile.

"Let me get out of the way," Shannon said, leaving the kitchen.

Gina watched Kim pour a glass of wine and smiled as she turned back around to face her.

"So have you been feeling bad or did something change?"

Gina looked into Kim's eyes and there it was. A look of pity crossed her face and then she smiled. This was the smile that said someone needs to take care of you and I'll do it.

"The disease has progressed and the doctor said it's time to get serious about finding a match." Gina was so tired of talking about her kidneys. "But you know what, I'd rather hear about you." This wasn't entirely true, but it was better than talking about her kidneys.

Gina tuned Kim out and could see her lips moving as she talked about her job and what had happened over the last few months. It was nice that she wanted to get tested, but if she was a match, how could Kim take that much time off work and keep her career path moving forward?

Besides, Gina didn't want someone to take care of her. Sure, there would be times she'd need help, but there would be times she'd need to help her partner, too. Wasn't that the way it worked in a relationship? She wanted to be an equal and wanted her and her partner to care for one another when it was called for, but also live and share their life together. All of it! Not just in sickness, but in fun and doing things together, exploring and trying new things.

Someone called Kim from the living room and Gina took the chance to get away. She snuck back to the bedroom and luckily no one was in the bathroom so she quickly slipped inside. She did her business and as she washed her hands she looked in the mirror. Her color didn't look bad, she didn't look sick. She dried her hands and let out a deep breath. No more kidney talk tonight.

She walked back into the living room and saw Kim still in conversation with several of Shannon's co-workers. Stepping onto the balcony, she closed the door and inhaled the crisp cold air.

"Are you hiding?" a sultry voice asked, followed by a chuckle.

She turned around to find Angel sitting in the corner of the terrace on one of the chairs.

"More like escaping," she said, sitting on the chair across from her.

"That's great that Travis and Shannon want to help you, but I thought I saw a look of discomfort pass over your face with all the attention," she said, staring into Gina's eyes.

"You are very observant. I really appreciate what they're doing and I'm grateful, but it can all be too much sometimes. And I would like to not talk about me or my kidneys the rest of the night. I'd like to know about you. Travis said you were new to his team. Have you been in New York long?"

Angel gave Gina an amused look. She studied her for a moment and then said, "I've been here a little over a month and the only people I know are on the team." She leaned toward Gina and said quietly, "Would you want to get out of here before the awkward stroke of midnight ritual?"

Gina hesitated for a moment, but knew this was a chance to get to know Angel better.

When Gina didn't answer right away, Angel added, "I promise I won't ask about your kidneys."

Gina's face lit up with laughter. "You promise?"

Angel nodded and held her hand over her heart.

"Then yes, I would love to sneak away with you, Angelica," Gina said, lowering her voice and using Angel's full name.

They were both grinning from ear to ear when they eased out the front door.

4

"Do you live far from here?" Angel asked as they walked out of the apartment building.

"Not too far. How about you?"

"I live more towards the financial district. Do you mind if we walk for a bit? Is it too cold?"

"Not at all. I'd like that."

"Have you and Travis and Shannon been friends a long time?"

"Shannon and I grew up together in Texas. My parents tried to have kids for a long time. They had pretty much given up and then I came along. They were in their late forties when they had me, so I don't have any siblings and my parents were a lot older than the other parents that had kids my age. When I was in fifth grade, Shannon, who doesn't have any sibs either, and I hit it off and have been best friends ever since."

"Was that hard, having older parents?"

"No. If anything they put me in too many activities to make sure I could try it all. Okay, it's your turn. You know way more about me than I do about you," Gina said, looking sideways at Angel as they strolled along.

"I am the oldest. I have two sisters and two brothers. I grew up in Arizona."

"Wow, that's a lot of kids. Did you grow up around the Grand Canyon or in the desert?"

"Kind of both. I used to go to the Grand Canyon on trips with an exploring group for at-risk kids."

"But now you're an IT wizard. How did you get into that?"

"I liked school. It was sort of an escape for me. I was always responsible for something at home and at school I was only responsible for me. And then…" she trailed off.

Gina looked over at her and could see her face was troubled. "Look, you know the horrible part of my childhood because that's when my disease was discovered. Believe me, you don't want to be the sick kid at school. Shannon was the only person that wasn't afraid to be around me. Some of my teachers even treated me weirdly. So, whatever happened next, I assure you, I would've been there for you. I know how it feels to be different."

Angel stopped and then turned toward Gina. "You would've been there for me? You don't even know what it is."

"I know it was upsetting and the way your voice quieted I know it hurt you. That tells me enough to know I would have been there for you."

Angel smiled and shook her head. "Your kidneys may not work so well, but your compassion organ is bigger than the Grinch's new heart."

Gina laughed. "When we're different we have to stick together, right?"

Angel chuckled. "Right." She considered her next words and then started walking again. "Those outings with that group let me hang out with kids from other schools. There was this one girl that really liked me and I liked her too. We were safe because we went to different schools and no one knew we were together."

"I take it your family didn't know."

"No one knew except for a couple of guys in the group. One night we were walking through this Christmas light exhibit and she grabbed my hand. We thought it was okay because it was dark and no one was paying any attention to us. What I didn't know was that my little brother was there and he saw us. Before I got home he had already told my parents."

"Oh no! What happened?"

"They forbid me to see her and made me quit the group. I could only go to school and work and for weeks they barely even spoke to me. I was a junior then, but I had a teacher take an interest in me and she helped me graduate early. I got a scholarship to college, packed my bags and never looked back."

"Oh Angel, I'm so sorry," Gina said, placing her hand gently on Angel's forearm.

"I worked hard and studied all the time. I was afraid to get close to anyone because of what happened in high school."

"But it wouldn't have been like that in college," Gina said.

"I didn't know that. I was a scared, poor, minority country girl. I studied and made good grades so when I graduated I had all kinds of job offers."

"Travis said you've been all over the world. Is that what you've done? Worked all over?"

"Yep. I thought the further away from home I was, the more I could be myself."

"Wow. Where all have you lived?"

"My worldly travels kind of started when I got a job in Spain. They thought since I had dark hair and light eyes that I was a native Spaniard that had gone to school in the U.S. So I was hired."

"Did you like it there?"

"Yes, it was beautiful. Of course, anywhere would have been beautiful to me after growing up in the rural desert; however, the desert can have its own beauty, too. After that, the same thing happened again, only this time it was in Brazil. They thought because of my appearance I was from there and hired me."

"I've got to ask," Gina said, giggling. "Do you have girlfriends all over the world?"

Angel smiled and looked at Gina for several moments before

answering. "I could ask you the same thing, Miss Gina. Do you have girlfriends from here to Texas?" She smirked.

Gina nodded. "That's fair. I do not. I had one serious girlfriend after I graduated and started working. There was a time when I got really sick and she had to take care of me. In hindsight, she probably would have stayed, but I pushed her away. I didn't want our life to be her taking care of me. I haven't had a serious girlfriend since. I won't let myself. I know that's a fucked up way to look at things, but that's me right now."

Angel let out a deep breath and nodded. "I can understand how you'd feel that way, Gina. For me, I haven't had a long term relationship. My parents made me feel so ashamed and afraid that every time I've even considered giving someone my heart, I can't do it. I just know I'll screw it up."

"Aren't we a pair," Gina said sadly. "We're so depressing!"

Angel exclaimed. "We really are!"

They looked at one another and then started laughing.

When they quieted Angel looked at her watch. "Hey, it's almost midnight. Would you want to toast the New Year with a coffee?"

"I'd like that. And look," Gina said, pointing ahead. "There's a stand with coffee and hot chocolate."

They walked over and each got a steaming cup of hot chocolate. Gina led them to a bench outside a neighborhood park and they sat and sipped.

"You are very easy to talk to," Angel said after a comfortable silence. "I haven't told anyone about my past in a very long time."

"I'm glad you felt like you could tell me. I think our pasts do shape us even if they weren't particularly good. I mean, I had a wonderful life growing up, but when you're different or treated differently it has an effect."

"I know what you mean. I sometimes wonder if I'm empty inside because of what my parents did and then in my own way I continued it by isolating myself. Fear can really do a number on you."

Gina thought about what Angel said. "I realize we've just met, but there's more inside you than you think. You obviously are good at your job and like to help people. Travis said you've already helped him."

Angel smiled and raised her eyebrows at the compliment. "I do like to help people, I guess. I hadn't really thought about it that way."

Gina sipped her hot chocolate and glanced at her watch. She looked over and smiled. "Happy New Year, Angel!"

Angel looked at her watch again and smiled. "Happy New Year, Gina."

For a moment they both looked into one another's eyes, unsure what to do next. Angel slowly leaned over and gently kissed Gina on the cheek. She pulled back and softly said, "I know I promised not to mention this, but I hope you find a donor this year, Gina."

Gina smiled. "Thanks, Angel. And I hope you find that someone to take a chance on."

"You think that's what I need to do? Take a chance?"

"I do. You said you were afraid."

"Hmm, didn't you say the same thing?" Angel asked.

Gina looked at her, confused. "What do you mean?"

"You said you didn't want anyone to take care of you. Isn't that like being afraid to let someone completely in?"

Gina furrowed her brow and considered Angel's words. "I guess you're right. Well then," she said, holding her near empty cup up to Angel, "here's to you and me not being afraid."

Angel's smile grew and lit her face even in the dark. They touched their styrofoam cups together and drank.

Gina was appreciating how nice this New Year was beginning when a thought suddenly occurred to her. "Hey, what are you doing today? Who are you eating black eyed peas with?"

Angel looked at Gina, seemingly confused. She shook her head and said, "What? Black eyed peas?"

"Yes, it's tradition. You have to eat black eyed peas on New Year's Day for good luck. Don't you do that?"

"I think I've heard of it," Angel said after a moment. "I'd actually planned to go in later and get some work done while everyone was home nursing hangovers."

"Oh no, you can't do that!" Gina blurted out. She caught herself. "I mean, you can, but you've got to have black eyed peas. Shannon and Travis are coming over this evening and we're having black eyed peas. Please come?"

Angel hid her laughter at Gina's exuberance. "Are you sure?"

"Yes! My mom used to cook corned beef, cabbage, and black eyed peas. Let's see," Gina said, looking up and remembering. "The black eyed peas are for luck and the cabbage is for money. I'm not sure what the corned beef was for," she said, shrugging.

"Maybe your mom and dad liked corned beef," Angel offered.

Gina chuckled. "Maybe. Shannon and Travis are coming over at 5:00. I'd really like for you to come too."

Angel hesitated.

"If you don't want to come, you've got to at least promise to eat some black eyed peas for luck," Gina said, insistent.

This time Angel couldn't hide her laughter. She threw up her hands. "Okay, okay. I'd love to come to your place this evening."

Satisfied, Gina sat back and smiled. "Good. I won't have to worry about you all year." She got up and said, "Come on. I'll show you where I live; we're almost there."

They threw their cups in the trash and began to walk.

Angel looked over at Gina and said, "When's the last time you had a real New Year's kiss?"

"Um, let's see," Gina said, thinking back. "I guess it'd be with Victoria, my ex I was telling you about. That would have been six or seven years ago. Dang, that sounds really sad. How about you?" she said, looking over at Angel.

"Well, I have celebrated New Year's in some pretty incredible places. There were a couple of clubs in Brazil and then there was one in Hong Kong that was crazy."

"Wow, you have to share your stories."

"I have stories, but they are mostly about places, not people. I mean, yes, I shared New Year's kisses, but they weren't like I knew I'd be spending the year with them. Last year I was in this rooftop club in Hong Kong and I remember thinking, you're thirty-six years old, you've lived in all these exciting cities and you don't have anyone you want to wish a happy new year."

"I think my New Year will happen when I get this kidney," Gina said earnestly.

"I get that. Asking that question has made me see how sad my New Years' were too."

"What do you mean? You've been to amazing places!"

"That's just it. I'm realizing I've missed out on people. They are much more important than places."

"I may not have had a real New Year's kiss in a long time, but I do have good people that I've spent it with. I'm lucky to have good friends."

"Yeah, you are. And now I can say I've spent New Year's with good people too," Angel said, glancing over at Gina.

Gina smiled and looped her arm through Angel's. "I'll introduce you to some good people tomorrow that weren't at the party tonight. We have a few friends that have kids and they always try to come by for black eyed peas even though they don't make the New Year's Eve party."

Angel smiled as they walked along and Gina slowly dropped her arm.

"This is me," Gina said, walking up to an apartment building and stopping outside the door. "I'd text you the address, but..." she said, not finishing the sentence. She took her phone and raised her eyebrows at Angel with a question.

Angel grinned and gave her the number. In a moment she heard her watch ping with an incoming text. She reached for her phone and found Gina's address and then a message. It read, *New Year's Angel*.

"Is that what I am? Your New Year's Angel?" she asked Gina.

"We'll see," Gina said with a flirty look on her face.

"Can I bring anything tomorrow? Well, today, I mean," Angel said, suddenly tripping over her words.

"Just yourself," Gina said, shyly looking away. After a moment she said, "Thanks for walking me home."

"You're welcome and thanks for making this a happy new year," she said, then quickly added, "Well duh, that didn't sound cheesy or anything did it?"

Gina laughed at their sudden awkwardness. "I'll see you in a few hours." She walked to the door and went in. Once inside she turned and gave Angel a small wave. Then she let herself on through to the elevators.

* * *

Angel watched her go inside and wave and then disappear inside the building. She couldn't remember when she'd had such a pleasant night. She had spent New Year's at some of the hottest spots in the world, but for some reason they didn't compare to the easy vibe of tonight.

There was always a little anxiety with meeting new people, but after meeting Gina Gray she continued to run into her at the party. And now that she thought about it, those were the best parts of the night. She definitely didn't feel so empty this New Year's.

5

Gina had fallen asleep last night with a smile on her face and awoke the same way. She had worked for a while that morning which wasn't unusual for her.

She was grateful that she could work from home. On days when her hands and feet would swell or she'd be tired from the lack of work her kidneys were able to do, she could still get her job done. She could lead her team from her couch just as deftly as from her office.

Once again she realized there was a small smile on her face. This had happened a few times throughout the day and Angel was responsible. What had begun as a mystery last night had become the opportunity to make a new friend. She liked Angel and last night when she got home, a plan had started to form in her brain to fill some of the emptiness Angel had told her about.

Maybe Angel could keep her mind off her kidney troubles. Shannon and Travis were determined to find her a match. She was grateful for them and their help, but she didn't want her life to be centered around a transplant. That sounded dumb, because her life depended on it in many ways. But with Angel she didn't have to talk about herself. Angel had seemed comfortable to open up about her travels and her childhood last night.

Who knows, maybe she and Angel could help one another. It was obvious that Gina wasn't looking for a relationship right now and Angel was so guarded. But they could spend time together and have some fun to get their minds away from work and other problems.

Her phone vibrated and began to ring on the table in the living room. She looked at the screen and saw it was Angel. She immediately smiled and swiped to answer.

"Happy New Year!"

"You told me that a few hours ago," Angel said, with amusement in her voice.

"I did and it's still happy. At least so far."

"That's good to know. Hey, are you sure you want me to come over later?"

"Yes. I wouldn't have invited you if I didn't want you to come."

"I know, but it sounds like it's a tradition with your friends and I don't want to intrude."

"You're not intruding at all. You'll know Shannon and Travis and me," Gina said cheerfully. She could hear Angel release a breath in relief.

"What can I bring? I can't show up without bringing anything."

"Yes you can. I have everything covered. All I want you to bring is yourself and maybe another story of some exotic place you spent New Year's."

"I'm not that interesting, I assure you."

"I don't see it that way. Look, this is a small, low key get-together. It's just people sitting around stuffing their faces and talking. Oh, and eating black eyed peas for good luck." She giggled. Her laughter must have been infectious because she could hear Angel chuckle.

"Okay then. I can use all the good luck I can get."

"Great. I'll see you around 5:00. Or you can always come over earlier if you want."

"Hey, I could come over and help you cook. I mean if you want me to," Angel said, her words running together.

Gina considered this for a moment, a little surprised. Angel seemed like a loner, but perhaps Gina was wrong. "I could put you to work, but are you sure? You're my guest."

"I'd love to help out. Really. How about I come over around 4:00?"

"That sounds great. See, it is a happy new year," Gina said, grinning.

"It's certainly starting off that way. Bye, Gina."

"Bye." The call ended and Angel's voice lingered in Gina's ear. She liked the way Angel said her name, the *gee* sound kind of rolling off her tongue. This made Gina smile again.

* * *

A few hours later Gina's phone pinged with a text. She grabbed her phone and a smile creased her face.

Angel: *Your New Year's Angel is here with treats!*

Gina: *Get up here!*

She walked to the front door and opened it after she'd hit the button to let her up. It didn't take long until she heard footsteps in the hall. Gina leaned out the door and grinned, liking the sight of Angel smiling and walking toward her.

Gina took a moment to appreciate Angel's stride. She was a couple of inches taller than Gina, but her legs looked like they went on for days. She was wearing faded jeans and a T-shirt with a jacket. The look was casual, but also attractive. Her dark hair was loose around her shoulders and she had sunglasses perched on the top of her head. Her smile made her light eyes appear to be dancing with mischief.

"What are these treats?" Gina said playfully.

"Well, you're going to have to let me finish them," Angel said, stopping in front of Gina.

"Come on in," Gina said, stepping aside. "Welcome to my little piece of the city."

"Thanks," Angel said, walking past her and into the living room.

"What do you have there?" Gina pointed at the sack Angel was holding.

"Well, I told you I couldn't come empty handed, so I decided to make a traditional little sweet bread my mother used to make for us."

"Oh my gosh, how nice. Tell me about it," Gina said, interested.

"Well, we used to have a *panaderia*, which is like a Mexican bakery. They had all kinds of *pan dulce* that translates to sweet bread and were part of our holidays. I'm not especially good at baking, but there is one pastry that I loved."

"I remember Mexican cookies and pastries during holidays growing up! There was a Christmas fair and one of the booths had these delicious crumbly Mexican cookies. What a nice memory," Gina said, her face softening as she recalled those family times. "Which one was your favorite?"

"Those crumbly cookies you're talking about were probably galletas. Were they different colors?"

"Yes, I remember pink, red, and maybe yellow?"

"Could've been. The ones I made are called oreja," Angel said with an accent. "It translates to ear. They're made from flaky dough and brushed with butter and sprinkled with sugar. I made the dough after I talked to you. I just need to roll them out and bake them, if that's okay?" Angel said, a hopeful expression on her face.

"Of course that's okay. I can't believe you did this, Angel. Thanks for sharing your childhood with me."

"I don't know what you've done, but I've had more happy childhood memories in the last day than I've had in years. So I wanted to share and contribute to this meal. Let's see, what can this pastry bring us?"

"Hmm, how about the promise of new friendship?"

"So the peas are for good luck, the cabbage for money, and the orejas for friendship. I like it," Angel said, nodding. "Now, if I could use a couple of your cookie sheets, we can get these rolled out and baked."

Gina went into the kitchen and put two cookie sheets on the counter.

"I see the peas on the stove. What else do we need to cook?" Angel asked as she unpacked the dough and turned the oven on to preheat.

"We have to make cornbread and then right before everyone gets here I'll start the fried cabbage. I wait until the last minute to make it so it won't get soggy," answered Gina.

"Fried cabbage? I've had it sautéed and boiled, but I'm not sure about fried," Angel said as she arranged the orejas on the cookie sheets.

"It's really easy. I promise you'll love it."

"You promise? I may hold you to that," she said jokingly.

"I don't promise unless I mean it," Gina said confidently.

Angel nodded. "Okay, these are ready for the oven." She took the cookie sheets with the orejas and slid them inside.

While the cookies baked they mixed two batches of cornbread and got them ready to go in the oven next.

"This is nice. Thanks for coming over early to help me," Gina said as she poured the cornbread batter into two pans to bake.

"You're welcome. I haven't cooked much since moving here, so it's nice to get back to it."

"Do you cook often?"

"Yes. I don't like to eat out alone. You'd think I'd be used to it, but no. Anyway, I'll cook for you sometime."

"I'd like that. I know what you mean about eating out alone. I pick up take out and bring it home," Gina said, locking eyes with Angel for a moment. She smiled and then started to get the ingredients ready for the fried cabbage.

The timer dinged and Angel took the cookies out of the oven. She put them on top of the stove to cool. "These go in next?" she asked Gina, indicating the two pans of cornbread.

"Yep," Gina said and reset the timer. "Would you like something to drink while those bake? We have a few minutes before we have to start the cabbage."

"Sure. How about water?"

"Water? I have wine, beer, soda, and sparkling water."

"I'd really just like a glass of water. You thought I was mysterious, but I'm really pretty boring," Angel said, grinning and shrugging.

Gina got them both a glass of water and led them into the living room. "Let's sit for a minute." She handed Angel her glass and added, "I don't think you're boring, but there's nothing wrong with that if you are. Look at me." She gestured around the room. "I work from home most of the time. I don't hang out with my friends very often because everyone is busy. So I'm pretty boring myself."

Angel eyed Gina for a moment. "You know, I stay to myself mostly, but maybe this new job and new city should be a reason to do things differently. Why don't we see if we can liven up our boring ways. Would you be interested?"

A smile crept onto Gina's face. "I don't know, you went to a party last night and you're at my place today. That doesn't sound much like a loner."

"I think the reason for last night and today is the company, if I'm being honest," Angel said as her face brightened.

"If I'm being honest, I could use a new friend that isn't always concerned about my health. And there's lots of things to do here that I haven't. So, I'm game on breaking out of this boring life."

Angel smiled and before she could say anything the timer went off. They both jumped up and went to the kitchen. Gina grabbed the oven mitts and pulled both pans of cornbread from the oven.

Angel put the cooled cookies on a plate as Gina's phone pinged.

"That's probably Shannon," she said, taking the mitts off and finding her phone. "Yep, she and Travis are here," she said, going to the door and buzzing them up.

A few minutes later they walked in and Shannon stopped when she saw Angel. "Well hi there. Has Gina put you to work?"

"Not really. I came a little early to help out. It's nice to see you again, Shannon," Angel said. "Hi Travis," she said, turning to him.

"Hi Angel, I'm glad you're here. You've made me think you're at the office all the time," he said.

"We're going to do something about that," Gina said, speaking up. "We have decided we are both somewhat boring and we're going to liven it up this year."

"Is that your New Year's resolution?" asked Shannon.

"I hadn't really thought about it that way, but I guess so," said Angel.

"Good for you both," said Travis. "I say that as someone who works too much, but has an extremely understanding girlfriend."

"Angel, you can help me out here. When you leave the office to do something fun with Gina, drag him out of there, too."

Angel smiled and said, "I'll see what I can do."

"Get something to drink and have a seat. I'm going to start the fried cabbage. The others should be here soon," Gina said, shooing them out of the kitchen.

Shannon poured herself a glass of wine and Travis reached for a beer. They went into the living room with Angel.

"Do you need any help?" Shannon asked before sitting next to Travis on the couch.

"No. Angel is my helper today," Gina replied over her shoulder. "If you want to see how this is made you'd better get in here."

Angel hopped up and went into the kitchen.

Shannon got up and leaned on the bar. "Hey, Kim asked where you ran off to last night."

Gina didn't look at Shannon, but said, "She did? That's nice."

"Did you even talk to her?" Shannon asked.

"Yes. You were with us in the kitchen," Gina said, looking away from the cabbage to make eye contact with Shannon.

"Okay. She seemed genuinely interested," Shannon said a bit defensively.

Gina sighed. "She offered to get tested and said she'd give me a kidney, but there's no way she could take the time off with her career and all. I appreciate her saying that, but I know how important that is to her."

"How long would it take?" Angel asked. "A lot of people work from home now."

"That's true," said Shannon, agreeing excitedly.

"I don't know for sure, but I've heard the surgery can be harder on the donor than it would be on me. I'd think it'd take at least two weeks away from the office and maybe even more."

"Hey Gina," Travis said, getting up and joining Shannon at the bar. "I have five people lined up to be tested from last night."

Gina turned to face Travis. "Really?" she said, surprised.

"I know all of this is hard for you and it was a bit overwhelming last night, but I'd like to kind of manage this project, if you will," he said carefully.

"Project? What do you mean by 'manage?'" Gina asked, with a curious look.

"Well, hear me out. I'd like to take a different approach to it. Let me ask our friends and co-workers to be tested. If someone is a match then you and I can sit down with them and explain the whole thing. That way there's no pressure for them to do the first part, which is to get tested. The real issue and question comes up if they're a match. I'm trying to make it easier for them, but also for you. I can't imagine how hard it would be to ask someone to do this."

Gina thought about what he said. "So, do I make a list of our friends and maybe my co-workers and go from there?"

"Yes!" Shannon said, nodding. "Travis and I have made a list, too. We will keep up with who we've asked."

"Won't they think it's strange that you're asking and not me?"

"Think about it. You don't want someone to say yes and then back out later. It would be hard to say no to you because you're the one that needs it. We can ask them, explain the situation, and then they can make an honest decision," Travis explained. He smiled at her with compassion and then raised his eyebrows and nodded, trying to convince her.

Gina couldn't help but return his smile, but she hesitated.

"As an analyst," Angel said tentatively, "this sounds like a solid strategic plan."

Gina quickly looked at her and stirred the cabbage and added seasoning. Part of her wanted to agree immediately, but then this was her problem, not her friends', and she didn't want to burden them. She knew Shannon would berate her for even thinking she was a burden.

As the tug of war continued inside of her she turned to her

friends and saw hopeful faces. Even Angel was looking at her optimistically. She knew she needed their help and honestly she wanted it. "Everything you've said makes sense. But have you considered the strain this could put on our friendship?"

"It's not going to put a strain on our friendship," Shannon said adamantly. "We have been living with this, too. Obviously, it's harder on you," she said seriously. "But come on, GG. You've had this practically since I've known you and it hasn't come between us."

"I truly want to do this," Travis stressed. "If we don't find a match among our friends and co-workers, we'll find another way. This is just the first step. If at any time you feel uncomfortable about it then we'll stop. Promise."

Gina let out a breath and looked at each one of them. "Okay. Let's give it a try and see what happens."

"Yes!" Travis exclaimed. "We can do this!"

"Thank you, GG," Shannon said, relieved.

"Enough," Gina said. "Let me finish this cabbage so we can eat. I'm going to need extra black eyed peas," she said, chuckling.

They all laughed with her.

6

Angel watched Gina sprinkle sugar over the sizzling cabbage and cover it. "Let me see if I have this right. You fried bacon in the pan, then took it out and crumbled it. In the same pan you put the shredded cabbage and let it cook until it began to soften. You stirred it and then added the crumbled bacon back. Then you sprinkled sugar on it so it would brown, and that's it."

"You've got it. It just cooks for a minute or two after you sprinkle the sugar," Gina said proudly. "I think you know more about cooking than you let on."

"Not really. This looks like something I could do though."

"Be prepared for it to stink up your place. Hopefully the taste will be worth it." Gina handed Angel a fork and nodded toward the cabbage.

Angel smiled and forked a small bite into her mouth after blowing on it. Her eyes closed in delight and then she smiled. "This is so good," she moaned.

Gina returned her smile. "I promised you. I'm glad you like it."

"I love it," she said, taking another bite. "You keep your promises."

Gina chuckled. "Let's put this in a bowl. The others should be here any minute."

Just as Gina finished the cabbage she heard her phone ping. "Shannon, can you get that?"

"Michael and Sarah Beth are on their way up," she said, buzzing them in. "Brandy and Dustin are with them."

"Thanks," Gina called from the kitchen.

A few moments later their friends came in and Gina's living room was full of people.

"Come on," Gina said, grabbing Angel's hand. "I'll introduce you to everybody."

The simple gesture sent a jolt through Angel that she hadn't felt in a long time.

"Hi everyone," Gina said as they walked into the room. "I'd like you to meet Angel Ruiz." She looked at Angel and smiled then continued. "She works with Travis."

"Hi Angel," Brandy said with a friendly smile.

"Nice to meet you," Sarah Beth said.

"She's new on Travis's team, but is becoming my new best friend because he isn't working as late," Shannon explained.

"What?" Michael asked with a confused look.

"She's right," Travis said. "Angel is a strategy genius and it doesn't take near as long to interpret data as it did before."

"Nice to meet you, Angel," Dustin said, walking over and offering his hand.

"Good for you, Angel," Michael said. "Travis works too much."

"It's nice to meet all of you," Angel said, smiling. She was a bit nervous to meet everyone and still couldn't believe she was here. Something about Gina and this group of friends made her usual unease in groups not quite so uncomfortable.

"Happy New Year, everyone!" Gina said. "Let's eat."

They took turns filling their plates in the kitchen and spread around the living room, enjoying their meal. Shannon entertained them with highlights from the New Year's party the night before.

Angel ate her food and observed everyone quietly, which was her usual behavior. She watched Gina's eyes sparkle when Brandy recounted the antics of her two kids. This made Angel smile and then

Gina looked over at her. A warmth spread through Angel's chest as their eyes locked. She looked away and busied herself with her food, not sure what had just happened.

The laughter continued and when the kid stories waned Travis began to tell them about his plan to find Gina a kidney donor.

"Oh no!" Brandy said. "I'm so sorry you're having to go through this. But Travis's plan sounds solid."

"It does. How do we sign up?" Dustin asked.

"I'll put you on the list," Travis said. "I'll email you the info."

"Please don't think you have to be tested. You're my friends, and this is a lot. I'll understand if you don't want to do it. Honestly, it won't change our friendship."

Michael stared at Gina. "Of course we want to be tested!"

Angel noticed Sarah Beth looked away and didn't say anything. She wondered if Gina noticed.

"I'll email all of you," Travis said.

"I appreciate it, I really do. But I hope you'll think about it before you get tested," Gina said. "That's enough kidney talk for one night. Angel made us some special cookies for dessert."

"And I can't wait any longer to taste them," Shannon said.

Gina smiled over at Angel and went into the kitchen. As she passed the orejas around she explained, "We decided that since the black eyed peas are for luck and the cabbage is for money then the orejas are for friendship."

"To friendship," they all echoed.

"These are wonderful," Sarah Beth said in between bites.

"Mmm, they sure are," Dustin agreed.

"Thanks," Angel said simply.

It wasn't long until the parents had to go. Angel helped Gina clean up the plates and put the food away. There were only three orejas left.

"You keep these," Angel said to Gina.

"Are you sure?"

"Yes. Thanks for inviting me and cooking everything."

"We've got to go, too," Shannon said, bringing in their glasses from the living room. "I'll call you tomorrow and let you know how the project is going."

Gina sighed. "Okay." They all walked back into the living room.

"What do you want to do this week for *our* project?" Gina asked Angel.

Angel furrowed her brow. "Our project?"

"Yes. We are no longer boring. Remember?"

"Oh yeah," Angel said hesitantly.

"I'll text you later this week with some ideas," Gina said.

Travis and Shannon put their coats on and said their goodbyes.

Angel got her coat and began to put it on. "Thanks again for inviting me today. It was nice meeting your friends."

"Thank you for coming over early and helping me."

Angel chuckled. "I didn't really help."

"You made dessert, which is now a tradition for our New Year's meal," Gina said, smiling.

Angel gazed at her with a forced smile. Her chest felt tight and she had an overwhelming urge to get out of there and now. She quickly went to the door. "I'd better go. Thanks again."

"Bye Angel," Gina said with a puzzled look.

"Bye." Angel hurried out the door and when she stepped onto the street a cold blast hit her face. She took a deep breath and released it. What was happening to her?

She began to walk and the thoughts swirling through her head were confusing. It had been a long time since she'd been interested in another woman. Is that what this was? Was she interested in Gina Gray?

She pushed her hands deeper in her coat pockets as the wind was chilly. An Uber or cab would be a lot warmer, but she wanted to walk and think. Her analytical mind chose to review the last two days and her unexpected behavior.

When she began a new job, she normally stayed to herself. Eventually, she might become acquaintances with co-workers, but rarely friends. She used dating apps to meet like-minded women that were focused on their careers, but also liked to go out occasionally for a meal and bedroom fun afterwards.

This protected her heart and kept her from becoming a total recluse. She could still feel the pain like a knife slicing through her heart from the night her dad told her she had shamed their family. He forbade her from ever seeing her girlfriend again and wanted to kick her out of the house, but her mom had intervened. She couldn't remember her dad ever looking her in the eye again.

The years had helped her pack this pain away. The few times she was interested in another woman and thought about taking a chance, the hurt would resurface just to remind her that she wasn't good enough for anyone else.

A part of her knew this was untrue, but the scars were many and ran deep. She got used to the emptiness she felt inside and hid the hole in her heart much like everyone hides their deepest sorrows, regrets, or secrets. On the outside people thought she was a quiet loner, not necessarily happy or sad. She engaged just enough with other people to appear like an intelligent strategist working her way up the corporate ladder.

When she began working on Travis's team she immediately liked him. He didn't try to micro-manage his team or boss anyone around. His expectations were clear and everyone did their jobs and the team excelled.

It wasn't long after she'd started that she found several ways to build better reports with better information that led to more profitable decisions. She thrived on challenges like this. The money or profits didn't necessarily drive her. She looked at these problems like puzzles and got great pleasure from solving them. This made her a team player and managers loved her.

She thought back to when Travis had invited her to the party. It didn't take her long to accept because she looked at this as a way to interact with her co-workers, giving the appearance not of a loner, but rather a new quiet team member.

And then she met Gina. Her kind eyes and welcoming smile immediately put her at ease. She was always on alert meeting new people and couldn't remember ever being this relaxed around someone she'd just met. A smile crept across her face; she may have been calm, but there was also something fluttering inside her chest. She'd escaped to the balcony and then Gina appeared. All of a sudden she'd asked her to leave the party and they did.

Instead of trying to hide behind her loner persona, Angel opened up, surprised that Gina managed to get her to talk about things she hadn't told anyone in years. And when she learned of Gina's kidney problem she didn't feel pity. Something inside her knew that Gina would make it through this. Why? She didn't know. It was a feeling. Thank goodness she didn't share this with Gina. That would have been hard to explain.

Then she'd found herself thinking of Gina that morning. She came over early to help and even made orejas. She hadn't thought about a *panadería* since leaving Arizona and then found herself baking! As she took a deep breath she thought back to the afternoon. The people she'd met were nice and included her in the conversation.

And then she remembered the conversation with Gina about their boring lives. In two days this woman had gotten her to do things she hadn't done in years. This realization had come to her as everyone was leaving. It frightened her and led to her quick exit.

The smart thing would be to put some distance between them. She knew Gina wasn't looking for a relationship. She made that very clear with the kidney transplant looming. So why was she wondering what Gina would plan for them this week?

A sigh escaped her lips and was loud enough for the man walking in front of her to look back. She smiled briefly and walked past him. The sigh came from the hole in her heart closing a little since having met Gina Gray.

Maybe a friend wouldn't be such a bad thing. They both had reasons to hold back, so a guarded friendship might be okay for a while. But Gina made her feel out of control at times, so she'd have to find a way to manage that.

She looked up and found herself standing in front of her apartment building. The fear had subsided as she'd talked herself through her behavior, but the lack of control still worried her. As she stepped on the elevator her phone pinged. It was a text from Gina.

You left quickly. I hope my disease hasn't scared you off. But I get it.

Oh wow, Gina couldn't be more wrong. Angel quickly texted her back.

Honestly, what scares me is how quickly I've opened up to you.

Angel couldn't believe she hit send. Within seconds she had a response.

I promise I don't want to beat up your heart. We're just trying to beat back the boring, right?

Angel chuckled. Beat back the boring; she liked it.

Right! I promise not to bring up your kidney.

I'm holding you to that! No kidney talk!

Deal! Sorry I left so abruptly. Thanks again for inviting me.

Thanks for helping and sharing. I'll think of something we can do this week.

Okay.

Angel put her phone down, shaking her head. Gina Gray was hard to say no to.

7

Gina had been thinking about Angel's quick exit on New Year's Day. What was it about the cautious woman that intrigued her? She was so guarded and openly admitted to her that she didn't do relationships or even friendships beyond acquaintances.

She planned to do something simple with her and wasn't surprised when she said she was working late all week. Instead of letting it go, Gina was pursuing this friendship even though Angel wasn't making it easy.

Angel was damaged just like her and maybe that's why Gina was interested. They both carried emotional scars. Granted, Gina's were from a physical disease. But it caused emotional pain too. Maybe that's what drew them to one another.

Whatever the reason, Gina was taking a chance as she walked into the building where Angel worked. She rode the elevator to the floor of Travis's office, hoping Angel's would be nearby.

When she walked into the open area usually full of team members pecking on keyboards at their desks, she didn't see anyone. She gazed to the back of the large room and saw Travis's office door was open, but the light was off.

On her way to Travis's office, she decided to walk along the perimeter where some office doors were open. Then she saw a light on in the office two doors down from Travis's. As she approached she could barely hear the sound of a mouse clicking.

She peeked her head in the doorway and was rewarded with the sight of Angel intensely staring at one of two computer screens on her desk. The movement must have caught her eye because Angel looked to the door.

When she saw Gina tentatively smiling, her posture immediately relaxed and a smile grew on her face. "What are you doing here?" she said, standing up.

Gina stood at the door and shyly looked down.

"Come in," Angel said, walking around her desk.

"I don't mean to interrupt," Gina began, stepping inside the office. "Well, I guess I do, but I hope you don't mind."

Angel chuckled. "I don't mind. Have a seat."

Gina sat down in one of the chairs in front of Angel's desk. "I came by to see if…" Gina said hesitantly.

"To see if I was really working late?" Angel said, finishing her sentence.

Gina's brow furrowed. "Not at all. I wanted to see if I could convince you to take a break. You've worked late every day since New Year's and I couldn't decide if you wanted to continue with your boring life," she said, pausing with a twinkle in her eye. "Or if maybe there was some other reason you keep saying no to my texts."

Angel grinned and looked at Gina, shaking her head. "So you don't take no for an answer, huh?"

"If you're interested, I have a theory on why you do that," Gina replied.

"A theory? I'd love to hear it," Angel said, obviously interested.

"I think you are so protective of that heart of yours that you naturally say no. It's hard for you to say yes because it's out of your comfort zone." Gina watched as Angel nodded slightly. She continued. "There's a solution to this. You simply have to practice."

Angel looked at her, amused. "Practice?"

"Yes. You have to practice saying yes now and then. The more often you do, the more comfortable you'll get. Eventually, when you see my texts you won't automatically reply 'no.'" Gina folded her hands in her lap and waited.

Angel gazed at her. "That makes sense except you're assuming one thing."

"What's that?"

"You're assuming that I've had a good time and will want to reply with a yes."

"I see. Good point. Let me ask you, did you have a good time at the New Year's party?"

"I did," Angel replied.

"And did you enjoy yourself at my place on New Year's Day?"

"Yes."

"Then I think it's safe to say that so far you have a good time when you're with me, so there must be some other reason you keep saying no."

Angel looked at her but didn't say anything.

"I might wonder if fear has something to do with your answers, so I offer this. My idea for this first 'beat boring adventure' was simply a quick dinner and a little conversation."

Angel tilted her head. "Really?"

"Really. Honestly, this hasn't been a great week, so I've been working from home. Today I felt better and wanted to get out for a bit." Gina could see the concern on Angel's face and could tell she was weighing her words carefully. "It's okay to talk about the kidney because I brought it up. You aren't breaking your promise."

Angel blew out a breath and smiled. "I'm sorry you haven't felt well. Is there anything you can do when that happens?"

"Not really. I work from home because my energy is so low that the idea of going to the office tires me out. But today is better and I thought maybe you could use a little something different than working late. So I took a chance and here I am."

Angel's face softened. "Tell me more about this quick meal you had in mind."

Gina's eyes lit up. "Well, I thought it would be fun to meet halfway between our apartments and find a place to eat. Nothing fancy, just some diner or restaurant that looked interesting. But," she said, drawing the word out, "I don't know where you live."

Angel smiled and went around behind her desk. She reached for a backpack on the floor, putting a notebook inside before zipping it up. She typed on her keyboard and then looked at Gina. "I'll show you my place on another adventure. But for now, come look," she said, motioning Gina around her desk.

Gina stood next to Angel and looked at the monitor. She had pulled up a map of the city.

"Here is where I live," she said, pointing to the screen. "And this is where you live."

"Okay," Gina said, studying the map. "Let's go here," she said, pointing to an area in between their apartments. "All it takes is one little yes," she said, trying to convince Angel.

Angel reached for her phone and pulled the map up on it and zoomed in on where they were going. She looked at Gina and smiled. "Yes."

Gina beamed.

Angel grabbed her backpack and they walked to the elevator. Once inside she turned to Gina, "Is it okay with you if we take an Uber or cab?"

Gina appreciated the suggestion because walking wasn't a good idea with her energy level just beginning to come back. "I'd like that."

Angel took her phone out and requested a car. When they walked out of the building their car pulled up. Gina looked at Angel and gave her an impressed look. Angel chuckled and opened the back door, allowing Gina to get in first.

During the ride they peered at Angel's phone and looked at eating options in the area. They had the driver drop them at an intersection and looked around when they got out.

"What do you think of that little place there?" Gina said, nodding toward a storefront that had an OPEN neon sign in the window.

"I think it looks just right," Angel said.

Gina smiled at Angel's approval and opened the door, waiting for Angel to enter first. They found a booth near the back and sat down. A waitress promptly brought them menus and took their drink orders.

"I don't know about you, but a place like this always makes me want to order a burger. They're usually greasy, messy, and delicious," Gina said, gazing at the menu.

Angel looked up from her menu at Gina's explicit burger description. "You really love a burger don't you?"

Gina laughed. "I guess you could tell."

"Nah, the expression of glee on your face gave it away," Angel said, laughing with her.

When the waitress came back with their drinks they both ordered burgers.

"How did I end up the lucky one tonight?" Angel asked as she sipped her drink.

"The lucky one?" Gina said, bewildered.

"You chose to have dinner with me. I'm sure Shannon or your other friends would love to see you."

Gina looked down and sighed. "If I had dinner with Shannon she would want to talk about the project," she said, doing air quotes with her fingers. "Three of the five people that offered to get tested at the New Year's party weren't a match."

"Oh," Angel said softly. "That must be hard to hear."

"You know, I'm pretty good at staying positive, but I will admit that when she told me, it did sting a little. Just knowing they were getting tested gave me hope."

"I'm sure it did," Angel said, narrowing her eyes at Gina.

Gina met her stare and could tell she was contemplating her words. "What?" she asked.

Angel let out a breath. "Uh, promise me you won't think I'm nuts."

"Okay," Gina said, her voice tentative.

"When you told me about your kidney disease and needing a transplant, I didn't feel sorry for you. I mean, I'm sorry you have to go through that, and this has happened to you, but..." she said.

Gina spoke up before Angel could finish. "I remember. That's why I immediately liked you. You didn't look at me with sadness or sorrow."

"But when you said it, I knew you were going to be all right. It was a feeling I had. I know that sounds crazy, but I do. I know you're going to find a donor, have the transplant, and be fine."

Gina looked into Angel's eyes, trying to see past her words. She saw assurance and kindness. A smile slowly spread across her face. "I don't think that sounds crazy. I'm going to remember this and when I get negative results it's not going to hurt me. I'll simply have to wait a little longer. Because I'm going to believe like you do that it's going to happen and everything will work out."

Angel returned her smile and before she could say anything the waitress brought their burgers.

"One more thing," Angel said before they started to eat.

Gina raised her eyebrows in question.

"I haven't broken my promise not to talk about your kidney since you brought it up first, right?"

Gina chuckled. "No, you have not broken your promise."

Angel nodded, picked up her burger and took a bite. She moaned with enjoyment. "This is so good," she said after swallowing.

Gina nodded because her mouth was full of joy. After a moment she said, "I told you. I knew this would be a good burger."

Angel laughed. "This will make me text yes next time," she teased. She took another bite and smiled as her hands got messy.

"Is there anything you'd like to see or do since you're new to the city?"

Angel wiped her hands and looked at Gina timidly.

"Tell me! I'd love to show you the city," Gina said, encouraging Angel.

"I'd like to go to the Statue of Liberty. I've been to New York several times, but I've never been there."

"I'd love to take you. I don't think I can get you to take a day off so it'd have to be on a Saturday or Sunday."

"Okay."

Gina thought for a minute. "If you wouldn't mind, let's go next weekend. I know I'll feel better by then. You'll want to walk up inside her and I probably couldn't do that this weekend," she said honestly.

"No problem. That would work out better for me anyway."

Gina nodded. She decided to push a little further. "Maybe we could meet for coffee near your apartment on Sunday."

"Hmm, you wouldn't want to see my apartment would you?"

Gina giggled. "Of course I do."

Angel chuckled. "I think I could find time for coffee with you on Sunday."

"You know, you can tell a lot about a person from where they live," Gina said, feigning nonchalance.

"Is that so?"

Gina nodded, biting into her burger.

Angel thought for a moment. "Your apartment is very welcoming, much like you. It may be small, but it didn't feel that way when all your friends were there the other day."

"Thanks. But it is small."

"Doesn't it fit you, though? Why would you need a bigger place?"

"I guess it does."

Angel smiled. "I love your place. It's not boring," she said, winking. "It's comfortable and happy."

"Happy? I don't know that I would describe it like that, but okay," she said, chuckling. "Now I'm really curious to see your place."

"You realize I haven't been here long, so it may appear a little stark."

"Don't say anymore. I'll reserve judgement until I see it for myself."

Angel finished her burger. "That was delicious. Maybe we need to go around the city and eat burgers at all the little diners."

"That's not a bad idea," Gina said, wiping her hands.

The waitress came over with their ticket and Gina snatched it before Angel could. "This time is on me. I came to your work and practically forced you."

"It didn't feel forced. I'm so glad you pushed me to do this. Thanks," she said earnestly.

"You're welcome. I've had a really good time, too. I'm glad I took a chance. You might learn from that," Gina said as she got up and went to the register to pay the bill.

Angel grabbed her backpack and watched her walk away.

Gina could feel Angel's eyes on her as she paid. She turned around and Angel held the door open for them.

Their rides arrived at the same time. Angel turned to Gina and said, "Thanks again. I think I could learn a great deal from you, Gina Gray." She opened the door for her and Gina got in.

"See you Sunday."

8

"Can I come over?" Shannon asked.

"Well hello to you," Gina said, answering her phone.

"Hello, so can I come over?"

"Why?" Gina said, drawing the word out.

"Because I haven't seen my friend in days and I miss her."

This made Gina smile. "It has been days."

"I'll pick us up something for dinner on the way over," Shannon offered.

"What about Travis?"

"Working," Shannon said. "I shouldn't complain because he's been home earlier the last couple of weeks."

"Because of Angel," Gina stated.

"And how would you know that?"

"Bring food and I'll tell you all about it."

"On the way," Shannon said, ending the call.

Gina laughed. Shannon loved to be right in the middle of her love life—when she *had* a love life, she thought.

It didn't take long for Shannon to get there. She walked in with several cartons of Chinese food.

"Is someone else coming over?" Gina asked as she watched her take carton after carton out of the sack.

Shannon chuckled. "No. I was hungry and figured you could use the leftovers."

"Thanks," Gina said, handing her a plate.

After they'd filled them and sat down to eat Shannon said, "Okay. Let's hear it. What have you been up to with Angel?"

Gina laughed. "I haven't been up to anything. I texted her several times last week to see if she wanted to do something and she said no every time. She always said she was working late. So I took a chance and went to her office after work."

"And?" Shannon said impatiently.

Gina chewed her bite of fried rice and swallowed before continuing. "She was the only one there. I guess Travis can go home now since she'll stay late."

"Not true," Shannon said, defending her boyfriend. "He stayed late to go over some reports with her, but that doesn't matter. What happened?" she asked excitedly.

"We went out for a burger."

"That's it? Come on, GG. I can see you want to tell me," she said, peering into Gina's face.

Gina couldn't help but laugh. "We had a nice time. We made plans to go to the Statue of Liberty next weekend."

Shannon nodded and looked Gina up and down. "Good for you. She seemed to fit right in New Year's."

"Don't get any ideas. We're just friends; well, we're becoming friends."

"What's wrong with her?"

"There's nothing wrong with her."

"Then you need to be more than friends."

"Oh okay. I'll tell her Sunday that Shannon has decided that we need to be together. I'll see if she wants to move in with me, or should I move in with her?" Gina said, glaring at Shannon.

"Hold up," Shannon said, raising her hand. " You're seeing her Sunday?"

Gina nodded. "Yes, we're going to meet for coffee."

"Look, you've told me over and over that you don't want to even think about a relationship until this kidney business is over, but that doesn't mean you can't have some fun. And when I say fun, I mean sex. There's absolutely nothing wrong with you and Angel having sex while you are 'becoming friends,'" she said, mocking Gina.

Gina let out a frustrated sigh. "Did you ever think that maybe I don't want to have sex, Shan?"

"What? Why in the world would you not want to have sex?"

"Because I don't feel good about myself and I have so much weighing on me with this transplant and donor search. That's why I like being with Angel. She never brings up my disease or the transplant."

"That's an even better reason. Nothing can relieve your stress like a good orgasm and Angel doesn't care if you're sick."

"She cares!" Gina said, raising her voice. "But she knows that I don't like talking about it so she promised me she wouldn't bring it up."

Shannon sat back and looked at Gina. After a moment she said, "You like her." She pointed her fork at Gina. "I can see it in your eyes. You like this woman."

Gina scoffed. "Well, of course I like her." When Gina looked up, Shannon had a smirk on her face. "Okay, okay," Gina said, holding her hands up, giving in. "There's something kind of mysterious about her. She's very cautious, but for some reason she seems to open up to me. She doesn't see me as the sick girl and that's really nice for a change."

"You know I'd take all this away if I could, GG," Shannon said softly.

"Of course I do," Gina said, looking up and smiling.

"Okay. I'll stop pushing you with your new mysterious almost-friend. For now," Shannon said.

"Thank you."

"Unfortunately, you do have to talk about your kidney with me. The other two from the party are not a match. Dustin and Brandy are set to be tested the first of next week and I think Michael is too. I don't know about Sarah Beth."

"Good to know," Gina said, taking her plate to the kitchen.

Shannon watched her and when she walked back into the room she said, "You're taking this rather calmly."

"I'm trying to. I admit I got upset when the first ones were negative, but I know this could be a long process. I'm trying to stay calm and hopeful."

"Good for you, GG." Shannon shook her head. "You have amazed me since the first day I met you and you still do."

Gina smiled. "You're pretty darn amazing yourself."

Shannon got up and hugged Gina. "We are," she said, hugging her a little tighter.

* * *

Travis sat back in his chair and stretched his arms over his head. He looked at his watch and turned to Angel. "I think I've had enough for tonight."

Sitting across from Travis's desk, Angel looked up from her laptop. "Shannon may be mad at me because you're working late," she said.

"Nah, I haven't really worked late since New Year's. Besides, she was going to Gina's."

Hearing Gina's name made her heart jump. "If you don't mind me asking, how's your project with Gina going?"

Travis chuckled. "You mean the great donor search? We had five sign up to be tested at the New Year's party. The first three weren't a match and I just heard today that the other two didn't match either."

"What will you do now?"

"The friends you met at Gina's on New Year's Day will be tested next week. Hopefully one of them will match."

Angel nodded. "What will you do if they don't match?"

"Then it will be time for Gina to ask some of her other friends that I don't know as well. We are starting with our tight little circle, but Gina has other friends through her job and volunteer work she does."

"She does volunteer work?" Angel asked, not surprised Gina would help others.

"Yeah, she used to volunteer at an LGBTQ+ youth center in her neighborhood. I'm not sure if she's still doing that. She's not able to do things like she used to. She gets tired easily sometimes. We've got to find her a donor," Travis said, sounding a little desperate.

"I'm sure you will," Angel said with confidence. "If I can help out with your research, let me know," she offered as she closed her laptop and stood up.

"Thanks Angel, I appreciate that. Gina is one of the best people I know," he said. "Hey, you left the party together and then you came to her place the next day. Have you seen her since?"

"Uh, yes. She came by here one night and we grabbed a burger."

"She came here?"

"Yeah, it's when I was working on that Phillips analysis and stayed late several nights. She surprised me."

Travis smiled and then his face lit up. "I wonder if Shannon is still there? Maybe it's your turn to surprise Gina." Travis grabbed his phone and sent Shannon a text.

Angel instantly began to think of a reason she couldn't and then she stopped those thoughts. There was no reason she couldn't go to Gina's. All she had to do was say yes.

Travis stared at his phone, waiting for Shannon to reply.

Angel felt a tingle inside her body. She didn't know if it was because she was actually planning to go with Travis or if it was the idea of seeing Gina again. Before she could figure it out, Travis smiled and looked up at her.

"She's still there. Do you want to surprise Gina?"

"I don't know. Some people don't like surprises," Angel said, her newfound confidence waning.

"I've never known her not to like surprises. Come on, it'll be fun. Isn't that what you and Gina are doing? Trying to add fun to your lives?"

"I guess that is what we're doing," Angel said, nodding. "Okay. I'm in. Let me get my backpack," she said, going to her office.

Travis texted Shannon to give him twenty minutes and he'd be there with a surprise. "Let's go," he said to Angel as he left his office.

They got a cab and managed to get there with a few minutes to spare.

Shannon opened the door and Travis kissed her on the cheek and then walked in, grinning at Gina. "I brought you a surprise," he said.

"Oh you did," she said, grinning right back at him. Then she saw Angel and her face lit up. "Well hi," she said, obviously happy to see her.

"I hope you don't mind that I came along," Angel said shyly.

"Not at all. What a nice surprise."

"Hi Angel," Shannon said, closing the door.

"Hi Shannon."

Travis noticed the food and walked over, looking in the cartons. "Were you hungry?"

"I may have been when I ordered. Do you want some?" Shannon answered.

"There's plenty for you both. I'll get plates," Gina said, going into the kitchen.

Angel followed her. "I wanted to tell you that this was Travis's idea, but I said yes." She was pleased with herself.

Gina tilted her head. "I'm glad you did." Then she added, teasing, "It didn't hurt? Saying yes?"

Angel chuckled. "No it didn't. I'm practicing what I learned the other night from a friend," she said, her eyes bright.

Their eyes locked for a moment and then Gina laughed. "Good to know." She handed Angel a plate and then took one to Travis.

They filled their plates and then Travis looked at Gina. "I guess Shannon told you we don't have any matches yet," he said tentatively.

"She did, but we'll find one, Trav."

"We will," he said firmly. "We have a few lined up for next week, but you may want to think about asking your other friends or co-workers. I know I told you I'd ask them and I will, but I need their contact info."

"Let's see what happens next week and I'll think about it," Gina said. "I appreciate all you're doing, but let's talk about something else now. Okay?"

"Let's talk about your exciting lives," Shannon said, taunting Gina and Angel.

"Very funny," said Gina, her face turning red.

"I'm going to see the Statue of Liberty next weekend and I am excited about it," Angel said, surprising Gina with her candor.

"Oh you are?" said Travis. "I haven't been to the statue in forever. Maybe we should come along," he said, looking at Shannon.

"We'll see," Shannon said.

Gina got up to get something to drink and Shannon followed her into the kitchen. "Hey, we're not crashing your fun with Angel next weekend," she said quietly.

"It's not a date," she responded.

"Yeah, but it could be," Shannon said, raising her eyebrows.

"Hey, did they give you extra fortune cookies?" Travis asked from the other side of the bar.

"Oh, I don't know. We haven't opened ours yet," Shannon said.

Travis looked in the sack and pulled out four fortune cookies.

"I guess since you ordered so much they thought there were four of us," Gina said, laughing.

"I told you I ordered extra so you could have the leftovers," Shannon said self-defense.

"Oh no," Angel exclaimed. "I think we ate it all."

"It's all right. I'm glad you joined us." Gina smiled at her.

"Me too," Travis said, patting his belly.

Gina laughed. "Pass out those fortunes. I need a lucky one."

Travis gave each one of them a fortune cookie.

Shannon quickly unwrapped hers and said, "'A hunch is creativity trying to tell you something.'" She looked at Gina. "I have a hunch if you don't find a donor soon then I need to put my creativity to work and design a media campaign."

"Oh, I like it, babe," Travis said. "Mine says 'A friend asks only for your time, not your money.'"

"What does yours say, Angel?" Shannon asked.

Angel took a bite of the cookie and uncurled the paper. "'A new perspective will come with the new year.'" She looked at Gina and raised her eyebrows.

"How about that," Gina said. "Maybe saying yes is giving you a new perspective."

"Maybe," Angel said softly.

"Your turn, GG," Shannon said.

Gina opened hers and smiled as she read it to herself. "'A lifetime friend shall soon be made.'"

"Hmm, maybe it will be a kidney donor," said Travis.

Angel looked at Gina, wondering if she could be the lifetime friend in Gina's fortune. Gina stared back and Angel wondered if she was thinking the same thing.

9

Gina was happy it was finally Sunday. Angel Ruiz had been in her thoughts off and on since she'd left her apartment the other night with Shannon and Travis. There was something about this woman that tugged at Gina. Sure, she was interesting and had traveled all over the world. But knowing she guarded her heart and had for years because of her family softened something inside Gina.

She was used to being the one that everyone else took care of, but with Angel it was different. Gina couldn't really ease the hurt her family caused, but she wanted to show her that not everyone wanted to hurt her. Gina certainly didn't. Angel had become someone she liked to be with, *preferred* to be with, if she was being honest.

She loved Shannon and talked to her nearly every day; Travis was always glad to see her, but still, she didn't like imposing on them. They never made her feel that way, nevertheless sometimes it happened. She found Angel to be a welcome alternative.

As these thoughts mingled in and out of her head, her phone rang. She looked at the name on the screen and smiled.

"You're not trying to get out of showing me your apartment are you?" she said.

Angel chuckled on the other end of the phone. Gina liked the sound of these little laughs. "No, I'm going to show you my apartment. But it's such a nice day I wondered if you'd like to meet at a park that's not too far from my place. We can sit and enjoy the weather or walk around for a bit."

Gina appreciated the fact that Angel didn't ask how she felt, thus keeping her promise to not bring up her disease. But she gave her options, knowing her energy could be good today or not. "That's a wonderful idea. I'd love to walk around or sit, doesn't matter to me."

"Oh good! I'll send you the location. How about we meet there in half an hour?"

"I'll be there."

"There are several places around there we can have coffee or get something to drink."

"See you soon." Gina ended the call with a smile on her face.

It wasn't long before Gina walked out the door and made her way to the park near Angel's. She looked down at her phone and then back up to make sure she was in the right place. The buildings along the sidewalk stopped and a fence began. Gina followed the fence with her eyes and could see Angel waiting at the gate to the entrance to the park.

When Angel saw her approaching, her face lit up and she waved. Then she began to walk toward Gina. "You found it," she said, greeting Gina.

"Hi. This is such a good idea. It's beautiful today."

"Come on," Angel said, walking back the way she came.

Other people had the same idea, but the park wasn't crowded. They walked around and ended up at an area with a basketball court. There were two teams of three playing one another. They sat down and watched.

"Do you play basketball?" Angel asked.

Gina laughed. "Not in a million years. I played when I was a kid and was on the team in high school."

"Me too. I don't know when I've shot a basketball since then.

Watching them makes me think I could run out there and keep up," Angel said, laughing.

"I'll sit right here and cheer you on," Gina said.

"You know, I've been thinking about that fortune cookie I got at your place."

"Oh yeah? What was it? Something about perspective?"

"Yeah. It said a new perspective will come with the new year. I think you've given me that new perspective."

"Me?" Gina said, looking at Angel in surprise.

"Yes, you. This idea of livening up our boring lives and saying yes has me looking at things differently."

"Really? How so?"

"Well, I wouldn't have gone with Travis to your place if you hadn't talked about practicing saying yes. And I wouldn't have had such a good time or gotten the fortune cookie. I wouldn't have been looking forward to today, either."

"You were looking forward to today?" Gina asked.

"I was."

Gina smiled and locked her eyes on Angel's. "I was, too."

Angel smiled, then nodded.

They sat back and enjoyed the sunshine and watched the basketball game. Gina noticed that they didn't have to say anything. The silence wasn't uncomfortable. As a matter of fact, it was nice to simply sit together and enjoy the day.

"Are you ready to see my place?" Angel asked after a while.

"Well, if you're not going to play we may as well go," Gina said playfully.

"Maybe another time. Those guys are a little out of my league. Come on," she said, getting up and offering Gina her hand.

Gina took it and immediately felt the warmth of Angel's hand encircling hers. It was as if her hand had been waiting on Angel's for a long time. She couldn't remember the last time she'd held hands with someone and it felt this good. Then she chided herself: Angel was just a friend offering her a hand.

But she didn't drop her hand until they went through the gate and started to walk toward her apartment. Gina instantly missed the feel of Angel's hand in hers. She didn't know where these thoughts were coming from—at least that's what she told herself.

"Here we are," Angel said, stopping in front of her building. They went inside and she led them to the elevator. "I have to admit that I'm a little nervous showing you my place."

Gina turned to her as they stepped into the elevator. "Why?"

"Because of what you said the other day about being able to tell a lot about a person from where they live."

Gina smiled mischievously. "Do you have secrets?"

Angel scoffed. "No."

The elevator door opened on Angel's floor and they stepped off.

Gina followed Angel to her door and put her hand on her arm before she could unlock it. "Before we go in, it doesn't matter what your apartment is like, Angel. I already know you're a person that I like spending time with and I hope we keep doing it."

A big smile grew on Angel's face. "Thank you for saying that." She unlocked the door, stepped inside and turned to Gina. "Welcome."

Gina walked into the wide open space. As much as Gina's place was small and cozy, Angel's was spacious and open, with high ceilings and a warehouse feel. Directly across from them was a wall of almost floor to ceiling windows. The view was of the neighboring rooftop and she could see down the street in the direction of her apartment. There was no need for window coverings because no one could see directly into this apartment.

"This is spectacular," Gina said, her eyes wide. She tore her eyes away from the windows and looked to her right. There was a long island that separated the kitchen area from the living space. To her left there were three doors.

Angel had a couch and chair arranged directly across from the widows. Gina imagined sitting here after a long day and taking in the night lights. Then she thought of how cautious Angel was all day and how exhausting that must be. She could come in, drop her guard and let it go, gazing into the evening sky. This space fit the Angel she was coming to know.

On one end of the windows was a TV and on the other was a tall bookcase full of books.

Angel walked around the couch to the windows and Gina followed her. "If you look down the street right here," she said, pointing, "you can almost see your building."

"No way!" Gina said following where she pointed.

"Well almost, if you use your imagination," Angel replied with an enchanted lilt to her voice.

"Oh, I see it now," Gina said, winking, but she wondered if Angel did in fact look out and imagine her building.

Angel smiled and started walking toward the kitchen.

Gina followed her and walked around the island, gently running her fingertips along the counters. "This is so beautiful. Have you been cooking more? I think this might make me want to."

"I've been cooking some. I don't think I've ever thought of a kitchen as beautiful," she said thoughtfully.

"Well, this one is."

"Thank you. I'll show you the rest." Angel walked through the living area to the first door that was open. She turned the light on and let Gina go inside first.

"This is a small room that I think may be for storage. I use it as a small office. You'd be surprised how distracting those windows can be."

"Oh, I believe you," Gina said, noticing how neat and tidy Angel kept the space.

"This next door is the bathroom. There's also a door through to my bedroom."

Gina walked into the bathroom. It was spacious with a sparkling shower and large mirror. Something tightened in her chest as she looked at the shower and she stopped her thoughts before her imagination took off.

"Let's go through this way," Angel said from behind.

She shook her head and followed Angel back out the door and then stopped at the bookcase. "Look at all these," she said in wonder. "You must love to read."

Angel stopped at the door to her room. "I do. I read mostly on my iPad now. It's gotten tedious moving all these books, but I'm not ready to let any of them go yet."

"I get that. My bookcase is in my bedroom. I'll show you the next time you come over and we can compare titles," Gina said, looking into Angel's eyes. She could feel something shifting between them. Suddenly, instead of enjoying the warm feeling tingling through her body, she hoped Angel's fear wasn't closing off her heart. Meeting and getting to know Angel had been such a wonderful surprise; she didn't want anything to threaten it.

Angel smiled. "I'd love that."

Gina breathed a sigh of relief and followed her into the bedroom. It was what she might expect from Angel. The furniture was simple, but polished. It felt warm and the king sized bed that dominated the room had a multicolor comforter that gave the room color.

"This is so you," Gina said, looking around the room.

"I'm almost afraid to ask what that means."

Gina turned to her. "It means it's beautiful. It's warm and inviting," she said, her voice trailing off. She could see Angel swallow and she didn't look away.

A smile began on Angel's face until it reached her eyes. "That wasn't so bad."

Gina saw an opportunity and said, "Sometimes you're afraid and you don't need to be." She hoped Angel understood that she had nothing to fear with her.

Angel stared at her a moment and then suddenly said, "We didn't get anything to drink. I can make coffee here or I have other drinks." She hurried toward the kitchen.

Gina watched her walk away. Something was definitely shifting.

10

"Let's see," Angel said, opening the refrigerator. "I have several flavors of sparkling water, pineapple juice, and water. I could make iced tea or hot tea or coffee."

Gina walked up behind her, looking into the refrigerator. "Have you ever mixed juice and sparkling water?"

Angel's brow furrowed. "Mixed them? No."

"Get out the pineapple juice and grapefruit sparkling water."

Angel did as Gina said and placed them on the island.

"Now two glasses, please."

Angel got out a glass for each of them and set them in front of Gina.

Gina took the pineapple juice and poured some in each glass until each was about a third full. "Do you have ice?"

Angel took ice from the refrigerator and added some cubes to each glass.

Then Gina opened the sparkling water and filled the glasses. While the fizzing bubbles died down, she asked Angel, "Do you have a straw or something I can stir with?"

Angel reached in a drawer and pulled out two metal straws and held them up.

"Perfect," Gina said, her eyes bright. She took the straws and stirred each drink then handed one to Angel.

They both sipped, looking into one another's eyes.

"Well?" Gina asked timidly.

"This reminds me of a tropical drink," Angel said, taking another sip.

"You can always add rum," Gina said, happy Angel liked it.

"Aren't you full of surprises?" Angel said.

"Not at all. I promise. What you see is what you get," Gina said, looking away. A painting next to the front door caught her eye. She walked over and studied it. There was a small house that looked over a field that backed up to a mountain. The sun was peeking out behind the mountain. She wasn't sure if it was sunrise or sunset. The colors were beautiful. The mountain was dark with red, orange, and purple from the sun just behind it. The sun painted a swath of light over the field to the house. There was a light shining from one of the tiny windows. The whole scene was tranquil and calming.

"Do you like it?" Angel asked.

"I do. It's so peaceful."

"Yeah. When I'm trying to solve a complex problem at work or if I'm feeling lonely, I can look at this and it soothes my heart and relaxes the tension."

"When you look at it you don't feel as lonely?" Gina said, making sure she heard her correctly. "How's that?"

"In a place like that, any problem would have to fade. And I don't feel as lonely because I imagine the woman I love is in the house with me."

Gina looked sideways at Angel and then back at the painting. "That's lovely," she said as a feeling of longing came over her.

"Maybe someday that will be my future."

"I can see why you'd want that."

"I'm glad you like it."

"I love your entire place," Gina said, walking back into the living area and sitting on the couch.

Angel joined her and they both gazed out the windows. "It's nice that I don't have anyone that can see in across the way. That gives me the luxury of not having drapes or blinds. When it's really cold I do have shades I can close to keep the heat in, but I don't have to do that very often."

"I'm sure it's beautiful at night too," Gina said.

"It is. When I first looked at this place these windows sold me immediately."

"I can see why."

"You know, my place may be bigger, but it's not better than your apartment."

Gina looked at Angel skeptically. "You're going to have to explain that to me."

"Your place may be small, but it's cozy. It feels…how do I explain?" she said, searching for the words. "It feels like a home. This," she said, raising both arms and spreading them out, "is simply a cool apartment."

Gina thought about what she said. "That's a really nice thing to say. You don't feel like this is a home?"

"Not really. It has my things in it and some that are dear to me, but it doesn't feel like a home."

This declaration pinched Gina's heart. It was one thing to be homesick and she knew that's not what Angel meant. To feel like you didn't belong or have a home was such a strong and torturous pain to carry around. Gina had to do something.

She sat up and angled toward Angel, their knees almost touching. "I know you don't mean you're homesick. If my place feels homey to you then you are welcome anytime."

Angel's face softened. "Thank you, that's really kind."

"What do we need to do to make this feel like home to you?"

"I'm not sure."

"I have an idea," Gina said, her face lighting up. "Since you made those orejas on New Year's Day, it's made me notice the Mexican sweet breads at my corner deli."

"Really?" Angel said, surprised.

"Yes! I enjoyed those cookies so much. I've found this coconut bar with pineapple that I love."

Angel smiled. "One of my favorites."

"And these little cinnamon cookies that are wonderful," Gina said, gesturing with one hand, her fingers making a small circle.

Angel chuckled. "I love them too, but what do they have to do with making this a home?"

"Maybe you should keep them around. Would they give you happy memories?" Gina watched as Angel considered her question.

"They would. Not all my memories from my childhood were bad. Going to the *panaderia* will always be a happy memory. I can't believe you've been buying sweet breads. I'm glad I shared with you and it made such an impression."

"It did." Gina looked at Angel's smiling face and gazed into her eyes. "You know, you were talking about your fortune cookie earlier. Do you remember mine?"

"I do. It was something about making a lifelong friend."

"That's right," Gina said, still looking in Angel's eyes. She hoped this didn't scare Angel away but she said it anyway. "When I read that, I hoped it was you."

Angel nodded. "I did too."

For a moment they stared at one another and then they both began to lean in as if drawn together by some hidden force.

When Angel's lips touched Gina's, her heart exploded into rapid beats and it took her breath away. But her lips didn't move; they were melded to Angel's. She felt Angel's hand cup her face and the softness of her lips along with the tenderness of her touch was the polar opposite of what was happening inside Gina. Every part of her body was tingling; her heart was fluttering furiously like hummingbird wings and she never wanted it to stop.

She felt Angel exhale and then slowly pull her lips away. Her hand was still on her face and then her fingertips were gone. Neither of them spoke as they stared into one another's eyes. Gina wanted to kiss her again, but hesitated.

Finally Angel said, "Was that okay? I know you told me in the beginning you weren't looking for a relationship."

Gina could see the doubt in Angel's eyes, but she didn't see fear. She smiled, hoping to ease the furrow in Angel's brow. "I wasn't looking for a friend either." Then she boldly leaned forward. This time her hand went to the back of Angel's neck and she firmly placed her lips on Angel's. She could feel Angel's hand glide up her arm then to her back, pulling her closer.

Gina opened her mouth slightly and ran her tongue over Angel's lower lip. She could feel Angel weaken and sink into the kiss. Then their tongues met and this was tastier than any of the sweet breads Angel had introduced her to. Arms encircled bodies, breathing became ragged, and tongues explored as the kiss went on and on and on. Gina heard an almost imperceptible moan escape Angel and pulled her closer.

Why had she not done this earlier? Their lips were perfect together and their arms fit around one another like they were made that way. And then Gina realized she had been guarding her heart just as Angel had. She wouldn't let herself look at Angel as more than a friend. But now, how could she ever go back? This kiss was the hottest, sweetest, most gentle and firm kiss she'd ever had. She liked the feeling of their lips crashing together and then softening, flooding desire through her body.

Their arms loosened and their lips softened and slowly they pulled away from one another. Gina looked into Angel's eyes. They were usually a very light brown, sometimes with a green tint. But she saw a deep dark brownish green that reminded her of a turbulent sea. Gina couldn't tell what she was thinking.

This kiss felt hopeful and gave her a peek at what could be. She hadn't felt hopeful in so long. So she chose to be brave and said, "You don't have to be afraid of me."

Angel's eyes bored into Gina's. "What about you?"

"Me? I'm not afraid," Gina said, not understanding what Angel meant.

"Aren't you though? When I met you it wasn't long after that you made it clear you weren't going to be with anyone until this kidney transplant was settled." Angel held up her hand and stopped Gina from speaking just yet. "And I'm not breaking my promise by talking about the transplant. I'm simply repeating what you said."

Gina narrowed her eyes and took a few moments to digest what Angel said. She'd never looked at it that way, but perhaps Angel was right. "So you're saying I'm scared to be with someone?"

Angel smiled compassionately. "I'm saying you talk about me guarding my heart and you're doing the same thing, although for a different reason."

Gina continued to wrestle with Angel's reasoning. Was she doing the same thing?

Angel continued. "You told me I needed to take a chance that not everyone is out to hurt me. I'm saying you need to do the same. Not everyone sees you as someone they might have to take care of. In fact, I don't see you that way at all."

"Now I'm scared to ask," Gina said, referring to how Angel felt earlier.

Angel smiled and took Gina's hand. "I see you as someone who puts on a brave face, who is always hopeful, and never shows weakness around others. But I know that you can't feel hopeful all the time and sometimes you doubt you'll get better. And those thoughts spin into doubting you'll ever find someone who would want a woman like you, and *those* thoughts spin on and on and on. Am I close?"

Gina nodded. She couldn't believe that Angel had described her so completely. Her cheeks reddened and she was speechless.

"I know how thoughts can spin because for years mine told me I wasn't good enough. No one would want someone like me. Our thoughts get so distorted they don't resemble us at all."

Gina kept listening, her heart pounding.

"What I'm trying to say is that we are a lot alike in how we see ourselves. And that we're wrong."

"We're wrong?" Gina said, unbelieving.

"Yes. I knew soon after I met you that you were someone I wanted to be around because you made me feel comfortable. I didn't have to be this quiet, aloof loner. I could be myself and I knew you would see my scars, but you'd look past them."

"And I knew you didn't look at me and see my disease; you saw a person."

"Exactly. We both are people that these other things happened to. But that's not all we are."

"What does all this mean then?" Gina asked cautiously.

"Well," Angel said, still holding her hand. "You don't want to commit to anyone right now and I happen to be the master of being noncommittal. So, I'd say we're a match made in heaven. No pun intended regarding your looking for a kidney match."

Gina snorted at Angel's explanation. "You know Shannon told me the other day there's nothing wrong with having a little fun."

Angel raised her eyebrows. "Fun?"

"Yeah, she meant the kind of fun we were just having before all this fear set in."

"Oh," Angel said, realizing what Gina meant. She searched Gina's eyes and began to lean toward her. When her lips were about to touch Gina's she whispered, "I'm not scared."

Gina met Angel's lips and they stopped talking.

11

What a week, Angel thought. She turned from the windows and looked at the couch. Her heart skipped a beat thinking about the best first kisses she'd shared with Gina days ago. But they had both been busy this week and were only able to text and occasionally talk on the phone. Gina was supposed to be here any minute for their adventure to the Statue of Liberty.

Angel smiled when she thought of the word adventure, because that's how she imagined this with Gina. From the beginning they both were able to look right through the guise they showed others and see deeper inside. It was like an adventure discovering Gina's fear and helping her tame it, but what she liked was the boldness that flew out of her at times. A knock at the door brought her out of her thoughts and around the couch.

She opened the door and narrowed her eyes at Gina before kissing her on the cheek. "I was afraid you might not come."

Gina walked in. "Why would you think that?"

"Well, you hopped up kind of suddenly Sunday and you've been working since."

"Does that mean you've been thinking about me?"

"Of course I've been thinking about you."

Gina reached for the front of Angel's shirt and pulled her in for a hot, wet kiss. She released her and walked around to sit on the couch.

Angel knew she had a silly smile on her face as she joined her.

Gina smiled. "It's been a crazy week. I have those sometimes. But you worked late every night this week, too."

"That's because I didn't have anything else to do."

"Oh really," Gina said, smirking. "I'm not the one that runs away."

"How do I know that?" Angel said, her brows raised playfully.

"I'm the one that came to your work, if you'll remember, and I'm also the one that sort of wiggled my way into you showing me your apartment," Gina explained.

"Yeah, but I thought you were just trying to be my friend."

"I am your friend," Gina said softly.

That soft voice and those rich brown eyes ignited a fire in Angel's chest. She moved closer. "Just so you know, I'm not going anywhere." She started the kiss slow and soft and then it quickly became full of fire as arms pulled each other closer and Gina moaned.

When they took a moment to breathe Angel said, "We don't have to see the statue today."

Gina leaned her head back on the couch and a low chuckle left her throat.

Angel was about to lean in and taste her beautiful neck when Gina sat up.

"No, we're going. You've always wanted to do this. I'm looking forward to exploring with you," she said with a gentle smile. She put her hands on both sides of Angel's face. "But we don't have to go right this minute," she said, capturing Angel's lips with her own.

Angel deepened the kiss and decided she could do this all day long.

Eventually Gina pushed her away. "Stop," she said, panting. She put her forehead on Angel's and said, "It's not that I don't like this because I really, really do. But we have a lady waiting on us."

Angel laughed and shook her head. She got up and reached her hand to Gina. "We can't keep her waiting."

They left Angel's apartment and made their way to Battery Park to catch the ferry. All of a sudden Gina grabbed Angel's arm. "Look! We have to have a knish." She led them over to a street vendor that sold hot dogs as well as knishes. "Have you had one?" Gina asked Angel.

"I haven't. I don't really know what that is," she said tentatively.

"You'll love it," Gina said as she turned to the vendor and paid for two knishes and a drink. Then she led them to a bench where they sat and unwrapped the baked treat.

Angel looked at hers and then at Gina.

Gina chuckled. "It's like a little burrito filled with mashed potatoes. Take a bite, you'll see." Gina encouraged her with a nod and a smile.

Angel took a small bite and as she chewed, the silkiness of the potato surrounded by the dough invaded her mouth with flavor. She looked over at Gina as her eyes grew bigger.

"I told you. It's good, isn't it?" Gina said as she bit into hers.

After swallowing Angel said, "I was not expecting that! It's so good. This dough is so light and the potatoes are seasoned perfectly."

Gina chuckled between bites. "You weren't expecting that from a street vendor, huh?"

Angel laughed. "I wasn't. But I should know better. Street vendors have been around forever."

They finished their treats and shared the drink. As they got up to throw their trash away it was their turn to board the ferry.

"Let's go upstairs," Gina suggested. They found the stairs and walked up to the top deck and went outside. The wind was brisk but not too bad as they stood next to the rail watching the Statue of Liberty get bigger. Angel stepped behind Gina and put her arm around her middle, pulling her close. She rested her chin on Gina's shoulder as they looked out over the water. She felt Gina lean back into her and she fit perfectly.

Angel could tell Gina was getting cold so she took her hand and led them back inside. The ferry wasn't full so they had their choice of seats. They sat down and Angel cradled Gina's hand between both of hers.

"It was getting chilly out there," Angel said, explaining their move.

"You want to walk to the crown, right?" Gina asked.

Angel looked at her, torn between asking if she felt up to it, thus breaking her promise not to mention her health. But she didn't want Gina to do this just for her and threaten her health.

Gina raised her eyebrows, waiting for an answer to her question.

Angel relaxed and said, "I know you're a smart person and wouldn't do this if it could have an adverse affect on you."

"That's right," Gina said plainly.

Why did Angel want to kiss her right now? She looked around and then did just that. She placed her lips on Gina's and she didn't pull away. Angel could still taste the flavor of the knish and smiled into Gina's lips.

"What was that for?" she asked.

Angel eyes widened and she shrugged her shoulders. "I just had to kiss you."

Gina grinned and then said a little shyly, "Feel free to do that anytime."

"I think I appreciate the fact that you wouldn't do something harmful to yourself just so I could have an experience. That means a lot to me."

"But it's not entirely true."

"What do you mean?"

"I told you earlier, I really wanted to do this with you. I want to see Lady Liberty through your eyes. I've never wanted to do that before. So it's important to me that you get the full experience. If I didn't think I could do everything, I would ask you to wait until I could. That's a bit selfish, isn't it?"

"I don't think so," said Angel. "It's thoughtful and it's telling me that you care."

Gina gazed into Angel's eyes tenderly. "I do care," she whispered. Her hand stroked Angel's face and their lips were about to meet when the ferry horn sounded, indicating they were preparing to dock. They both jumped and then laughed.

Once off the ferry they walked past the gift shop, café, and information center.

"I have tickets so we can go up in the pedestal and then walk up the steps to the crown."

"You do? I had no idea you had to have tickets."

"Stick with me, sweetheart," Gina said playfully, grabbing her hand as they walked up to the screening area.

They made it through security and then began the climb.

"I wanted to do this first because I was afraid we'd have to wait, but this line isn't bad at all. I can't believe there aren't more people here since the weather is so nice," Gina said.

The two made the steady climb up and when it was their turn they walked through the crown, stopping to look out at the skyline and harbor.

"That was cool even though it was brief," Angel said as they started back down.

"I know, but you can say you did it and that's something."

Angel agreed, but as she followed Gina and looked down on her rich auburn hair as it bounced around her shoulders, what mattered to her was that she'd done this with Gina.

She was quickly realizing that Gina Gray was something special. Angel smiled to herself because she'd known this all along, but that unwavering habit of guarding her heart wouldn't let her feel it. Not anymore. Gina had started opening Angel's heart the first night she met her and every time they were together, she pried it open that much more.

When they got back down, Angel led them into the restroom and looked around. Surprisingly no one else was in there. She gave Gina a flirtatious look and pulled them both into a stall. Her lips found Gina's instantly and she kissed her with purpose and passion. She slipped her tongue in Gina's mouth and moaned quietly. Gina pulled her closer and Angel could feel both their hearts speed up.

Angel pulled away and said quietly, "Lesbian perk #7, sneaking into the same bathroom stall for a much needed kiss."

They heard the door open and both froze, their eyes wide. Angel covered Gina's mouth with her own to stifle a laugh. When they heard the person enter a stall further down, Angel pulled back and unlocked their stall door.

They walked in front of the sinks and looked in the mirror. Gina put her hand over her mouth and headed for the door. They burst through to the hallway, both laughing.

"I don't know why we're acting this way, we didn't do anything wrong," Gina said, still giggling.

"There was absolutely nothing wrong with that kiss!" Angel exclaimed.

Fits of laughter overtook them again as they made their way to the museum. Later they walked the grounds and went to the gift shop. Gina bought Angel one of the small replicas of the statue.

"You didn't have to do that," Angel said, holding the sack with the statue and refrigerator magnets inside.

"I most certainly did. You need one of these. And now we both have magnets for our fridges. We may turn into New Yorkers yet," Gina teased.

"I don't see that happening," Angel said, squinting her eyes and wrinkling her nose.

"Nah, me neither," Gina agreed. "Let's get a drink," she suggested as they left the gift shop and entered the café.

They sat together sipping their drinks, looking out over the water to New Jersey.

"This has been the best day." Angel sighed.

"Has it? I'm so glad you enjoyed it," Gina said, sounding pleased.

"The best part is because I've spent the day with you," Angel said, gazing into Gina's eyes.

"If I didn't know better I'd say that hole in your heart is filling up," Gina said carefully.

"You could be right since you seem to see right through to the middle of it."

"Do I? Just as you see right through to mine?"

Angel stared and waited for Gina to continue, seeing she wanted to share something.

"Shannon, Travis, and I have exhausted our joint friends network and didn't find a match," she said, a bit defeated. "So the next step is for me to reach out to a group of friends I volunteer with and my work friends. They are going to reach out to more of their work friends that weren't at the party."

"When did Travis and Shannon get tested?"

"A long time ago. Shannon got tested when we were in college. She's been ready to be my donor since we met," she said, chuckling. "Unfortunately she doesn't match. Travis doesn't either. It wasn't long after they started dating that he got tested."

"I've wondered about that and didn't want to pry," Angel said.

Gina reached for her hand. "It's okay to ask questions. The reason I could do all of this today is because I'm on a new medication. I don't get as tired. We'll see how I feel tomorrow." Gina looked down at their hands.

Angel tipped Gina's chin upward. She pointed to her own eyes. "Look at me," she said softly. Then she smiled and her eyes crinkled. "I get tired, too. And when that happens, I like to laze around on my couch and watch a movie. Sometimes I even fall asleep."

Gina smiled back. "Is that an invitation?"

"It certainly is." Angel couldn't think of anything she'd rather do than enjoy a lazy Sunday with Gina.

"You seem to have a way that brightens me up."

"There's nothing wrong with feeling down, it happens. But I've noticed when I'm with you there is no down, it's all up. So if I brighten you it's because you've taken me there."

Gina narrowed her eyes. "Oh no, you've got charm too." Gina threw her arms around Angel's neck and hugged her. "You are my New Year's angel." she said quietly into Angel's hair.

Angel hoped so.

The ferry sounded the horn, announcing it was time to board. They walked hand in hand to the top deck once again and gazed at Manhattan as the ferry prepared to leave.

Angel had such a good time, but suddenly it dawned on her that Gina hadn't asked her to get tested. She couldn't help but wonder why.

12

Gina cuddled into Angel a little deeper. They'd watched a movie and now napped on Angel's comfy couch. Gina was tired today, but for her it was a good kind of tired. She knew it was the result of a wonderful day yesterday with Angel, exploring the Statue of Liberty. She smiled into Angel's chest, recalling how she'd swept her into the bathroom stall and kissed her thoroughly.

Since that first kiss it felt like Angel's heart had opened and let Gina in. She could hear it beating and imagined the scars it carried. She hoped that maybe spending time together had caused them to fade. Angel had certainly changed Gina's life. She no longer had the burden of the kidney transplant playing in the back of her mind. Angel made it seem like a certainty; it was simply a matter of when.

So instead of worrying about her kidneys, now she thought of things they could do together under the cloak of making their lives less boring. What they both wanted was to just spend time together; maybe they were trying to fool both of their hearts. Whatever it was, Gina was happy that neither of them were running away; it felt more like they were strolling forward. Gina wanted to believe it was to something joyous, but fear kept her from wanting too much.

They still had her health and Angel's fear of commitment to overcome.

Angel stirred and mumbled, "I can feel the thoughts whirling through your brain." She yawned and tightened her arms around Gina. "I thought you were tired."

Gina raised her head. "I am, but I couldn't stop listening to your heartbeat."

"Oh," Angel said, now obviously awake. "And what was it saying?"

"You don't know?" Gina said, unsure, propping her head on her hand.

Angel smiled at her. "Remember the night we met, when I told you my heart felt like it had a hole in it?"

Gina nodded.

"Well, it felt like it was empty. I'm not an unhappy person, but as you know I'm very cautious. You said yesterday that you thought the hole was smaller. That's not exactly true because even if the hole is gone it could still be empty inside."

"Okay," Gina said, drawing the word out, waiting for her to finish.

"But my heart fills up a little each time I'm with you. It doesn't feel as empty and it can *feel* again. Does that make sense?"

Gina smiled and nodded. "It does. What does it feel?"

"Right now it feels content holding you like this."

Gina leaned in and kissed Angel gently. "What does it feel now?"

Angel's brow furrowed. "I'm not quite sure. Maybe you should do that again."

Gina sat up and straddled Angel. She looked down at her with one eyebrow cocked. Then she crashed her lips into Angel's and her tongue explored all of her mouth. Angel moaned and Gina kissed her harder. She raised up and said, "How about now?"

Angel's eyes had fire in them. "It feels like it's going to explode if you don't do that again," she said, panting.

Gina was about to bring their lips together again when her phone began to ring on the table. She gazed over and could see it was Shannon. She reached for it, but not before she kissed Angel quickly.

"Hey Shan," she said.

"Hi GG. I'm at your apartment, where are you?"

"You are? I'm at Angel's, watching a movie," she said, getting off Angel and sitting on the edge of the couch, winking at her.

"Oh yeah? Is there something you need to tell me?" Shannon probed.

"Not right now," Gina said in a sing-song voice.

Shannon laughed.

"I'll call you when I get home."

"Can't wait," Shannon said. "Tell Angel hi for me."

"I will. Bye," Gina said, ending the call.

Angel was sitting next to Gina now. She bumped shoulders with Gina and said, "My heart is full of happiness, but my stomach is empty. Are you hungry?"

Gina bumped her shoulder back. "I am a little hungry."

"How about pizza?"

"Sounds good. What kind?"

"Your choice?"

"Anchovies and onions," Gina said, trying not to smile.

Angel looked at her, eyes wide. "Seriously?"

"No!" Gina laughed. "Do you like pepperoni?"

"Yes," Angel said, relieved.

"Someone told me if you like pineapple on a pizza that it's even better with pepperoni. Wanna try it?"

"Let's do it," Angel said, grabbing her phone and placing the order at a nearby pizza place.

It wasn't long until the pizza arrived. Angel already had plates out and drinks for them both.

Gina reached for a piece and took a bite before setting it on her plate. "Mmm, this is good."

Angel did the same and began nodding. "This *is* good. I'm glad we tried it."

"Me too," Gina said, taking another bit. "You know what else I'm glad we tried?"

"What's that?"

"This," Gina said, leaning over and kissing Angel on the lips.

"Me too."

While eating the pizza they talked about yesterday and their visit to the statue. Then they talked about their upcoming week and finally it was time for Gina to go home.

She put her coat on and got her bag.

Angel walked her to the elevator and grabbed the lapels of her coat. She gave her a big smile and kissed her softly. "I'm so glad you came over today."

"I am too. This was the best Sunday I've had in a very long time."

The elevator dinged and the doors opened. Angel gave her one more kiss and then Gina stepped on the elevator.

At the last minute Angel jumped on with her.

"What are you doing?" Gina exclaimed.

"I'm riding down with you to make sure your ride is there."

Gina smiled and grabbed Angel's hand and squeezed.

When they walked off the elevator Gina saw a car at the curb. It was her Uber. She stopped Angel from walking out with her. "You don't have a coat on. I'll text you when I get home," she said, kissing her one more time.

Angel waited and watched her drive away. Her heart was full. She knew what it was, but couldn't admit it just yet.

* * *

Gina walked into her apartment, threw her coat on a chair and put her purse down. She smiled, thinking about her afternoon and her ride home from Angel's. The Uber driver had commented on how she smiled the entire drive to her apartment. He said something like whoever she'd spent the day with was worth keeping if they put that smile on her face and it lasted that long. Gina had to agree.

She texted Angel that she'd made it home and sat down to call Shannon.

"Hey, GG. I have been patiently waiting all afternoon for you to call."

Gina chuckled. "Why is that?"

"Don't be coy with me. You know exactly what I'm talking about. I'm guessing the trip to the statue was great. And…" Shannon squealed into the phone. "Oh my God, you didn't spend the night, did you?"

Gina laughed. "No, I didn't spend the night!" She stopped for a moment, wondering what it would feel like to wake up next to Angel. She quickly shook her head. "We did have a great time yesterday. But I should back up a little."

"Have you been holding out on me?" Shannon asked.

"Not really. I was busy last week if you'll remember."

"I do, so was I. What was going on? Travis worked late, too. Anyway, continue please."

Gina grinned. "Well, do you remember last Sunday Angel and I were meeting for coffee?"

"Yep."

"We met at a little park near her place and then she gave me a tour. You should see her apartment, Shan. It has this one wall that is all windows. It's so beautiful. The whole place is so sleek and contemporary."

"Not surprised. I'm sure she's loaded; Travis said they were lucky to get her."

"It's not that, Shannon. It's really a cool place and feels like her."

"So why don't you tell me what you mean? Give me details!"

Gina exhaled into the phone, feeling a bit defensive. "You know I don't care about how much money she makes."

"Yes, I know that. But I can tell you care about her and that means something to me!"

"Slow down." She chuckled. "I like her, Shan, a lot. It's kind of snuck up on me, but I'm not denying it."

"What happened?"

Gina sighed. "It's like she's opened her heart to me. You know how I always feel like someone is trying to take care of me."

"Yes. It's not always true, but that's what you see."

"I feel like I'm caring for her. She's been hurt so deeply and won't let anyone get close to her heart, but somehow I have. So, I'm taking care of her instead of the other way around. And it feels so good."

"You sound happier than I've heard in a long time."

"I am. When she was showing me around her place I could feel something changing between us. I think it was there from the beginning but we were both scared, you know."

"I know exactly what you mean."

"I couldn't help thinking about what you said about it being okay to have a little fun."

"Oh my gosh, you actually listened to me."

"I did and you're right. We've been having fun."

"Oh really," Shannon said seductively.

"Not that much fun, yet." Gina chuckled.

"What are you waiting on?"

"It's new, Shannon. I don't want to scare her away by jumping into bed. Besides, I don't feel like it's a good idea to get so serious before I have the transplant. You know that."

"I know, but it doesn't mean I agree with it."

"I don't want to hurt her. She's been hurt enough."

"What? You're not going to hurt her, GG. Stop fighting it. Who knows, you may just fall in love."

Gina didn't say anything. Those feelings had been humming around quietly in her heart. She'd pushed them down and ignored them, but they were taking up more and more space, as well as getting louder.

"GG?"

"It's way too soon for that."

"When are you seeing her again?"

"I've got to go to the youth center one day this week to ask my fellow volunteers to get tested. I thought I'd ask her to go with me." When Angel told her about how empty her heart felt, she thought this might be a way to fill it. There was so much she had to offer these kids, especially those with parents like hers.

"I've got a list that I'm starting on this week at my work. We'll find you a donor. Don't worry."

"I'm not worried yet. This new medicine has made a difference for now. I don't get nearly as tired as I did."

"So I'm thinking you and I need to surprise Travis and Angel at work one of these days."

"That's a great idea."

"Okay, let me know how it goes at the center and I'll check in with you on my list in a few days."

"Thanks, Shan. And thanks for doing this."

"Stop. You know I'm doing this because I'm selfish. I need you."

"I love you, too." With that Gina ended the call and sat back.

She replayed Shannon's words, 'stop fighting it and you may fall in love.' She understood why they called it falling now. Every time she was with Angel she did feel like she was falling and when their arms were around one another or their lips met, she felt anchored, secure, settled.

She wondered if Angel felt the same.

13

Gina finished her last email of the day and closed her laptop. She looked at her watch and saw she had plenty of time to change. Angel had texted her earlier and wanted to come over. She was a bit mysterious about it, but Gina didn't care. All that mattered to her was that she'd get to see Angel. Ever since her conversation with Shannon she couldn't get Angel out of her mind. What she really wondered was if Angel was having the same feelings.

She got up and was about to go into her bedroom when her phone pinged. It was Angel and she was here! Gina looked down at her favorite comfortable sweatshirt and yoga pants. She had on socks, but no shoes. Her finger hit the buzzer and let her in. Quickly she went to the bathroom and at least ran her fingers through her hair and smoothed it down some so it wasn't sticking out every which way.

As she walked into the living room she heard a quiet knock at the door. She took a deep breath and opened it a crack. She looked out with one eye and there was Angel dressed in a fitted suit. Her hair fell down to her shoulders, straight and sleek. She looked beautiful and handsome and all Gina wanted to do was grab her and kiss her.

"You do realize you're early," Gina said through the crack.

Angel eyebrows were raised and her expression went from surprise to amusement. "I thought that would be a good thing."

"I worked from home today and was just about to change."

"Oh," Angel said, staring at Gina's one eye. "It doesn't matter what you're wearing."

"You have no idea how good you look right now, do you?" Gina said, looking her up and down.

"Can I please come in so you can show me?"

Gina smiled and opened the door a little wider so Angel could see her face. "That was a very good answer."

Angel chuckled. "But it was a question."

Gina opened the door so Angel could step inside.

She looked Gina up and down. "You do realize that is what I would be wearing had I worked from home."

Gina smiled. She didn't care what she was wearing now that Angel was here. She grabbed her hands and pulled her into the room. They both sat on the couch, still holding hands.

"Thanks for letting me come over," Angel said, leaning in and kissing Gina softly.

"I'm glad you're here."

Angel sat back and said, "Have you heard of Montauk Point out on Long Island?"

"Sure, there's a lighthouse at the end of the island."

"You can ride the train out to it. I was checking and wondered if you'd want to ride the train with me. We could explore the point and then catch the train back. It'll be a full day, but I love lighthouses and would like to see it."

"I love lighthouses too. When I was a kid I wanted to live in one," Gina said, laughing at herself. "I'd love to do that with you."

Angel gave her a big smile. "Good. I know it's winter, but it's supposed to be nice again this weekend."

Gina looked at her, surprised. "You want to go this Saturday?"

"Do you have plans? Whenever would be good for you is fine," Angel said quickly.

"No, I don't have plans. Saturday would be great."

"You're surprised I came up with an idea, aren't you?" Angel said, proud of herself.

"Not surprised—happy." Maybe Angel did feel something, too.

Angel sat back on the couch looking comfortable.

Gina remembered what Angel said about her place feeling homey. "You're staying for dinner, right? I can make us something or we can order."

"I'd like that."

Gina eyed Angel, thinking how relaxed she looked and how she belonged there.

"What?" Angel asked as Gina stared.

"You look kind of cozy."

Angel smiled shyly. "I've felt a little lonely today. But not anymore since I'm here with you."

Gina tilted her head and eased closer. When her lips hovered over Angel's she said, "You're welcome here anytime." Then she pressed her lips to Angel's. Her heart immediately began thumping in her chest. Angel's lips were so soft and kissable. But when Gina touched her tongue to Angel's she felt electricity zap through her and down to her core.

Angel wrapped her arms around Gina and pulled her closer. They were both breathing hard and fast as the kiss went on and on.

Gina pulled back, panting. She looked at Angel's darkened eyes and could see want. She wanted Angel too, but mostly she wanted to chase the loneliness from her heart. Gina slowly got up from the couch and reached out her hand to Angel. She took it and stood up.

Gina turned around and led them into the hall and then to her bedroom. She turned around and saw Angel taking the room in. She gazed over at Gina's bookcase, then turned and looked around the neat room.

Angel gently ran her thumb along Gina's cheek. "This is exactly how I pictured your bedroom," she said softly.

"It is?"

"Yes, it's beautiful, like you. But there's an electricity sparking around this room."

"I feel it," Gina whispered. She stared into her eyes as she reached up and gently eased Angel's blazer off her shoulders. She briefly looked down then back into Angel's eyes as she unbuttoned her shirt. Her hands reached up and pulled the shirt from her shoulders, but trapped her arms behind her. She pulled Angel into her chest with the shirt and looked at her lips and back to her eyes. She nibbled at Angel's lower lip and could taste desire as her tongue slipped inside Angel's mouth.

Gina had to slow down, but she couldn't remember wanting someone like this, almost desperately. She pulled back and Angel pulled her shirt tail from her pants and let the shirt fall to the floor.

Gina smiled at the tan bra with a touch of lace at the top, nestled against Angel's bronze skin. She started to bring her finger up to trace right above the lace, but Angel grabbed the bottom of her sweatshirt and pulled it over her head.

A smile grew on Angel's face as she saw that Gina wasn't wearing a bra.

Gina shrugged slightly, but then her hands quickly went to Angel's pants. She stopped to look back into her eyes, suddenly needing affirmation that this is what she wanted. Was this just sex or would Angel let her into her heart? Gina realized it mattered to her. She didn't want to be just sex to Angel.

Angel's face softened as if she'd read Gina's thoughts. "Fill my heart, Gina," she breathed.

Gina stopped unbuttoning her pants and cradled Angel's face with her hands. She slowly and tenderly brought their lips together. In this kiss she poured respect, affection, friendship, and healing into Angel. But then they couldn't stop the passion and lust as the kiss ignited into more.

They quickly removed the rest of their clothes and faced one another as they lay on the bed. Gina stroked Angel's cheek and gazed into her eyes. "I want you. All of you," she said softly. She slowly rolled on top of Angel and fit right between her legs. Their lips met in one of the most passionate kisses Gina had ever tasted. It was rushed and then languid, hard and then soft, Angel's tongue bathing

Gina's mouth before Gina's did the same. Nothing else existed but this kiss.

Gina felt Angel open her legs wider as her hands stroked up and down her back. Gina began to move her hips to the same rhythm of Angel's hands. Oh it felt so good. Slow and steady and so sensual.

But Gina couldn't wait any longer to taste every inch of Angel's brown body. She started at her neck and nuzzled and nipped. She licked and sucked and then kissed lower and lower until she circled one of Angel's darkened nipples that was pebble hard. She couldn't resist taking it into her teeth and biting down gently. Angel gasped and her hands went to Gina's head.

"Oh yes, Gina. That feels so good," she purred.

Gina kissed her way to Angel's other nipple and gave it the same attention. And then she put her lips where she could feel Angel's beating heart. She sucked on her skin, imagining drawing the loneliness out of Angel's heart and then she laid kiss after tender kiss over the spot, filling Angel's heart with all she had. It couldn't be love, no, it was too soon for that. But it was tenderness and like and affection.

Angel moaned and if nothing else Gina knew she was filling her with pleasure. She replaced her lips with her hands on Angel's breast and continued her descent. She kissed Angel's stomach and gently ran her tongue over Angel's hip. She heard Angel gasp and smiled against her warm skin.

"You like that, huh?"

"Very much," Angel gasped again.

Gina knew she was going to like this even more. She'd made it between Angel's legs. She ran her hands down either side of Angel's body and down along her outer thighs. Angel bent her knees and Gina ran her hands up her inner thighs and spread her legs a little more. She looked up at Angel, knowing she was in a vulnerable position. All she wanted to do was reassure her.

"You are so incredible," she said, peering into Angel's eyes. "Let me show you."

Angel barely nodded her head.

Gina leaned down and breathed in Angel's aromatic scent. She couldn't wait to taste her, so she ran her tongue from Angel's opening up and through her folds. This was the most wonderful taste of sharp and tangy goodness. She moaned as she lavished Angel up and down and around. Angel moaned right along with her.

"Oh Angel," Gina said, glancing up to look at her quickly. Then she put her head down and took Angel's clit in her mouth and sucked.

"Oh my God, Gina. Yes!" Angel exclaimed.

Gina wanted more. She circled Angel's opening with her finger as she did the same to her clit with her tongue. She gently pushed her finger inside and Angel's hips bucked. Gina could feel Angel's velvety softness and moaned into her clit.

"Gina," she gasped.

This sparked Gina on even more. She could feel her own wetness, but pushed another finger inside Angel as she sucked her clit into her mouth again. Her other arm was wrapped under and around Angel's leg, holding her in place. She began a rhythm of in and out and thought she might come right there. But Angel was who mattered right then. Sweet, scarred Angel who had opened herself to Gina even though she was afraid.

Gina continued her rhythm and sucked even harder as Angel moaned and panted.

"Oh Gina, Gina, Gina," she screamed as she came undone.

Gina felt Angel stiffen and held her fingers in deep. She slowly made her way up Angel's body. She felt Angel's arms encircle her and hold her close.

"My God, Gina," she breathed out.

Gina was elated and raised her head and smiled.

"You look very pleased with yourself," Angel said.

Gina chuckled. "You look pleased."

"Oh no. You don't get to have all the fun," Angel said, leaning up to kiss Gina.

As much as Gina wanted it to last, she knew when Angel touched her she'd explode. Angel opening herself and trusting Gina was such a turn on it had every nerve in her body buzzing.

Angel rolled Gina over and gazed down at her. "How did you make me feel like that?"

"Like what?" Gina said seductively.

"Cared for, adored."

"Is that what you felt? I hope so."

"I did, Gina."

"That's so much better than lonely. Isn't it?"

"I'm about to show you how much better it feels."

Gina put her arms around Angel's neck as their lips met. Oh God this felt good.

Somehow Angel knew just how close Gina was to a spectacular orgasm. She took her just to the edge and brought her back, again and again. It was luscious and it was frustrating. But then Angel would do it again and it felt so good. She used her fingers, she used her tongue, she used words, she used sounds, and then she looked at her. The orgasm began to build, but when Angel looked at her then kissed her, it was all over. She fell over the edge and held on for the most amazing pleasure to wash over her. Now her body was humming with contentment.

"Why are we just now doing this?" she said, exhaling, her body all warm and loose.

"I wondered the same thing," Angel said.

They looked at one another and started giggling and then laughing.

"I'm so glad you came over," Gina said, cuddling Angel to her chest.

"So am I," she said happily.

14

Angel knocked lightly on Travis's open door.

"Come in," he said, looking up and then smiling when he saw it was Angel. "Hey Angel. What's up?"

Angel smiled tentatively. "I wanted to ask you how the project for Gina's kidney was coming along."

It was late in the day and Angel knew Travis was just about ready to go home. "If you've got a minute I'll show you. I'm open to any suggestions. I really thought I'd have her a donor by now, but we haven't even found a match." Travis clicked on a spreadsheet that was full of names and columns.

Angel walked around his desk and looked at the monitor.

"I have their names, when they were tested and the results," he said, explaining the sheet. "I also have them grouped where they came from, like here are Shannon's work people, our friends, Gina's friends. You get the idea."

Angel nodded as she scanned the list.

"We've got to get the word out to more people. The more we have tested, obviously the more likely we'll find a match."

"But you're not sure that if you find a match they'll be willing to donate," Angel stated.

"Oh, I get that, but finding a match is the first step. And I really thought I'd have a match or two by now."

"Gina mentioned asking another group of friends. I'm sorry, but the only people I know work here," Angel said, sounding dejected.

"You and Gina have become friends," Travis stated.

"We have," Angel said, not able to keep from smiling.

Travis grinned. "We haven't known one another long, but your face sure lights up when you talk about her."

Angel looked down shyly and then looked back at Travis. She liked Travis and could tell he was a good guy that cared for Gina. "I really like her."

He continued to smile. "You've changed over the last month or so."

"I have," she said, knowing what he said was true.

"You seem happier."

"She has a way of looking inside you and at first it was a bit unnerving," Angel explained.

"But then you feel safe," Travis asked.

"Yeah, she makes it easy to trust her. Does that make sense?"

"Yes. It's as if she's caring for you instead of you having to care for her. I think she does it and doesn't even realize she's doing it," Travis explained.

"Do you think it's because of her situation, her health?"

"Not necessarily. She has been sick a long time and there are days when she needs help, but I think..." Travis hesitated.

Angel looked at him expectantly. "You think?"

"I don't want to overstep."

"You're not. I thought we'd become friends?"

Travis smiled. "I think the same."

"What were you going to say?"

"I think she sees you as a kindred spirit of sorts. You've both been through some tough times."

"True."

"She is so adamant about someone not having to take care of her that she can't see that's what two people do in a relationship. Well, a good relationship. You nurture one another. I know for Shannon and me, some days she takes care of me, some days I care for her. It's so varied and depends on what's happening in our lives."

"It's surprised me how easy it is to trust her. Or maybe it's how easily I have trusted her. I don't do that."

"I know. I can tell," Travis said, chuckling. "But let me say, you can trust Gina. She and Shannon are the best people I know. They are fiercely independent, but they love completely. In the last few years though I think that's changed for Gina."

"How so?"

"The progression of this disease has made her more cautious. She'll love you completely, but may not let you do the same."

"Is that why she's alone?"

"Maybe. I think she hasn't met anyone that challenges her."

Confused, Angel looked at Travis.

"What I mean is, being with her obviously comes with her health issues, and she doesn't want that to be the center of attention. I think she wants to be challenged, to give all of herself to someone. Shannon and I have talked about this at length."

"You have?"

"Yes, we want her to be happy, but she makes it hard. She doesn't want to be a burden and whomever she ends up with will have to show her she isn't. And the way her mindset is right now... I don't know how you do that."

Angel nodded, her brow furrowed in thought.

"I don't know why I'm telling you all of this. Unless..." Travis didn't finish.

Angel looked up. "Look Travis, all of this is happening quite fast for me. I'd convinced myself that I'd always be alone. And Gina has swooped in and shown me that may not be the case." Angel studied him and then decided to continue. "I think about her all the time!"

A big smile grew on Travis's face.

"The interesting part is that I don't think about her kidney transplant or about what happens if she can't find a donor. I don't see her that way."

Travis narrowed his eyes. "You do know it's inevitable. She's going to have to have it or go on dialysis."

"Yes, I know. I understand that," Angel said assuredly. "But I also know she'll get the transplant. I've felt it all along. You'll find her donor."

Travis sat up. "I certainly like your confidence. And I'm going to trust it because I know your exceptionally bright, analytical mind wouldn't let you say that if it wasn't true."

"I'm not so sure it's my mind that has the confidence," Angel muttered.

"Uh oh. Gina's gotten into your heart."

Angel looked resigned. Travis was right, Gina Gray was in her heart.

"You're not disputing it. So what are you thinking?"

Angel sighed. "You're right, she's in my heart. The question is: how do I get in hers?"

Travis nodded, clearly wondering the same thing.

*   *   *

"It's going to be a beautiful day," Angel said, looking out the window of the train.

Gina leaned over to see what she was looking at and saw the city whizzing by. "It already is a beautiful day from where I'm sitting," she said, looking at Angel.

Angel met her eyes, realizing what she meant, and her cheeks reddened.

"Are you blushing?" Gina said rubbing her thumb along Angel's cheek.

Angel's heart skipped a beat at Gina's touch. She had been looking forward to this all week. Her imagination had been running wild, picturing them walking hand in hand on the beach, exploring the lighthouse and surrounding area, stealing kisses and laughter, lots of laughter. She decided this was a good time to steal one of those kisses and leaned in, touching her lips to Gina's. These little kisses could quickly turn into more, making them both hot messes, and she looked forward to it.

Gina pulled back, smiling at Angel. "Have you got an idea of what you want to do today?"

Angel smiled with friskiness in her eyes. "I know exactly what I'd like to do when we get back, but I know you don't mean that."

Gina giggled. "Now you're trying to make *my* cheeks red, but it's good to know we're on the same page," she said, looking at Angel boldly.

The fire inside Angel simmered. It had been there since leaving Gina's the other night. She looked at Gina and thought she saw the same thing in her eyes. This trip may not last as long as she'd planned.

"Stop looking at me like that or we may end up in the restroom again," Gina said, her eyebrows raised.

Angel chuckled. "We could join the mile post club."

"The what?"

"The mile post club. You've heard of the mile high club on planes. The mile post club is for trains," Angel explained.

Gina narrowed her eyes. "Are you making that up?"

Angel laughed. "I promise I'm not. A couple of friends told me about it in Spain. We rode the train a lot to different places on the weekend."

"Hmm, that might be a fun club to be in," Gina said, wiggling her eyebrows.

They both laughed, then sat back and watched as the city changed to towns.

"Hey, I was wondering," Gina said, reaching for Angel's hand and holding it in her lap. "I'm going to ask another group of friends if they'd get tested and wondered if you'd go with me. I volunteer at an LGBTQ+ youth center, and the director and other volunteers are friends."

"Sure. I'd love to go."

"I was thinking about what you told me before about your heart being empty. I don't know how you feel about volunteering, but I think with your history and past experience with youth groups that you'd have a lot to offer these kids. That could fill your heart."

Angel hadn't really thought about it, but maybe she could help. "You think I'd relate to them?"

"Yes!" Gina said emphatically. "There are lots of kids that have parent problems just like you did. Imagine the example for them when they see a successful woman who made it through that."

"But I don't know anything about counseling."

"They have counselors that do that part. You simply listen, tell your story, and hang out."

"Is that what you do?"

"I'm one of the lucky ones who has accepting parents, but I can empathize with feeling different."

"I'd love to help, if I can."

"Oh good," Gina said, turning toward her and still grasping her hand. "If you don't like it that's fine too. Volunteering isn't for everybody. No pressure."

Angel beamed at Gina. She wondered when a heart was full, where did the extra go? Gina Gray was filling her heart and she had no doubt it would be overflowing before she was finished.

15

Gina and Angel trekked up the sidewalk to the Montauk Point lighthouse. The weather was cooperating. The sun was shining and of course it was windy on the point.

"Let's tour the lighthouse first and then the other buildings," Angel said as they walked uphill.

"I'm surprised there aren't more people around," Gina said.

"Me too. Maybe it's because it's winter," Angel said, looking at Gina sideways. "Can you imagine coming here in the spring or summer?"

"Maybe this is the time to come and people just don't know it."

"We're about to find out," Angel said, opening the door for them to enter.

A park attendant took their tickets and gave them a little history and a map. They asked about the lack of visitors and sure enough, winter kept people away. He explained that there were only two other people there and they had already been in the lighthouse.

"Let's go to the top then," Gina said, excited.

They decided to come back through the exhibits that included the Keeper's quarters, communications room, and oil room. Step by step they walked to the top.

"There aren't near as many steps as last weekend," Angel said, leading them to the top.

"We can take the time to look out since there isn't anyone behind us," Gina added.

"Oh Gina, look," Angel said as she looked out over the water.

"It's beautiful!"

"You can see where the ocean meets the sound. Look how the water is flowing," Angel pointed out.

Gina walked up next to Angel and put her arm around her waist. She rested her head on her shoulder and sighed. "Can you imagine the views at sunrise?"

"Or during a storm?"

Angel turned to Gina and looked into her eyes. "Thanks for doing this with me." She took Gina's face in her hands and touched their lips together. A spark flew through her and spread over her body. Gina parted her lips slightly and Angel slid her tongue inside. When their tongues met they both forgot where they were. Angel's tongue swirled and caressed as she could hear her heartbeat throbbing in her ears. Gina pushed back and danced her tongue into Angel's mouth, claiming it as hers.

When they pulled back panting, Gina's eyes were gleaming and Angel knew she'd felt that spark too. "This sea air is intoxicating," Angel whispered.

"I don't think it's the air," Gina whispered back, her arms around Angel's waist keeping her close.

Angel rested her forehead on Gina's, closed her eyes and exhaled, then she opened them again. She quickly kissed Gina's lips and pulled away. "Let's see what we missed downstairs."

Gina winked at her and led the way. At the bottom of the stairs there was a small public restroom. She reached back and grabbed Angel's hand and pulled them inside. When the door closed Gina locked it. She turned around and Angel pinned her against the door. Gina gasped, but couldn't stop the smile spreading across her face or the fire shining in her eyes.

Angel's chest was heaving. Hearing that door lock had turned the fire inside her into a roaring inferno. She crushed her lips to Gina's, inducing a moan. Her hand was under Gina's shirt before she could even think. She cupped Gina's breast and could feel her hardened nipple through her bra. "Gina," she whispered.

Her other hand slid into the waistband of Gina's leggings and inched lower and lower. Their lips were still pressed together and they were both breathing hard by now.

Gina tore her lips away and softly moaned, "Yes."

That's all Angel needed to hear. She began kissing Gina's neck and nibbling her earlobe as her finger was met by the most glorious wetness.

"Good God, Angel," Gina gasped.

As much as Angel wanted to take her time this wasn't the place. She slid two fingers inside Gina and flattened her palm against her throbbing clit. She covered Gina's mouth with her own, swallowing a loud groan.

Then she started a brisk steady rhythm and whispered in Gina's ear, "You are so fucking amazing."

Gina's response was immediate. Angel felt her walls tighten around her fingers and she pushed deeper.

That's all Gina needed as she pulled Angel's lips to hers and growled her climax into her mouth.

She pulled away, panting, and then looked into Angel's eyes, shaking her head. "Wow," she said, exhaling, her head hitting the door behind her.

Angel gently removed her hand. "What are you doing to me?"

"Uh, excuse me? I think you are the one that pushed me against this door," Gina said, smirking. She walked into the one stall to clean up and Angel walked over to the sink to wash her hands.

When Gina walked out she was grinning. "I think we have a problem with public restrooms."

Angel looked at her, relieved, and smiled. "I think you're right."

They unlocked the door and stuck their heads out and looked around. There was no one in sight.

Gina reached for Angel's hand and they walked out to explore the rest of the Keeper's quarters.

"Let's get some lunch," Angel said after they'd seen the rest of the buildings around the lighthouse.

"I'm ready."

They ate at the Lighthouse Grill and talked about all they'd learned.

"Do you still want to live in a lighthouse?" Angel asked in between bites.

"That ship sailed," Gina said, laughing at her word choice. "A long time ago. But I do love the beach."

"Let's go walk along the beach below the lighthouse when we finish."

Gina nodded and continued eating. "I'm going to the restroom," she said, getting up. She pointed at Angel. "You stay right here." Her face was serious and then she winked.

Angel chuckled. *I'll never forget this day*, she thought.

* * *

Gina washed her hands and looked in the mirror. She smiled, thinking back to what they had done in the lighthouse restroom. Angel made her do things she'd never done before. Her face fell as the same dark thought swirled around the back of her mind. *I don't want her to have to take care of me.* She shook her head, trying to do the same to the darkness. This had been such a fun day and it wasn't near over.

When she walked out of the restroom Angel looked up at her and smiled. That smile, Gina thought; she could look at it forever.

She sat down and a couple with two little kids walked in. She noticed Angel watching the kids and smiling. Gina turned to get a better look.

"Aren't they cute?" Angel said softly. "Look how the older sister is helping the younger one."

"I imagine you did the same for your little brothers and sisters," Gina remarked, watching Angel.

Angel nodded. Still watching the kids she said, "Do you want kids?"

Gina sighed. "Sometimes I do and then I think about my health and it's unrealistic."

"No it's not," Angel said firmly. "After your transplant you're going to be a lot better."

"I hope so, but still. What about you? Do you want kids?" Gina said, wanting to get the focus off her.

"I used to, but as my life became more about work, that idea kind of faded away."

"That's changing, isn't it? You're not all about work anymore."

Angel looked at her and smiled.

Gina gazed into Angel's eyes and for just a moment imagined having kids with her. That couldn't happen though, not with her damn fucked up kidneys, she thought. She couldn't bear to look at Angel any longer and pretended to pick at her food.

"Hey, are you okay?" Angel asked, concern on her face.

Gina looked up and tried to smile. "Yeah, I'm fine."

The door to the cafe opened again, drawing Gina's attention. She saw a man helping a woman inside. She could tell they were married and looked to be long past retirement. The man held the woman's hand and had his arm around her waist as he led her to a table. He pulled a chair out and helped her sit down. Then he went to the counter and ordered for them both.

"Isn't that sweet," Angel said, watching the couple.

Gina didn't say anything. To her it was a look into the future. Someday, that could very well be her and someone would have to help her like that. Her stomach dropped and for a moment she thought she was going to be sick.

When it passed, she looked at Angel. She was still watching the older couple with a smile on her face. "Are you ready to go?"

"Sure," Angel said, gathering their trash and throwing it away. "Are you sure you're okay?"

"Yeah. I feel like I need some fresh air," Gina said, walking to the door.

They walked down the path to the beach. Angel reached for Gina's hand and entwined their fingers.

Gina squeezed Angel's hand, but couldn't stop the dread and doubt that had blanketed her since the restroom at the cafe. Her heart sped up and she could feel her face begin to burn with heat. Suddenly she felt overwhelmed and dropped Angel's hand and began to run. Tears burned her eyes and her chest heaved.

She could hear Angel calling her name and then she was in front of her, grabbing her upper arms, stopping her.

"Gina! What's wrong?" Angel yelled over the wind, fear in her voice.

Gina looked at Angel with tears stinging her eyes. "I can't do this, Angel."

"Can't do what?" Angel said, confused.

"This," Gina pointed between the two of them. "Us. I can't stick you with me!" she said, forlorn and distressed.

"What? Stick me? What are you talking about?"

"If we keep seeing one another I know what's going to happen and then you'll be stuck with me and I can't do that to you!"

Angel still held Gina's upper arms as she shook her head. "I won't be stuck with you. I choose you."

"What?" Gina said, looking just as confused as Angel had been moments ago.

"Right now, it's a choice and I choose you. If we wait until later down the road it won't be a choice anymore. I'll have to have you; have to be with you. I know that's where we're going so right now, don't feel guilty; you're not sticking me with you. I'm choosing you. That makes a difference." She had to shout over the wind.

"You're choosing me?" Gina asked as tears rolled down her cheeks..

"I'm choosing you!" she shouted again. Then Angel spun them around and yelled to the sky, "I choose Gina Gray!" She turned them to face the ocean and shouted, "I choose Gina Gray!"

Gina couldn't help the tears streaming down her face, but now they were happy tears. She shouted to the ocean, "She chooses me!"

Angel smiled through her own tears and kissed Gina hard. She pulled back and stared into Gina's eyes. "But what do you choose?"

Gina stared back and knew she had to be honest with Angel. "I want to be with you, but these thoughts are always in my head, sometimes louder than others."

"Then you need to choose to forget them. Give me a chance. Give us a chance. You don't know what's going to happen, neither do I. But Gina, you've changed something inside of me. You opened my heart and I don't want to close it off again."

Gina put her hand on the side of Angel's face. "It's not a choice for me. I'm already down the road. I have to have you. I pushed you away because I let you get too close."

"You have to have me," Angel said, smiling. "Those are the sweetest words I've ever heard."

"You think I've changed you. Well, you've changed me too. I haven't let anyone this close to my heart in years," Gina admitted.

Angel put her arms around Gina's waist and pulled her close so she wouldn't have to shout. "It seems to me that you want to take care of my heart, but not let me take care of yours."

"I do want to take care of your heart," Gina said.

"Then let me take care of yours!" Angel pleaded. "It's got to go both ways."

Gina put her arms around Angel's neck, narrowing her eyes as a grin grew on her face. "Would you hold my hand and help me walk into restaurants?" she said, referring to the couple in the cafe.

Angel smiled. "Yes, and I'll even order for the kids."

Gina's eyes widened. "The kids?"

Angel laughed. "How about we slow down and start with a real date?"

"A real date! We haven't done that."

"Exactly. How about next Friday?"

"I'd love to." Gina's face turned serious. "I'm sorry I ran away from you."

Angel's face softened. "Thanks for letting me catch you, but please don't do that again."

"I won't. I'll tell you what's going on in this fucked up brain of mine."

Angel let out a breath and pulled Gina close. They held one another tight as the wind whistled around them and the waves rushed to the shore.

They had said everything but the "L" word. Weeks ago Gina had told Angel she had to get the kidney transplant done before she would even consider a relationship. And Angel had told Gina she didn't do relationships because she wouldn't let her heart be hurt again. Yet, here they were as this relationship blossomed and they'd just promised to give it a chance to grow.

16

On the train back into the city, Angel sat cradling Gina's hand in her lap. Gina had her head on Angel's shoulder as they watched Long Island whiz by.

"Are you sleeping?" Angel asked quietly.

Gina raised her head and smiled. "No. I was just thinking about the day."

"Ah, and what were you thinking?"

"I was thinking that this has been a really good day."

Angel smiled. "Whew," she said, running her hand over her forehead, faking wiping sweat. "I had a really good day, too. But it's not over yet."

"No, it's not."

Angel kissed the back of Gina's hand. "I've been thinking about the couple in the cafe."

"Okay..."

"You were so focused on the man helping her that you missed how they looked at one another."

"I did?"

"Did you see how he looked at her? He had joy on his face. He wanted to help her and obviously loved doing it. Have you ever thought that maybe someone would like helping you? It might mean the world to them," Angel said with her eyebrows raised.

Gina gazed into Angel's eyes.

"Let me ask you something," Angel said with a hint of a smile. "Do you like filling my heart with happiness? Because that's what you do."

Gina smirked. "You know I do."

Angel nodded. "Isn't that a way of taking care of me?"

"Is my New Year's Angel trying to make me look at things differently?"

"It's a new year; why not a new perspective?"

"Is that what you're doing? Looking at things in a new way?"

"That's what you've made me do. And I have to tell you," she said, lowering her voice and leaning closer to Gina, "I like this new way of thinking."

Gina giggled. "You do? Then I must try it. Will you help me?"

Angel leaned back and put her hand to her heart. "You're asking for help!" she said playfully. Then earnestly she said, "There's nothing that would make me happier."

Gina chuckled then leaned in closer and said seductively, "I know something that makes you happy and I'll show you when we get back to my place."

Angel leaned her head on the back of the seat. "How much further?"

Gina grabbed her chin and pulled her down for a quick kiss. "Now you have something to look forward to."

They sat back and enjoyed the rest of the ride. Leaving the train station, they caught a cab to Gina's apartment.

"What a day," Gina said, sighing as they walked into her place.

"Are you tired?" Angel said, taking off her coat.

"A little. Actually I'm hungry."

"Let's order in. I have a question," Angel said, plopping down on the couch.

Gina straddled her. "Don't look at me so surprised. I said I was hungry, but not for what." She bent down and kissed Angel tenderly.

Then she slid off, resting her butt next to Angel with her legs in her lap. She leaned back with her head on a pillow. "What's your question?" Gina asked, resting her hands under her head.

"Last Saturday when we went to the Statue of Liberty, we lazed around Sunday and watched TV. Would tomorrow be another lazy day perhaps?"

"Would you like for tomorrow to be a lazy day with me?"

Angel cut her eyes sideways as she ran her hand up and down Gina's leg. "I would." She began to massage one of Gina's calves, squeezing the muscle. She looked down at it. "No wonder you were so fast. Look at this muscle. I think you've been holding out on me. You may need a kidney, but it certainly hasn't affected your speed."

Gina whipped one of her legs up and over Angel's head and rested it on the back of the couch, wiggling it down between the couch and Angel's back.

Angel grinned and turned sideways, leaning toward Gina and placing a hand on each side of her chest. Gina wrapped her other leg around Angel and clasped her ankles together, holding Angel to her.

"I'm strong enough to handle you the rest of the night," she said, snaking her arms around Angel's neck and pulling her down for a kiss. It didn't take long for those lips to open, allowing her to explore. Gina squeezed Angel tighter with her legs. Angel moaned, knowing she was already wet, remembering the lighthouse restroom from earlier. How this woman could make her melt and light her on fire all at once.

Gina pushed Angel up. "Let's go into the bedroom where there's more room. We can order later."

Angel had a seductive smile on her face as she stood and offered her hand to Gina. "Wait."

Gina lay back down and looked at Angel expectantly.

"Do you have any idea how sexy you are lying there like that? The only way to make it better is if you were naked."

Gina stretched back and gave her a seductive smile. "Let me up and your wish will come true."

Angel grabbed Gina's hand and yanked her up.

Gina yelped and laughed as she hurried to the bedroom, taking off clothes with each step. "You'd better be doing the same thing behind me," she said, not looking back.

Angel chuckled and followed her, leaving a trail of clothing.

Gina threw the covers back on the bed and jumped on it. She patted the space next to her and Angel joined her.

In one move Gina was on top of Angel on all fours. She kissed up Angel's neck and ran her tongue around the inside of her ear. She felt Angel shiver.

She hovered over Angel and looked deeply into her eyes. Her face turned serious. "Tell me what you want."

Angel smiled. "I think we're pretty good at this already."

"We are, but I want to make your heart feel better than it ever has before," she said softly.

Angel's eyes were on fire. "I have never felt more wanted," she whispered. She could see the desire in Gina's eyes, but she also saw more. On the beach Gina said she had to have Angel. This was more than want and desire. Was Gina falling in love with her?

Gina gently placed her lips on Angel's and she couldn't think any longer. All she could do was feel. She felt Gina's tongue tenderly caress her mouth. This had to be the best feeling in the world. But then Gina's hand found her breast and squeezed. She pinched her nipple just enough to make Angel moan.

Gina kept kissing her and touching her and Angel felt light headed. This all felt so good. "Gina," she whispered.

"Tell me, my Angel. What do you want?" Gina breathed in her ear.

"More of you," she gasped. "Everywhere."

Gina began an onslaught of kisses from Angel's lips to her neck and down across her collarbone. Angel could feel her tongue glide along where her lips had kissed. Her heart was about to beat out of her chest. Gina's lips kissed a path around her breasts and her nipples. Angel couldn't help arching her back, begging Gina to take her into her mouth. When she sucked her nipple inside her mouth,

Angel couldn't believe the exquisite pleasure along with just a hint of pain as she bit down.

"Oh my God, Gina," she groaned with fervor.

This seemed to encourage Gina because then she began to kiss her way across Angel's stomach, not missing a spot as Angel's skin was on fire.

"Is this what you want?" Gina asked, hovering over Angel's center, her breath warm. She looked up into Angel's eyes.

"Yes, Gina. Love me," Angel said softly. She couldn't believe the word escaped her lips.

Gina's face softened and Angel could read the love in her eyes. Then she felt her tongue, just the tip, barely touch her. Angel's hips bucked and begged for more.

Just as she had caressed Angel's mouth with her tongue that's how she started on these lips. Her tongue teased and explored and lapped Angel up.

This wasn't just sex; Angel felt worshipped and treasured. Gina was circling her clit with her tongue as she did the same with her opening and the tip of her finger. Angel dug her head into the pillow and exhaled. She knew what was coming and the expectation was delicious. Electricity surged through her body. It was like she was humming, ready for Gina to come inside and fly away with her.

When she finally slipped her finger inside, Angel groaned loudly. "Yes Gina," she said over and over. And when Gina added another finger and curled them upwards while sucking her clit into her warm perfect mouth, Angel exploded.

"Don't stop," she begged.

Gina didn't. She kept her hand right where Angel needed it. Then Angel was pulling her head upward. Her mouth needed to be on Gina's mouth.

She tasted herself, but she tasted the sweetness of Gina, too. Their tongues danced and she feasted on the boldness that was Gina, her Gina. When the last wave from that soul shattering orgasm Gina had just given her rolled through Angel's body, she relaxed, spent.

Gina gently removed her fingers and rested her head on Angel's chest. She tenderly kissed where her neck joined her shoulder and stilled.

Neither said a word. They let their breathing slow down and Angel swore she could hear and feel their hearts beating in unison. Angel knew Gina was in her heart, she just had to let her stay.

17

"Thanks for coming with me," Gina said to Angel as they walked hand in hand up to the LGBTQ+ Youth Center.

"Thanks for letting me," Angel said, bumping shoulders with her.

"Suzanne is incredible and maybe some of the kids will be here. I'd love for you to meet them."

Gina pushed the door open and held it for Angel. She looked to where four kids were sitting at a table working on a jigsaw puzzle.

"There you are." A woman, who looked to be in her fifties, came out of an office, smiling.

"Hi Suzanne," Gina said, returning her smile. She turned to Angel. "I'd like you to meet Angel Ruiz."

"Hi Angel, it's nice to meet you."

"It's nice to meet you, Suzanne."

"I never know whether people want to shake hands anymore," she said, looking from Angel to Gina.

"I know what you mean," Angel said. "It's fine."

"Come in," Suzanne said, walking back toward her office.

They followed her in and sat down.

"This is awkward and difficult to talk about, but here goes." Gina took a deep breath. "As you know, I suffer with kidney disease and from time to time it keeps me from doing the things I love which includes coming here."

Suzanne sat up. "Oh no. What's happened?"

Gina appreciated her concern. "It's progressed to the point that I need a kidney transplant."

"Damn, Gina. I'm so sorry. What can we do?" Suzanne asked immediately.

"That's the awkward part. Would you get tested to see if you're a match?"

"To see if you could have my kidney? Where do I go? I'll do it tomorrow!" Suzanne said excitedly.

"Wow!" Angel said, unable to keep quiet.

"That's amazing, Suzanne," Gina said appreciatively. "I can't thank you enough."

"Fingers crossed we match. Just in case, I'll pass the word to all the staff and volunteers. What do I need to tell them?" she said.

"I'll text you a link. It has all the information you need on where to go, how to schedule the test, and what happens if you match," Gina said, her voice full of hope. She reached for her phone and sent the info to Suzanne.

"Okay. I'll read it over and schedule a test. I really hope I match. I can't think of anyone I'd rather give a kidney to," she said, looking at Gina compassionately. "If you get my kidney I wonder if you'll get some of my traits," she said thoughtfully, looking at the ceiling. "Maybe you'll love beer, like I do," she said, her eyes bright.

Gina and Angel didn't know what to say and stared at her.

Suzanne erupted in laughter. "I was just kidding," she said, catching her breath. "You should've seen your faces."

Gina shook her head and laughed with her. Soon Angel joined them.

"I think there are some people out there that would love to see you," Suzanne said as they quieted.

"Thanks Suzanne," Gina said, getting up. She went around and hugged the generous woman.

"It was so nice meeting you," she said to Angel, patting her on the shoulder. "Gina will introduce you," she said, nodding to the group at the table.

"Thanks Suzanne. It was really nice meeting you."

They walked over to the table and one of the girls looked up. "Gina!" she exclaimed. "We've missed you."

"Hi Maddie," Gina said affectionately.

"Where's your girlfriend, Shannon?" the other girl asked.

"She's not my girlfriend. She's been my best friend since I was in elementary school. You know that," Gina said, sighing loudly to their giggles. "Hey, I want all of you to meet Angel," Gina said. "This is Maddie, Camila, Isaac, and Dario." She pointed to each one.

They all quietly said hi and Angel said, "It's nice to meet you." She put her hand up pretending to tell them a secret. "I'm trying to be the girlfriend," she said, looking at Camila.

Camila smiled. "Good for you!"

Gina looked at her and smiled with her eyebrows raised.

"You've got to be honest," Isaac said.

"And talk. Don't be scared to communicate," said Dario. He stood up and grabbed two more chairs so Angel and Gina could sit. "Join us." He turned to Angel and said, "We call ourselves the Rainbow Warriors because we're all colors. Obviously, Isaac is Black, Camila is Hispanic, I'm Italian, and Maddie is our white girl."

Angel smiled and sat down. "I'm not very good at puzzles."

"Do you mean that literally or figuratively?" Camila asked. "Cause Isaac can help you with this puzzle and I'll help you out with the puzzle that's Miss Gina."

"Ohhh," Dario said, covering his mouth.

Gina's eyes widened. "So you know all about me, huh?"

"I didn't say that. I know enough to help Angel out, though."

"That's right, we both do. Why don't you go talk to Suzanne so we can help Angel?" Maddie said.

"No way I'm leaving her here with you. She'll be a Rainbow Warrior by the time you're done."

The kids laughed. "You're just jealous because we said you were too bright to be one." Isaac chuckled.

"You know they were kidding, right?" Maddie said.

"You'd better be," Gina said, putting a piece in the puzzle.

"So you want to be her girlfriend, huh?" Dario said quietly to Angel.

Angel grinned. "I sure do," she said just as quietly. She quickly looked over at Gina to see if she'd heard, but she continued to work on the puzzle.

"You know Valentine's Day is this Friday," Camila added.

Gina's jaw dropped. "It is?" She looked over at Angel. "I didn't realize."

"Yes, we are still going on a date Friday," she said to the group and to Gina.

"Here's your chance. Don't mess it up," Isaac said.

Angel smiled, gazing at Gina. "I know. This may be the most important date of my life."

"You'd better start planning," Maddie said, bumping her shoulder to Gina's.

Gina looked over at Angel with panic in her eyes.

"It'll be fine," Angel said, reassuring her.

"Come on, Gina. There's nothing to be afraid about," Camila said, snapping a piece of puzzle in place. "I think Angel's got this. And if she doesn't, we'll come for her," she said, piercing Angel with a look.

Angel swallowed, her brows raised. Then she said to the group, "Let me ask you something. Should I go for fancy and expensive, or sweet and special?"

"Whatever you do, make it romantic," Dario said, pointing a piece of puzzle at Angel.

"Fancy and expensive can be fun if you haven't done that," Camila said. "Imagine getting all dressed up and being waited on in a nice restaurant."

"Yeah, but you can make something really special if you put some thought into it," Maddie said. "And Gina likes special."

"I may be getting uncomfortable with how well you all know me," Gina said tentatively.

"It's all good," Isaac said. "We want only the best for you. You've always had our backs, it's our turn to have yours. So Angel, don't let us down."

Angel sat up a little straighter. "I won't. We'll come back next week and tell you how much fun we had."

Dario and Isaac nodded at Angel in approval.

"Are you going to start volunteering?" Camila asked.

"I'd like to," Angel said carefully.

"Did you have a kickass homelife like Gina?" asked Maddie.

"Wow, right to the point. My homelife was more like kick *my* ass," Angel said honestly.

"Your folks didn't like you being gay?" asked Dario.

"They shamed me and barely talked to me after they found out. That lasted about a year. I studied hard and graduated from high school early so I could get away."

"I hear you," mumbled Camila.

"Gina, I visited my grandmother over the weekend and we had an actual conversation," said Dario. "She is upset with the way my dad is treating me and is trying to get him to talk about it."

"That's awesome, Dario," said Gina.

Dario looked at Angel. "That's why I told you communication is important. My Nonna asked questions and listened to me."

Angel nodded seriously. "Thanks Dario."

"I'm so glad to see you all. I've missed you," Gina said.

"I'd give you my kidney," said Camila. "We all would."

Gina looked at her, shocked.

"I overheard you talking to Suzanne. I was going to say hello, but you were talking."

"It doesn't matter how we found out. We'd like to help," Isaac said.

Gina had tears in her eyes. "You all are something else. Thank you."

"What do we do to get tested?" asked Maddie.

"Actually, you have to be eighteen to donate."

"No way!" exclaimed Dario.

"Well, if you don't find a donor, I'll be eighteen in nine months," said Camila.

"I'll remember that, Camila. Thank you," Gina said, putting her arm around her shoulder. "Enough talk about me. We're supposed to be talking about you all."

"We are all fine," Isaac said. The others agreed.

"Time to go anyway," Maddie said, getting up from the table.

"We expect both of you back next week for a Valentine report," said Dario.

"That's right," Maddie added.

"It was nice to meet all of you," Angel said, putting their chairs back.

Dario leaned over and said softly, "Good luck."

Angel smiled and nodded.

The kids left and Angel waited until they were out the door to turn to Gina. "They are amazing! I wish I'd had a place like this when I was growing up."

Gina smiled, looking at the door fondly. "They are amazing.'

"Let me clarify, I wish I'd had someone like you to talk to," she said, squeezing Gina's hand.

"Did you realize Friday was Valentine's Day?" Gina said, changing the subject.

"I didn't when we made plans, but I noticed it Monday."

Gina faced Angel and gazed into her eyes. "You said we're still going. Do you have something in mind?"

"I do. I'll let you know more tomorrow, okay?"

Gina smiled and put her arms around Angel's neck. "I can't wait, girlfriend." She touched her lips to Angel's in a soft, sweet kiss.

18

Angel got off the elevator on Gina's floor. She'd never been this nervous around Gina. The calm she normally felt was long gone and she knew why.

This was a special night. Sure it was Valentine's Day, but Angel had been thinking about taking Gina on this date since the first time she'd made love to her. Angel could still remember it. She hadn't been that vulnerable or let anyone in her heart like she had that night. Gina knew it too because Angel could see it in her eyes. They didn't really talk about it and they hadn't talked about the "L" word slipping out the other night when they got back from Montauk either. Tonight may well be the night that happened.

This night wasn't about expenses as far as money went. Tonight was about emotion and trust and discovering one another. Discovering love.

Gina's door was ajar and Angel knocked on it gently, pushing the door open. She walked in and Gina was standing there with her hands on her hips and the most seductive smirk on her face.

She had on a black dress that came to a vee on top and showed just a hint of cleavage. Her gaze slowly traveled down Gina's body and paused when she saw those muscular calves. She wore black high heels to finish the outfit. Angel looked back up and stopped at those ruby red lips. When she pulled her eyes higher she could see the humor in Gina's eyes. She knew she looked good and she knew what it was doing to Angel.

Angel's mouth was dry and she ran her teeth over her bottom lip. It took her a moment to speak and Gina patiently waited. "You look incredible," Angel said, exhaling.

Pleased with Angel's reaction it was Gina's turn to peruse her date's appearance. Angel watched her look from her shining dark hair, down her face to the black fitted suit coat. She saw Gina pause to look at the lace camisole top almost hidden by the white scarf that hung from her neck. Her eyes kept going down the fitted pants that made her legs look even longer than they were and finally stopped on the high heeled boots on her feet.

"You look good enough to undress," Gina said, her cheeks becoming red.

Angel smirked. "Maybe I'll let you later."

Gina laughed and came over, putting her arms around Angel's neck. She gazed into her eyes and then softly placed her lips on Angel's. "You look beautiful. Thank you for wearing that suit. You remembered how much I like it," she said, pulling back.

Angel nodded. She couldn't take her eyes away from Gina. "You *are* beautiful." She kissed her just as softly back.

Finally they both exhaled and the spell was broken, or at least put on hold for the time being.

"You didn't give me much information so I wasn't sure what to wear," Gina said.

"That's perfect. Do you have your keys?"

"I thought we were ending up at your place since you had me drop a bag off there yesterday."

"We are, but I meant your keys to Travis and Shannon's. Travis said you had a key to their place."

"We're starting off at their place? I thought they had plans."

"They won't be there. If you'll trust me, it will all be revealed," Angel said mysteriously.

Gina smiled, narrowing her eyes. "I do trust you. Lead the way."

They made it to Travis and Shannon's and Gina unlocked the door. Once inside Gina was taking her coat off when Angel said, "You might want to leave that on. Come on," she said, taking her hand and leading her to the balcony door.

Angel unlocked the door and they stepped onto the balcony. The fairy lights were on and sitting on the table were two stemmed wine glasses and a can of grapefruit sparkling water. Gina looked at Angel and smiled.

"I thought we would celebrate tonight by revisiting the places we had dates that we didn't call dates because we were afraid, apprehensive, unsure, or stubborn," Angel said playfully. "But also," she said more seriously as she poured the sparkling water into the glasses, "these are the places where you slowly opened and then filled my heart."

She handed Gina a glass and looked deeply into her eyes. "This is where you first showed me kindness." She clinked her glass to Gina's and took a sip.

After Gina swallowed she said, "There was something about you. I had to know more. You were so mysterious."

Angel chuckled. "You thought I was mysterious, but really I was just scared for anyone to see who I really was."

"But I saw you."

"You saw me."

Angel set her glass down and pulled out her phone. She scrolled and then music began to play.

"One thing we haven't done is dance. May I?" she asked, holding out her hand.

Gina took it with a huge smile on her face. "I'd love to."

Angel put her hands on Gina's waist as Gina slid her arms around her neck. The song started off slow and they held one another close. Then it began to speed up and Gina pulled back.

"I know this song. Is this Benny Blanco?" she said, raising her arms and moving her hips to the beat.

Angel grinned. "Yep. It's 'I Found You.' I thought it worked for both of us."

Gina grinned back and they danced with abandon. She twirled and backed into Angel.

Angel's hands immediately grabbed Gina's hips as they swayed. By the end of the song they were face to face, arms around one another.

"This was fun," Gina said. "Why haven't we done this before?"

"I don't know. We can now."

"Yeah we can," Gina said. She leaned up and kissed Angel sweetly. "Thank you for this."

Angel smiled. "This is just our first stop. Shall we?" Angel led them back inside the apartment.

They took an Uber to the bench they sat on that first night. When they got out of the car they went to the little stand where they'd gotten hot chocolate.

The guy handed Angel a bag and said, "Happy Valentine's Day."

Gina followed Angel to the bench shaking her head in bewilderment.

Angel reached in the bag and pulled out two small plastic wine glasses and an airplane sized bottle of wine.

She handed Gina both glasses with the happiest grin on her face. She opened the wine and poured it into the glasses. She put the empty bottle in the sack and set it next to her. Gina handed her a glass and smiled with raised eyebrows.

"This was where we were when this new year started," Angel said, holding up her glass.

"Can I toast this time?" Gina asked.

Angel nodded, still smiling.

"If I remember, we toasted to not being afraid that night. Here's to my New Year's Angel. While I was trying to get her to be brave she made me brave instead," Gina said, clinking her glass to Angel's.

They both took a drink which almost emptied their glasses.

"I kissed you on the cheek that night," Angel said, leaning over and repeating the kiss. She put her hand on Gina's face and then kissed her firmly. She could taste the wine on her lips and the promise of what was to come. It was delicious.

When Angel pulled her lips away Gina said, "As much as I'm loving this, please tell me the next stop is your place."

"One more stop," Angel said, winking. "Aren't you hungry?"

Gina cocked one eyebrow.

"Don't answer that," Angel teased.

A car pulled to the curb and Angel got up, finishing her wine. Gina followed as she put her cup in the sack and they threw it in the trash as they walked to the car.

When the car stopped Gina knew where they were having dinner. They were on the corner in between their apartments where they'd had that first burger together. Since then they had eaten there several times and it had become their place.

"Now I know this isn't the fanciest place to have Valentine's dinner," Angel began.

"This is the perfect place for *us* to have Valentine's dinner," Gina assured her as she walked through the door. Towards the back in the booth they always sat in, there was one candle flickering, beckoning them to their table.

Gina stopped and turned to look at Angel. She leaned in and said so only Angel could hear, "You are making me swoon."

Angel grinned, winked at her and led them to their table. They slid into the booth as their waitress walked up.

"If it isn't my favorite customers. Happy Valentine's Day," the waitress said.

"Hi Tammy," Gina said, shrugging out of her coat. "Sorry you have to work tonight, but I'm glad you're our server."

"Don't you worry, my Valentine is waiting on me at home," she said with a wink. "Don't you both look nice."

"Thanks," Angel said. "It's kind of fun to get dressed up," she said, looking at Gina.

"Let me guess, you want Valentine's burgers tonight," Tammy said.

"I've tried other things, but your burgers are the best. What's wrong with a burger on Valentine's Day?" Gina said.

"Not a thing! There's something to be said for knowing what you want," Tammy said, looking at each one of them with raised eyebrows.

"I'm not sure you're talking about burgers, Tammy," Angel said suspiciously. "But that's what I want, too."

Tammy smiled at them. "I'll have them right out. Let me get your drinks."

Gina reached over and grabbed Angel's hand. "This has been so much fun. Dates that weren't dates. But you've added to each one."

"I'm glad you're having a good time. I know Valentine's kind of snuck up on us both and we haven't really been seeing one another for long, but I can't remember what I used to do before you," Angel said honestly.

"I do. We were boring people that didn't do anything. You can't say that now."

Angel chuckled. "No you can't."

Tammy brought their food and set their plates down.

"Would you look!" Gina exclaimed.

Angel threw her head back and laughed. The meat and bun of their burgers were heart shaped.

"Did you plan this too?" Gina asked her.

"No! Tammy, did you do this?"

"It was all the cook. He happens to like you, too," she said, grinning.

"Please thank him for us," Angel said.

"I will. Enjoy. I'll be back to check on you."

They dove into their burgers. Gina looked at Angel as she chewed.

"What?" Angel said.

"I'm learning that you are quite the romantic," Gina stated. "And I like it."

Angel swallowed. "I didn't think I was, but I guess I want to be with you. There are a lot of things I want to be with you, it seems."

Gina's eyebrows raised. "Is that a good thing?"

"Oh yeah, it's very good."

Gina's cheeks reddened. "You've certainly made me see things differently."

They finished their burgers and Tammy cleared their plates.

"I have something for you," Angel said. "I know we're just getting to know one another, but I wanted you to have this." Angel slid a tiny sack over to Gina. "Go ahead, open it."

Gina reached inside and pulled out a coin. She gasped when she looked at it. "It's an angel!" The coin had an angel on one side and the year engraved on the other.

"I wanted you to have this to remind you that I'm always with you if you need me."

"Oh Angel. I love it," Gina said softly, turning it over in her hand. "This year," she said, looking up at her and nodding.

"It's been good so far."

"It sure has," Gina said, continuing to turn the coin over and over. "I got you something too," she said, reaching for her purse. It was her turn to slide a small box over to Angel.

Angel raised her eyebrows and slowly took the lid off the box. She pulled out a small heart shaped box. It was made of wood and the lid came off of it. Angel looked inside and could see a slip of folded paper. She looked over at Gina quizzically.

"I thought we could put our wants in the box," Gina explained.

"There's one in here, I see," Angel said.

Gina nodded. "If I knew what you wanted I'd try to give it to you," she said affectionately.

"So I put my wants in here and then we read them?"

Gina nodded.

"I like this idea. Can I read this one now?"

"Sure."

Angel unfurled the paper and her eyes widened. It said *I want to be naked with you*. "I like this one. If that's what you want then that is what you will get," she said matter-of-factly.

Gina chuckled. "Your turn."

"We get to use these over and over?"

"It's your box; you make the rules."

Angel grinned. "I think they need to stay in the box because I hope this isn't the only time you want this."

Gina laughed. "I assure you it won't be the only time."

Angel looked around and waved to Tammy.

She came over. "What do you need?"

"I need a pen and small piece of paper if you have it, Tammy."

She pulled a pen out of her apron and tore off the bottom part off one of the tickets she used to write orders on. "There you go." She saw the box and exclaimed, "That's so cute! The wood is beautiful."

"Gina gave it to me. It's a want box."

"Oh. Do you put what you want in there and then Gina gives it?" she said, winking at Gina.

"Not exactly. It goes both ways. I put the first one in," Gina said.

"Can I see?" Tammy asked sweetly.

"Sure," Angel said, looking at Gina.

Tammy read the paper and looked at Gina then Angel and said, "What are you still doing here?"

Angel chuckled. "It's my turn to put one in and then we're out of here."

"I'll get your check. Be right back," Tammy said, walking away smiling.

Angel quickly wrote something on the paper and put it in the box. "You can read this when we get to my place."

"Okay. It's your box," Gina said, winking.

Tammy brought the bill. "I know you're going to have a good night, but I'm wishing you happiness anyway."

"Thanks Tammy. Same to you. Happy Valentine's Day," Gina said.

"Yeah, and thanks for making ours special," Angel added.

"Oh honey, you've got that covered."

They left Tammy a big tip, paid their bill and waited for their Uber hand in hand. Neither said anything; the anticipation was palpable, their desire simmering.

19

Angel opened the door so they could walk into her apartment. Neither had said much since leaving the restaurant.

Gina took her coat off and laid it on the back of the couch.

"Would you like a drink? I have wine," Angel offered.

"Can I have my own bottle?" Gina teased.

Angel spun around in the kitchen as she reached for the bottle of wine. "Your own bottle!" She saw the smirk on Gina's face and visibly relaxed. "Oh, I get it. No, this is a real bottle, not like at the bench." She poured them both a glass.

Gina walked over to the window and could see the lights of the city twinkling. Across the street, lights shined in windows and she wondered if people were celebrating Valentine's Day over there as well. She took a deep breath and let it out.

Angel walked up next to her and handed her a glass. "Are you okay?"

Gina took a sip and turned to Angel. "Why does this night seem so important? Does it to you?"

Angel smiled. "Yes. It feels like that to me too. And it's not just the pressure Dario put on me to make it special."

Gina chuckled. "Don't you worry, I'll give them a good report." She put her glass on the coffee table. "You've made this very special."

Angel set her glass down and reached for Gina. She put her hands on her hips. "I know this isn't the most romantic Valentine's…"

Gina put her finger over Angel's lips. "Don't say that. What you've done and how we've opened up to one another is more romantic than the finest restaurant. We've both opened our hearts and that's what's made this night so important."

Angel leaned in and kissed Gina softly.

"Can I look at the want you put in the heart box?" Gina asked sweetly.

Angel chuckled. "Of course." She went to get the box and opened it in front of Gina.

She looked inside and picked out the piece of ticket Tammy had given Angel. She read aloud, "'I want to kiss you all over.' That will go nicely with mine, don't you think?"

Angel smiled seductively and wiggled her eyebrows. She took Gina's hand and led her to the bedroom. Once inside Angel began to light candles around the room.

Gina kicked off her shoes and took a deep breath. She'd been looking forward to tonight. Not because it was Valentine's Day, but because she knew they'd have all night and then she'd get to wake up in the morning with Angel next to her. That's what she wanted. That's what she should have put in the heart box. She wanted to wake up next to Angel, not just on weekends, but every day.

This realization had become clear as the night went on, but she wasn't sure Angel was ready to hear it.

Angel reached down and took her boots off. She slowly walked toward Gina, removing her scarf, then her jacket. She stood in front of her and reached around behind Gina and unzipped her dress. Her eyes never left Gina's until she slowly pulled the sleeve of her dress off her shoulder. Angel bent down and kissed her shoulder up to her neck. Gina shuddered.

Angel slid both sleeves down and pulled Gina's dress down her body so she could step out of it. Gina could see how dark Angel's eyes had become. They felt like lasers traveling up and down her body as Angel appreciated her matching black lace bra and underwear. Gina could feel her skin heat up under Angel's intense stare.

She didn't want to rush this, but the sight of Angel in that lace camisole made Gina's insides melt that much more. She reached for the hem and pulled it over her head, dropping it on the floor. Next she unclasped her bra and soaked in the beauty of her breasts as she took a deep breath.

Gina put her hands on Angel's shoulders and slowly ran them down her chest and held each breast, running her thumbs over her nipples, watching them harden. Then she looked up into Angel's eyes. "You are so beautiful, Angel."

Angel smiled at her and unbuttoned her own pants, dropping them to the floor. She guided Gina over to the bed and made quick work of her bra and underwear. Angel eased her down to sit on the edge of the bed. She quickly removed her underwear and kneeled between Gina's legs.

Gina pulled Angel to her and wrapped her arms and legs around her. She held her close and could feel as well as hear their labored breathing. "Kiss me all over," she whispered into Angel's ear.

Angel started on one shoulder and kissed over to her neck across the base of her throat and over to the other shoulder.

Gina leaned her head back and felt Angel's soft lips and silky tongue leave a trail of pleasure over her body. She leaned back on her elbows and started to climb up the bed.

Angel watched her and followed her movements. She kissed the inside of Gina's ankle and then up to her calf, to the inside of her knee, and then the middle of her inner thigh.

Gina gasped. Now she was at the soft sensitive crease where her leg met her body, then her stomach and up between her breasts until she hovered over Gina, staring into her eyes.

"This night is important because Gina, I've fallen in love with you. Let me love you with my body, let me in your heart, let me love all of you," Angel said softly.

Gina held Angel's face in her hands. Angel loved her, she wanted all of her. She knew Gina's problems and still wanted her; it was almost unbelievable. "Love me, Angel," she whispered.

Angel pressed her lips to Gina's gently at first and then passion took over.

When Angel's tongue slipped into Gina's mouth she lost her breath. She needed Angel closer, so she wove her arms around Angel's neck and held on. Then she wrapped her legs around Angel as the kiss deepened. With her body wrapped around Angel, Gina didn't think she'd ever experienced a better kiss. She could feel Angel's love flowing into her heart and spilling over everywhere.

Then Gina felt Angel's hands. She caressed up and down the side of her body and then slid one hand between them. Gina released her grip and opened her legs wide. She wanted Angel like she'd never wanted anyone before.

Angel's hand began to stroke up and down the inside of Gina's leg.

"Please, Angel. I need you."

"I'm right here," she whispered, staring into Gina's eyes. She kissed her again as her hand found Gina's wetness.

"Oh yes. Love me, baby," Gina groaned. Angel's fingers circled her most sensitive bud and slid through her lips making her feel nothing but pleasure. Then she teased her entrance and slowly pushed inside with one finger and then added another.

Gina groaned loudly. "Oh Angel," she gasped.

Angel began a steady rhythm as Gina's hips matched it.

"Oh, you are so good at this," Gina moaned. She grabbed Angel's face again and looked at her eyes. She'd never seen them this dark. Gina felt like she was drunk with desire, lust and love. She pulled Angel down and kissed her hard, her passion uncontrollable. She was so close.

She pulled back, panting as Angel continued her rhythm. Their eyes were locked together.

"I love you, Angel. I love you," Gina said as the orgasm burst through her. She held onto Angel as wave after wave of pleasure washed over her. For a moment she thought she might lose herself, but Angel had her. She knew Angel had her.

As Gina's breathing quieted she gently stroked Angel's back as she lay on her chest. She sighed and raised up on her elbow, facing Angel. "I love you."

Angel smiled back. "I think you said that."

"Yeah, but I want you to know that I mean it."

"I believe you."

Gina stroked Angel's cheek. "I did what you wanted. I gave you all of me. You're in my heart." She had tears in her eyes as she emotionally kissed Angel's lips.

"Do you remember when we were at Montauk and you said you had to have me?" Angel asked.

Gina nodded. "You said that was the best thing you'd ever heard."

"I was wrong. When you told me you love me, that was the best."

"Get used to it because I like saying it," Gina said, kissing her again. She couldn't seem to stop kissing this beautiful woman.

"I thought saying it would scare me to death, but it was a relief. I had to tell you."

"It's a little hard for me to believe because I come with problems," Gina said. "But I do believe you."

Angel scoffed. "You think I don't come with problems? You've seen them and still you wanted to be with me."

"I do," Gina exhaled. "And you know what else," she said, sitting up. "We're going to stay here more often. It's feeling kind of homey to me, how about you?"

Angel looked around and then pulled Gina back on top of her. "It feels homey because you're here."

"Mmm," Gina said, kissing her. She deepened the kiss and it wasn't long until they were both breathing hard. "I can't stop kissing you," Gina said, exhaling.

"I don't want you to," Angel said, pulling her back down.

* * *

As Gina stood at the big windows looking out she thought back to that morning, as she'd begun to wake up. Before she'd moved a smile crept on her face because she was pressed up to Angel's back with one arm around her stomach holding her close. She could feel Angel's hand wrapped around hers, keeping it in place. Last night they had not only professed their love out loud, but they had also shown it to one another with their bodies and their hearts. They couldn't get enough of one another and had finally fallen asleep, spent.

Angel walked up behind her and kissed her neck. "What has put that pleased smile on your face?"

"You have," she said, turning to face her. "One of my favorite things is waking up next to you. It all started on this couch," she said, nodding toward it.

"On the couch?" Angel replied, her brow furrowed.

"Yes, we were watching a movie and fell asleep. I remember waking and feeling your steady breathing."

"Hmm, I remember that."

Gina turned back around to face the window and leaned back into Angel's arms. "Is that the park we met in the day you showed me your apartment?" Gina asked, gazing out the window.

Angel peered over her shoulder. "Yes, that's just the edge of it. The basketball courts are behind those trees."

"We need to go back there when the weather is nice. You can show me your basketball skills."

Angel chuckled and Gina could feel the sweet timbre vibrate through her body. "That won't take long."

Gina's phone began to ring on the coffee table. She glanced over at it and thought about letting it go to voicemail, but it could be her dad. When she picked it up she saw it was Shannon.

"Hi Shan," Gina answered.

"Hi Valentine," she said in a sing-song voice. "Did you have a good time last night?"

Gina chuckled. "I sure did. How about you?"

"Yes! I can't wait to show you the necklace Travis gave me. But I want to know about your night. Angel wouldn't tell us what she had planned."

This made Gina laugh. "From your house it just got better and better."

"You're still at her place, aren't you."

"Yep," Gina said, smiling.

Shannon laughed. "I'll make this quick then. You can tell me all about it tomorrow. Travis's brother has rented a place on Long Island for a weekend, but he has to leave town for work. He's letting us have it. We want you and Angel to come with us."

"Oh fun! When?"

"It's the first weekend in March."

"Hold on," Gina said. She told Angel about the weekend and she nodded enthusiastically. Gina laughed. "We're in. Let me know what we need to bring."

"We'll get together before then and plan everything. I'm hoping Michael, Sarah Beth, Brandy, and Dustin can come too."

"This will be so much fun!"

"I know. Go back to doing whatever it was you were doing," Shannon said, her voice low and sexy.

"Don't you wish you knew what that was," Gina said back just as seductively.

Shannon laughed. "I have a pretty good idea. Have fun! Bye GG."

"Bye Shan," she said, ending the call.

"This sounds like fun," Angel said. "Some of those places we saw from the train looked amazing."

"I know." Changing the subject she said, "Did you want to do anything today?"

"I don't know. It looks nice outside with the sun shining, but it's cold. You mentioned movies on the couch earlier and that sounds really good."

Gina sat into the corner of the couch and patted the space next to her. "I have a place just for you," she said with a wink.

20

"Would you look at them," Shannon said to Gina. She was watching Travis and Angel try to figure out the grill on the back porch.

"If they can't figure it out no one can," Gina said. They'd driven to the beach house the night before, arriving with just enough time to unpack and eat the food they'd picked up on the way. It was dark so they hadn't been able to see the view, but they could hear the water as it met the shore in a rhythmic melody.

This morning they could see the sand reaching out to the ocean, glistening in the bright sunshine. If nothing else the weather promised to cooperate for the weekend. Gina felt sluggish and attributed it to yesterday's hectic pace to get everything done so they could leave for the weekend. However, a tiny bit of doubt was lurking at the back of her mind.

"I've missed you lately, but I've never seen you this happy. I can't be mad at Angel for taking so much of your time."

"I've missed you, too. I have to blame part of it on work. It seems like the nights you're free, I'm with Angel and when I'm not, you've got Travis. We'll figure it out."

"One thing I've noticed is that you're not focused on your kidneys for a change."

"Believe me it's still there, but Angel keeps me from obsessing over it. However, I'm doing exactly what I said I wouldn't."

"What's that?" Shannon asked.

"I wasn't going to be with anyone until I got this transplant done and here I am head over heels in love with a woman who doesn't commit, yet she's committed to me. Go figure!"

"Love does what it wants and it's taken you two and turned your very deliberate, exacting lives upside down. It's been fun to watch." Shannon giggled.

Gina scoffed. "You make it sound like we aren't very flexible."

"You are now. Isn't it funny how you can find time to see one another?"

"Why wouldn't I want to be with her? Have you seen her!" Gina said eagerly.

Shannon laughed. "I have, but I've also seen you. I'm telling you, GG, Angel is the lucky one." She walked over and embraced Gina.

"Thanks Shan. Did I tell you she's been going to the youth center with me? Of course the kids love her. And they've asked about you, too," Gina said, hugging her close.

"I'm not surprised. She knows what they're going through. Hey, are you feeling okay?" Shannon said before letting her go.

"Yeah, just feeling a little slow this morning."

"Am I going to have to embarrass Angel and tell her you need your sleep at night?" Shannon threatened.

"Don't you dare. It's not her fault," Gina said, giggling.

"I love seeing you like this."

"I love being like this!"

Travis and Angel came in the back sliding door. "It's going to be a nice day," Travis reported.

"Did you tame the grill?" Shannon asked.

"We're ready. Gourmet burgers are on the menu later today," Angel said, putting her arm around Gina.

"I knew you could do it," Gina said, kissing her on the cheek.

"When are the others supposed to be here?" asked Travis.

"Anytime now," Shannon answered.

"Are you okay, babe?" Angel softly asked Gina.

"Yes, I just can't get going this morning," Gina said a bit defensively.

"Okay," Angel said quietly.

"Sorry. Shannon just asked me the same thing. Do I look bad or something?"

"No," Travis chimed in. "You always look good."

"See why I love this guy?" Gina grinned at him.

Just then the front door flew open and Brandy and Sarah Beth came rushing in, full of exuberance.

"Give me a mimosa!" hooted Brandy.

"Me too," shouted Sarah Beth. "No kids weekend!"

Michael and Dustin followed them with their arms full of bags. Angel jumped up and began pouring. When everyone had a drink they raised their glasses.

"To Travis's brother for letting us have the place for the weekend," Shannon said.

They all cheered and took a drink.

"What a sweet layout," Michael said, gazing around the room and out the windows.

The large open concept room looked out over the beach and the ocean. A large island separated the kitchen from the living area. It was full of snacks and drinks. There were games ready to be played on the table between the couches that faced each other.

"I see cornhole out on the patio," Brandy said. "We've got to play later. Sarah Beth and I are the reigning champions."

"Are you sure about that?" said Shannon. "I recall Gina and I kicking your asses."

"Nope. We won on the last toss." Sarah Beth put her arm around Brandy.

Gina narrowed her eyes and stood next to Shannon. She said

quietly, but loud enough for them to hear, "I don't believe them, but they're rather scary looking. So let's let them have this one."

Brandy laughed. "That's a wise decision, my friend. The kids have been terrors this week."

"So was Chloe," said Sarah Beth. "Was something in the air or Mercury in retrograde or whatever it does?"

Shannon chuckled. "Here, let me refill these," she said, taking their glasses.

Brandy walked up next to Gina and put an arm around her. "How's the search going?"

Gina smiled. "Not so great. Well, I shouldn't say that. We just haven't found a match yet. I know we will," she said, looking over at Angel.

Brandy followed her gaze. "Sorry I didn't match. But I love your attitude. Would someone or something have anything to do with that?"

Gina grinned. "Someone sure would."

"Angel, I'm glad we finally get to see you again," Brandy said. "You must be pretty special if Gina's let you stick around."

Angel couldn't keep from smiling at Gina. "I'm the lucky one."

"Ohhh," said Sarah Beth. "Tell us more!"

"Be nice," Gina said, sidling up next to Angel and putting her arm around her.

"I've got to pace myself," Shannon said, putting her glass down. "Anyone want to go for a walk on the beach?"

"I'm in," said Brandy, walking toward the door with Shannon.

Gina looked at Angel, her eyebrows raised. "Do you want to go? Maybe it'll help me perk up."

"Sure. What could be better than walking on the beach with your girl?" Angel said, smiling.

"I heard that," Sarah Beth said, leaning in. "I couldn't agree more; however, I'd add hand in hand." She gave them a wink and went to join the others.

Gina held out her hand to Angel and they followed.

The guys stayed behind to set up the cornhole game while Shannon, Brandy, and Sarah Beth ran toward the water. Gina and Angel walked along holding hands, in no hurry.

"You would tell me if you didn't feel well, right?" Angel said, a hint of concern in her voice.

"I would."

"How do I say this without being a bother?" Angel murmured, thinking out loud.

"Honey, you're always bothering me," Gina teased.

Angel looked at her, troubled. "I do?"

"Yes. I have a hard time focusing when you're around because I want to be doing this." Gina stopped them and kissed Angel soundly on the mouth.

Angel was smiling when she pulled away.

"I will tell you if I don't feel well. I'm hoping I'm just tired and it isn't anything more, but you don't have to worry or keep asking me. Okay?"

"Okay."

"Thanks, my Angel," Gina said, bumping shoulders with her. "Let's see if we can find some pretty shells."

Later, they met back at the house to compare the treasures they found on the beach.

"Look at these," Shannon said, placing several small shells on the table.

"Nice." Sarah Beth picked one up and examined it.

"I have a few," Brandy said, adding to the others.

"Check out these rocks Angel and I found." Gina held them in her open palm. "Look how smooth they are."

"They remind me of the ones we saw on Montauk," Angel commented.

"When did you go to Montauk?" asked Dustin.

"It was a few weeks ago."

"Wasn't it cold?" asked Michael.

"We lucked out with the weather. It was a nice day," Gina added.

"I love to go there in the spring," said Brandy. "I've never been in winter."

"We went up in the lighthouse and I felt like I could see forever," Gina said. "One thing about going in winter, there wasn't a crowd."

"We practically had the place to ourselves," said Angel.

"Yeah we did." Gina smiled at Angel. Flashbacks of the lighthouse restroom blazed through her mind and her cheeks began to color.

"I think there's a story there," Shannon said. After a moment she added, "Well?"

"No story. We had fun," Gina said nicely.

"Let's have lunch and start this cornhole tournament," said Travis.

"We brought everything for build-your-own sandwiches," said Sara Beth.

"I'll help get everything out," said Shannon.

Back inside, they spread everything out on the island and began constructing their custom sandwiches.

* * *

Angel couldn't help the uneasiness in the pit of her stomach about Gina. She just didn't seem like herself. There was something off. She knew there were times when Gina didn't have much energy, but she hadn't seen her like this. Gina assured her she would say something if she felt bad, though, and Angel trusted her.

"Do you remember we were about to team up that first night we met?" Gina said, pulling Angel down to sit next to her on the couch on the deck.

"I do. You and Shannon had just defeated me and Travis. If I remember correctly, it was your idea for us to team up."

Gina had a wicked smile on her face. "It was."

"But sadly we never got to play that game."

"I'd say everything worked out all right, wouldn't you?"

Angel chuckled. "You mean you didn't want to team up with me because of my vast knowledge of trivia?"

"There was that." Gina laughed playfully. "But there may have been another reason." She wiggled her eyebrows.

"I'm so glad you left that party with me," Angel said softly, kissing her on the cheek.

"Me too." Gina gazed into her eyes.

Angel looked into those rich brown eyes and could feel the love radiating to her.

"Come on love birds," Shannon said. "You're up first."

Angel didn't break their stare, but after a moment Gina smiled and looked away.

"Okay," Gina said, getting up. "Who are we beating first?"

"Oh no!" laughed Travis. "Trash talking Gina is back."

"Come on Travie, let's see what you've got," Gina said, walking to one end of the game.

Shannon and Angel took their places at the other end. Angel used this opportunity to talk to Shannon while Gina and Travis took their turns.

"I don't think Gina feels well today," Angel said quietly. "We've had days that we hung out on the couch because her energy was low, but this seems different."

"Are you sure you weren't hanging out on the couch for another reason?" Shannon asked, unable to resist teasing Angel. Angel's cheeks started to brighten. "I think you're blushing," she said as the others cheered a good shot by Gina.

Angel smiled shyly.

"I'm sorry," Shannon said, touching her arm. "You're right. This morning she said she was tired. When this happens sometimes it lasts for a day or two."

"Or?" Angel asked, hearing Shannon's hesitancy.

"Sometimes longer."

"She said she'd tell me if she felt bad. What should I do?"

"Nothing. If she said that, she will, Angel," Shannon assured her. "Don't hover. That's the worst thing you can do."

"I know. I'm not hovering; I'm concerned."

"Of course you are, you love her. It'll be all right. She won't push too hard. She knows her limits."

Angel sighed. "We've got to find her a kidney."

"We will," Shannon said.

"Okay partner, it's your turn. Let them have it!" Gina yelled from her end of the game.

Angel couldn't help smiling at Gina.

"Our turn," Shannon said, looking at Angel. "You go first."

21

"I can't believe it," Travis said, staring at the bean bag. "What is keeping it from going through that hole?"

"Sorry, Travie. If that little baby would fall you'd win. But we've been standing here for over a minute and it ain't going anywhere," Gina said.

Travis sighed and looked up at Shannon. "Sorry, babe. We were so close."

"Come on Travis," Michael said, putting his arm around him and looking back at the others with a smile.

"Okay, the next two teams are up," Shannon said.

Gina grabbed Angel's arms and pulled her away from the others. "Will you come inside with me?" she said, continuing to walk up the steps to the back door.

"Sure."

Once inside she led them to the bedroom they were staying in, sat down on the bed and looked up at Angel. "I'm going to lie down for a little bit." She smiled at the concern in Angel's eyes. "I'm okay, it's nothing serious. I simply need to rest. You know how after we went to the statue and Montauk, the next day we took it easy?"

"Yes," Angel said tentatively.

"It's like that. I just need to rest." She patted the bed next to her and Angel sat down. Gina put an arm around her. "I'm so glad we won. I knew we were a good team."

Angel grinned at her. "I knew we were too."

Gina cupped the side of Angel's face with her other hand. "I need you to go back out there and scout those other two teams."

Angel's brow wrinkled and she started to speak, but Gina stopped her with a tender kiss. "I'm fine. Let me rest for a while and I'll be ready for those gourmet burgers you and Travis have planned."

Angel's heart was pounding in her chest. She didn't want to leave her, but understood that rest was what Gina needed right now. She released a steadying breath, knowing Gina was being honest, and then she smiled. "I love you, Gina."

Gina gave her the sweetest smile back. "I know you do. Thanks for doing this for me, for us."

"I'll be back for another kiss in a little while," Angel said.

"I'll have one waiting."

Angel got up so Gina could stretch out on the bed. She smiled down at her then walked to the door. She stopped and looked back; Gina already had her eyes closed. As she left she pulled the door shut and stood there for a moment. She felt such a profound feeling of belonging and togetherness. It was as if her heart was where it was supposed to be.

She hesitated to use the word *home* because of the bad memories conjured up by the past. Maybe all the globe trotting and job placements were simply the path to Gina. There was not even a tiny piece of her that wanted to go back to what was her home. That wasn't her home; that was simply a house where she stayed while starting her education. Her family hadn't reached out to her, so were they really a family or just people she'd stayed with on that journey?

Gina was her truth. Gina was her absolute. That was where this path had led. They had found one another and there was no way anything could get between them. Not even sick kidneys.

Suddenly Angel felt settled, less afraid. She was still concerned that Gina felt badly, but something inside her knew it was all going to be all right. Just like on New Year's Eve when Gina told her she needed a kidney—she had the same feeling. Now she knew that feeling included her, too. *They* were going to be all right.

She peeked back into the room and saw a peaceful look on Gina's face. Then she turned to go back outside with a full heart beating with a new purpose, exactly where it belonged.

* * *

Gina closed her eyes and felt calm descend over her body. She knew Angel was nearby and that comforted her. The heaviness and dullness she felt inside wasn't going away anytime soon. This she knew. Her hope was that she could make it through the rest of the evening and she and Angel could go home earlier than planned tomorrow.

She slipped into sleep and felt like she was floating. There was no heaviness, no fatigue; she was light and ethereal. Something supported her; she felt safe and content. Then she realized what it was. Angel's love was wrapped around her. That's what held her and it felt magical, perfect, and true.

There was no fear, no worry, no anticipation or apprehension. She let go of it all surrounded by Angel's love; surrounded by all she'd ever need.

* * *

Angel went back outside and everyone immediately noticed Gina wasn't with her.

"Is she okay?" Brandy asked.

"She's a little tired, so she's napping for a bit," Angel answered, her face relaxed.

"I thought she looked tired this morning," said Shannon. "She'll be all right."

"She wanted to rest so she'll be ready for those burgers you promised, Travis," Angel told him.

"I think you were in on that promise, too," Travis said back at her.

"Let's finish this game," Michael said. "You're going to make me hungry again."

They went back to the game and Angel joined in and was welcomed like she'd known them for years. When the games finished, the group came back inside, some to snack and others to drink.

Angel looked in on Gina and saw she was peacefully sleeping. She smiled at her fighting the urge to touch her.

When she walked back into the living room Sarah Beth looked at her. "How is she?"

"Sleeping. I'm sure that's what she needed," Angel said, sitting down on the end of the couch.

"Be careful," Brandy said, sitting across from her. "She can be wary of people taking care of her."

"Oh I know. She told me all about Victoria," Angel answered with understanding.

"Yeah well, we like you and want to keep you around," said Michael. "So don't let her push you away."

Angel smiled. "She's better about that."

"Do you think you've changed her?" asked Dustin skeptically.

"I know she's changed me," said Angel.

"See I'm not sure I get that. You fall in love with someone, so why would you want to change them?" he said.

"For me it wasn't so much change, but opening up. Before Gina, I would've been sitting in the corner not adding to the conversation."

"I get that. Love can make you change. Sometimes you know early, like Dustin and Brandy," Michael said. "But for me I had to be in love a few times and get my heart broken to learn how to be a good partner."

"Thank you to all those that came before me," Sarah Beth said, looking up.

Several chuckles echoed around the room.

"It took me a little longer," said Travis. "I was serious about a couple of girlfriends, but I didn't fall in love until I met Shannon. It was love at first sight. I mean I felt like something had knocked the breath out of me."

"Aww, babe," Shannon said, kissing his cheek.

"Of course it took her a little longer," he said, laughing and putting his arm around her.

"I'm kind of with you, Travis," Angel said. "I had a girlfriend in high school and was falling for her, but when my parents found out it was ugly. I lost my girlfriend, my parents, and my family. That hurt so bad I wasn't about to open my heart."

"Dang, Angel. I can see why you'd close it off!" exclaimed Brandy.

"But not with Gina. It began to open the first time I met her," Angel said, shaking her head. She looked around the room and couldn't believe what she was about to say.

"Honestly, this is going to sound weird. I haven't even told Gina this because I've just now realized it," she said.

"Well don't stop now," Shannon said.

Angel looked up. "I used to think all this jumping from Spain to Brazil to Hong Kong was me running away. But now, I think it was the path to Gina. No one has made me feel safe like she has. I am so glad I came here."

"So am I," Gina said from behind Angel. She reached down and kissed her cheek and then walked around and squeezed in next to her on the couch.

"When did you all get so philosophical about relationships?" Gina said, grinning.

"Did we wake you?" said Shannon.

"Not at all. I kept dreaming about burgers."

Travis hopped up. "Then let's get to it!"

Everyone else got up to help and Gina stopped Angel before she could join Travis.

"Hey, thanks for how you're taking care of me," she said quietly, pulling Angel close.

Angel nodded. "I love you."

Gina smiled. "I love you too." She brought their lips together for a quick kiss. Then she pushed her away. "Now go light that fire!"

Angel tipped her head and raised her eyebrows seductively.

Gina chuckled. "You can light my fire later."

Angel kissed her then hopped up and was gone. Gina patted the empty spot next to her and Shannon sat down.

"Everyone really likes Angel," Shannon said.

"So do I," Gina said, wiggling her eyebrows.

Shannon chuckled. "You're going to have to let her help you this week."

"I know," Gina said sadly. "Something isn't right. I can feel it."

Shannon nodded. "Let's have one of these burgers our significant others keep bragging about and worry about the rest tomorrow."

22

Gina turned her Angel coin over and over in her hand. This had become a comforting routine for her when Angel wasn't with her or even if she was. It had been over a week since they'd returned from the beach house. Gina had let Angel stay with her.

She was able to work from home just enough to keep her team running smoothly. It had been a wise choice to wait for and hire the right people when she was putting her team together. The benefits were huge when she was sick like this.

Angel had been wonderful. Gina tried to get her to go to the office, but she and Travis assured her she could manage from Gina's place. Her face softened when she thought about Angel. She didn't hover, but was right there if she needed help. On several afternoons Angel went by her place or ran to the store to make herself scarce for a little while. There were times they both needed their space and these little errands were the perfect escape.

Her doctor had adjusted her medication and she hoped she would feel more like herself by the end of the week. Gina could feel her energy begin to creep back and smiled as she remembered last night.

Angel had been patient with her and held her close at night and snuggled on the couch with her in the evenings. But they were still in the honeymoon phase and Gina longed to touch Angel and make love to her; she simply wasn't up to it. Angel had come up with a perfect alternative.

Last night she'd filled the bathtub with steaming hot water and lit candles all around the bathroom. She added bath salts that not only smelled heavenly, but also made her skin feel luxurious and soft. She led Gina into the bathroom and slid her robe off and offered her hand. Gina stepped into the tub and waited. Angel shed her robe and stepped in behind her. She sat down in the tub and eased Gina down in between her legs.

Gina slowly reclined and could feel Angel's nipples harden against her back. Before she could move, Angel had her arms around Gina, holding her to her chest.

"Isn't this nice," Angel moaned. "I could hold you like this forever."

"I want to do so much more than hold you," Gina said, turning her head to look at Angel. The love she saw shining in Angel's eyes made her lose her breath.

"Sometimes," Angel began softly, "we get so excited we speed through a touch, a caress, a stroke." She gently ran a finger down the side of Gina's face. "We're so focused on the ultimate end. This is an opportunity to embrace these intimate touches and hold on to them, savor them, live them."

Gina closed her eyes and leaned back into Angel. She ran her hands along the outside of Angel's thighs; her legs bent at the knees. She felt encompassed by Angel in every way. Her arms and legs made a nest for Gina's healing body. She could feel Angel's love wrapped around her heart. And somehow she could perceive their future. They were enveloped around the other protecting, thriving, and happy. That was it; Gina could feel them swathed in happiness.

Angel ran her hands down Gina's arms and then back to her shoulders and massaged gently. She reached under her arms and rested her hands on Gina's stomach. Gina let her head fall back until it rested on Angel's shoulder and they nuzzled cheek to cheek.

They took deep cleansing breaths over and over until they were finally chased from the now chilly water. They got to their feet and stepped out of the tub.

Gina grabbed a towel and wrapped it around Angel's shoulders. She stepped into Angel's extended arms as she wrapped them around her. They stood, mesmerized by the intimacy. Gina could feel her heart beating with Angel's.

She stepped back and Angel dried her then did the same to her own body. She quickly blew out the candles.

They walked out of the bathroom and climbed under the sheets. Gina pulled Angel into her arms and whispered, "I love you so much."

She could feel Angel smile against her chest before she heard, "I love you, baby."

It wasn't long until they both fell asleep. When Gina woke up in the middle of the night they were still holding one another. She felt more rested at that moment than before she became sick. She would never forget sharing this act of love with Angel.

Gina was snapped back to the present when her phone rang. It was their regular night to go to the Youth Center and Angel had gone with Gina's insisting.

"Those kids need you," she'd told her earlier.

"You need me too," Angel had replied.

"You'll be gone a couple of hours. I promise not to do anything but miss you while you're gone," Gina had said, laughing.

Angel went begrudgingly. Gina smiled, recalling the glum look on Angel's face as she'd left.

"Hi honey," she said.

"Hey babe. Whatcha doing?"

"I'm just missing you, like I promised."

Angel laughed. "Can you go to the living room window and look out?"

"Sure," Gina said.

She looked down and could see Maddie, Isaac, Dario, and Camila waving up at her.

"Hey! It's the Rainbow Warriors," she said into the phone, waving down at them. "What are they doing here?"

"They missed you. When I explained you weren't feeling well they knew seeing them would cheer you up."

"Aren't they humble," Gina said, laughing.

"We can see how big your smile is all the way down here," Dario yelled into the phone.

This made Gina's smile grow even more. "Tell them I'll be back next week."

Angel relayed the message and the kids waved and took off down the street.

Gina was still looking out the window when Angel walked in.

"Hey," Angel said, taking her coat off.

Gina sat down on the couch and sighed.

"I thought they cheered you up," she said, sitting down next to her.

"They did," Gina said with a forced smile. "Sometimes I just wish I could be a regular person, not a sick one. Those last few months were so good; I almost felt like I wasn't sick—except for all the medication I take. I mean with you," she said, grabbing Angel's hand and continuing. "We did things like people do and went places and had fun and had amazing sex. Why in the world do you want to be with me? You could have a healthy beautiful girlfriend!" Gina threw Angel's hand out of her lap and got up and went to the bedroom, tears running down her cheeks.

Angel took a deep breath, slowly got up and walked to the bedroom door. Gina was on the bed, tears rolling down her cheeks.

"I have a healthy, beautiful, girlfriend," she said quietly from the doorway.

Gina looked at her like she'd lost her mind.

"Healthy encompasses a lot of things," Angel began. "If you'll remember, when we met I wasn't the healthiest of people either.

Mine may not be physical, but it hurts just like yours does. You have made me better; please let me help you get better."

Gina's anger quickly turned to remorse. "I'm sorry I yelled at you."

Still in the doorway Angel said, "I know this is hard. But please don't ever talk trash about my girlfriend again. I love her very much and she's the perfect person for me."

This made Gina smile. She looked down and then back at Angel. "I'm sorry. I won't do that again. Are you mad at me?"

Angel scoffed. "No, I'm not mad."

"Then will you come hold me?"

Angel smiled, climbed on the bed and took Gina in her arms.

"Sometimes it becomes too much."

"Honestly, I'm surprised you haven't blown up before now," Angel said. "I would have."

Gina raised up and looked at her, surprised. "You would?"

"You are so brave," Angel said, stroking the side of her face. "I can't imagine how hard this has been for you all these years. I'm so glad to be here with you so you have someone to yell at. You can yell at me anytime. Just know that I'm not going anywhere. I'm in it. With you!"

Gina kissed Angel with more passion than she'd had since becoming sick. The kiss continued until they both had to breathe.

"I love kissing you," Angel said breathlessly.

"Then don't stop."

"I want to savor your kisses just like the touches last night."

Angel leaned in and pressed her lips to Gina's. When their tongues met Gina moaned and lost herself in the most supple, passionate, never-ending kiss. It went on and on, soft then hard, smooth here and nips there, moans and groans.

"Mmm, I could do this all night," Gina said, nibbling on Angel's ear lobe.

"I'm not stopping you," Angel said, panting.

They had found another unforgettable way of loving one another.

23

Gina continued to improve and felt stronger every day. On Friday afternoon she knew Angel was going to run by the office and then to her apartment.

"Would you put this in the want box for me when you go to your apartment?"

Angel took the slip of paper, but didn't open it. "Should I look at this now?"

"Why don't you wait until this afternoon. I'll call you," Gina said mischievously.

"Ah, a little mystery, huh?"

"I won't make you wait too long," she said, planting a kiss on her lips.

"I'll be gone a couple of hours, so soak up this alone time," Angel said, grabbing her bag.

"I'm about ready for time out of this apartment."

"Let's plan something for tomorrow," suggested Angel. "I can tell you're stronger."

"Feel how strong I am," Gina said, straining her voice playfully and wrapping Angel in a bear hug.

Angel giggled and then stopped and stared at Gina.

"What?"

"The joy is back in your eyes and it makes them shine."

Gina kissed her again. "Go! So you can get back."

Angel hurried out the door and Gina went to change. She had a surprise planned for Angel this afternoon.

She waited an hour and was about to leave when her phone rang. A picture of her and Shannon, arms around each other's shoulders, appeared on the screen. Gina smiled.

"Hey you," she said.

"Someone is feeling better," Shannon said a smile in her voice.

"That would be me. The last couple of days I've improved exponentially."

"I'm so glad, but it's about time!"

"I know! This one lasted too long."

"Don't they all," Shannon said. "What are you doing? I thought I might drop by."

"I'm about to go surprise my girlfriend."

"Oh you are? I love hearing you say that."

"Which part? Go or girlfriend."

"Girlfriend. There's something in your voice when you say it."

Gina chuckled. "She's not my first girlfriend, Shan."

"I know that, but you sound different when you say it now. You can hear happiness in your voice."

"Because I am."

"Well, go have fun. You deserve it after being in that apartment for so long. Maybe we could get together this weekend."

"I'd love that! We'll come to you."

Shannon laughed. "Okay, call me tomorrow. Before I forget, Travis has another ten people signed up to get tested."

"Oh good. Where does he come up with them? He's not handing out flyers on the street is he?"

"Not yet, but don't put it past him. He's very optimistic. I think these came from another team within his company."

"I'll thank him tomorrow. Fingers crossed."

"You know it."

"Bye Shan."

"Bye GG."

Gina let out a big breath. She hoped her donor would be in this group. Enough about kidneys, she thought. A smile grew on her face as she grabbed her bag and walked out the door.

What a beautiful day. The sun was shining and she couldn't believe the wind wasn't blowing since it was still March.

She walked into the little park not far from Angel's apartment. One end of the basketball court was empty and there were a couple of balls under the basket. She walked over and picked them up and went to the bleachers. From there she could look up and just see Angel's windows. She took her phone out and called her.

"Hey babe," Angel said, picking up on the second ring.

"Hi honey. Are you through at the office?"

"Yep, I'm at my apartment and about to leave."

"Oh good. Did you put my want in the heart box?"

"I did," she said, chuckling. "Are you checking up on me?"

"Nope. Why don't you read it now?"

"Okay. Let me get it."

Gina could tell she was walking into the bedroom because she kept the box on her night stand.

"It says, 'I want to shoot baskets with you.'"

"Remember when we watched those people play basketball at the park near your apartment?"

"Yeah, you said you'd cheer while I played," she said, chuckling.

"Look out your window toward the park," Gina instructed.

"What?" Angel said.. Her face appeared in her window. "What are you doing?"

"I want to shoot baskets. I'll still be your cheerleader, but I want to shoot some too. Come down before someone takes our end of the court."

Angel quickly made her way downstairs and over to the park. She hurried up to Gina and hugged her, spinning them around.

"I didn't realize you felt this much better," Angel said, putting her bag next to Gina's.

Gina bounced her a ball and they went to their end of the court.

"Here goes," Gina said, throwing her ball up. It hit the backboard and bounced away. "Okay, your turn," she said, chasing after her ball.

Angel threw hers up and it hit the rim, but bounced out.

They both began shooting and working the rust off from not playing for so many years. Before long they were both making baskets to go along with their misses.

"Hey, Shannon called and said Travis has ten more people that signed up to be tested."

"Yeah, he told me about it when I went by the office," said Angel, chasing after her ball.

"Hopefully, one will be a match. I'm ready to get this done. Oh, I told her we'd come by and see them tomorrow, if that's okay with you."

"Tired of your apartment?"

"Aren't you?" Gina said, chuckling. "Yes!" she said when her ball went through the hoop.

"You know I like your place."

"I know, I know. It's homey. But we'd made yours feel more like a home before I got sick."

Angel made a long shot and it went in. "Woo hoo!" she yelled.

"Way to go Angel baby!" Gina cheered.

"Angel baby?"

Gina laughed. "I don't know where that came from. Wait!" she said, grabbing her ball, a memory in the back of her mind. She dribbled the ball trying to recall. "I can remember my parents dancing in the kitchen to a song." The tune was somewhere, trying to come forward. "I can't remember it all, but it was something like 'You're my angel baby, yes you're my angel baby, for the rest of my life.'"

"Hey, listen to you. I didn't know you could sing," Angel said, impressed.

"That's because I can't," said Gina, laughing. "I'll try to find that song later. Isn't it funny how memories pop into your head sometimes?"

"Yeah it is," Angel replied, watching Gina.

"Why aren't you shooting?"

"You're incredible, did you know that!" Angel said.

"What? No I'm not. You just haven't seen me happy like this in so long you don't recognize me."

Angel grabbed her around the waist from behind and Gina squealed. She turned in her arms and threw her head back laughing.

"Don't recognize you? I'll always know you, I'll always see you," Angel said, breathing hard. "Till the end of time."

Gina stilled and looked into Angel's eyes. They had suddenly turned serious and desire darkened them. "Let's go to your place," Gina said hoarsely.

Angel grabbed their bags and they raced to her building and into the elevator.

Gina backed Angel up against the wall and kissed her until they were both gasping. She gave her a sexy smile and said, "We have some catching up to do."

The elevator doors opened and Gina sashayed to Angel's door; she reached for Angel's key, unlocked the door and pulled her inside.

24

"I am glad it's April," Gina said, walking next to Angel, holding her hand.

"Me too. It feels like spring today," Angel said, swinging their hands.

Gina looked over at her and bumped shoulders, a wide grin on her face.

"Gina?" a woman said as she walked up to them.

Gina turned her head and stopped. "Victoria!" she said with surprise in her voice.

"I'm so glad to see you," Victoria said, smiling affectionately at Gina.

"You too," Gina smiled. She looked over at Angel. "Victoria, this is Angel, my girlfriend," she said easily. Gina felt Angel squeeze her hand and smiled.

"So nice to meet you, Angel," Victoria said politely.

"It's nice to meet you."

Victoria paused and looked at Gina, then smiled. "I don't mean to make this awkward, but I don't know when I'll see you again." She looked from Angel then back to Gina. "It was hard to move forward, but I want you to know that I understand now what you were trying to make me see."

Gina nodded. "I've learned some things, too."

"You look happy," she stated.

"I am," Gina said, glancing over at Angel with a smile.

Victoria looked at their clasped hands and then to Angel. "Hold on tight, she's worth it."

"Oh I know," Angel assured her. "I intend to."

"Do you want to join us? We're meeting Shannon and Travis at the East Side Diner," Gina offered.

Victoria chuckled. "I just left there. I'm actually on my way to meet my fiancée." She held her left hand up and wiggled her ring finger. "I'm engaged."

"Congratulations," Gina said, genuinely happy for her.

"It was really good to see you, Gina," Victoria said. "And again nice to meet you, Angel," she said, making eye contact. "Tell Shannon and Travis hello."

"I will," Gina said.

Victoria walked past them and they went into the restaurant and found a table.

After sitting down Angel said, "So that was Victoria."

"Where?" Shannon said, walking up with Travis. They both had a seat.

"Hi," Gina said to them both. "We ran into her outside the restaurant."

"How is she?" asked Shannon. "Still wanting to take care of you?"

"She didn't even bring it up," said Gina. "She looked good; she's engaged."

"She wants to take care of you?" Angel asked, confused.

Gina looked up at her. "Victoria took very good care of me when I was sick. The problem was she wouldn't let me do the same for her. That's how our relationship is different. You let me nurture and care for you, too. It's balanced."

"If I hadn't let you nurse my damaged heart we wouldn't be together right now," Angel said. "I realize that. I may not have known it was happening at the time, but I do now. It was simply my turn when you started feeling bad."

Gina smiled. "That's what Victoria meant when she said she understood now. I tried to explain it to her. And that's why I was afraid she'd end up resenting me. After she left it was hard to let anyone help me because I was afraid the same thing would happen. You made me see that sometimes people like taking care of others; it's not a burden and I get that now."

"That's right. It takes us both," Travis said. "Sometimes I feel like Shannon gives a lot more than I do, but I know it will even out because she'll tell me if it doesn't."

"I'm such a hard ass," Shannon said, smiling at him and reaching for his hand.

"No you're not. It's called communication. You call me out when I'm not paying attention."

"That doesn't happen very often though," Shannon said.

"And of course she's always paying attention, right Travis?" Gina said, chuckling.

"Right, Gina," Travis said, nodding and winking at her.

"Ha ha," Shannon said sarcastically. "Hey, did Brandy text you?"

"Nope," Gina replied.

"They want us to come out Saturday, hopefully for a picnic in their backyard if the weather cooperates. I just got the text when we walked in."

As if on cue, Gina's and Angel's phones pinged.

Gina laughed and read it out loud, "Party in the borough. Hope you and Angel can come."

"Mine says, it's time to meet the kids," Angel said, looking up. "That's so nice she texted me."

"I'm tempted to ask if I can bring someone else, just to mess with her," Gina said with a devilish grin.

"Ohhhhh, do it!" Shannon said.

"Let's see," Gina said, beginning to type. "Do I have to bring Angel?" she read and then hit send.

Angel shook her head and narrowed her eyes at Gina. "You've got a mean streak."

"Not really," Shannon said. "Brandy is always pulling shit on us."

Travis laughed. "It's true. She's the one with the mean streak."

Gina's phone pinged with a response. She started laughing and then read aloud, "If you mess this up, Gina Gray, I promise I will yank both of your bad kidneys out with my bare hands!"

Shannon laughed loudly and asked Gina what she was texting back.

Gina looked over at Angel and grinned, then read aloud as she typed. "I'm not letting her get away. Don't worry."

"See," Travis said, nudging Angel's arm. "She doesn't have a mean streak."

"Will Sarah Beth and Michael be there, too?" Angel asked.

"Oh yeah. You'll get to meet Chloe, too," said Travis. "She's a little sweetheart."

Angel had a grin on her face and Travis said, "Do you like kids?"

"Sure. Who doesn't like kids?" she replied.

"We do. How many are we having, babe? Five or six?" Travis asked. Then he winked at Angel, waiting for Shannon's response.

"You may father five or six, but this woman ain't birthing them," Shannon said firmly.

They all laughed, and enjoyed the rest of their time together.

* * *

Later that evening Gina and Angel sat on her couch.

"That was fun this afternoon at the restaurant with Travis and Shannon," Angel said. "Have you noticed how he looks at Shannon? At work he's so serious and focused, but when he's with her he relaxes."

"He has always looked at her like that. When they first met, he made his intentions known and clear."

"That doesn't surprise me about him at all." Angel chuckled.

"Did that bother you, meeting Victoria today?" Gina asked.

Angel looked over at her. "Why do you ask?"

"I felt you squeeze my hand when I introduced you as my girlfriend and then again when she told you to hold onto me."

Angel had a sly grin on her face. "I did have a moment that made me tighten my grip and hold on."

"Why?"

"I don't know. A moment of insecurity. I mean, Victoria is beautiful and here you are with me."

"She is beautiful, but so are you! Not just this beautiful face," Gina said, grabbing her chin and kissing her on the mouth. "There's so much more in here that is beautiful." She held her hand to Angel's heart.

"I wasn't fishing for compliments. What I meant was, for a moment there I wanted to hang on to you as if to say, you're mine. Ugh," Angel sighed, exasperated. "I don't mean that you're a possession, but you gave me your heart and that's real. I treasure it and will always value it and honor it and hold it dear."

"Oh honey. I understand what you mean. When you let me squeeze into your heart, I knew I had to be careful and appreciate it, but I also adored it and wanted to fill it with joy and happiness and love. That's why it was so easy for me to introduce you as my girlfriend. I'm proud that you are, that we are. I wanted you to know that."

"I do," Angel said softly.

"Hey, there's something I want to show you," Gina said, hopping up. She threw Angel's coat to her, put on her own and walked to the door.

"Where are we going?"

"Not far. It's a surprise." They got on the elevator and Gina punched the button for the roof.

Angel looked at her, perplexed. Gina raised her eyebrows and grinned with a 'trust me' look on her face.

They walked up a short stairway and opened the door to the roof. Stars dotted the sky and Gina led them to the middle of the roof.

"I didn't know you had a deck up here," Angel commented.

"It's not much of one, but you can see the stars. Look," Gina said, lifting her eyes to the sky.

"It's beautiful."

Gina grabbed her hand and led her to a small enclosed block abutted against a small square room on the roof. It was just perfect to sit on.

Gina leaned back against the wall and looked up. "I know we don't talk about it very often, but some days it gets to me that we haven't found a donor yet. Today is one of those days." She continued, "I know everything is going to be all right. I believe that, I truly do. But the waiting and no energy days weigh on me."

Angel kept her gaze on the stars. "It's hard to stay positive and optimistic all the time. Sometimes I can tell when you're feeling like this and other times I'm not sure. Thanks for telling me you're feeling down. Just know that I'm here and if you need picking up I can do that or if you need someone to be blue with you I can do that too."

"I'm glad you understand. I didn't want to say anything because I was afraid you'd think I was doubting you." Gina turned to Angel then and looked at her profile. Her heart swelled with love. "I could never doubt you."

Angel looked at her and slowly leaned in, pressing their lips together.

Gina could feel the love, the promise, and the assurance that joined them.

25

It was such a beautiful day for a picnic. The same group that spent the weekend on Long Island was back together only this time the kids were there, too.

Gina watched as Angel and Travis played with all three kids in the backyard while Michael and Dustin tended to the grill.

"You look so much better than our last gathering," Brandy said, putting an arm around Gina.

"I feel better, too."

"I had a feeling Angel would be great with kids," she commented, watching them.

"She really is."

"Maybe you two should have a few of your own," Brandy suggested.

Gina stiffened. "Slow down, Brandy!"

Brandy laughed. "I was just messing with you," she said, bumping her with her hip.

"You'd be a great mom," said Sarah Beth, who'd been listening.

"Thanks. But I have other things to take care of first," Gina said firmly.

"No luck on the donor I guess," said Sarah Beth, fidgeting from one foot to the other.

"Not yet. I'm usually positive about it, but this week has been hard."

"Have you felt bad?" Sarah Beth asked. "You look great."

Gina scoffed. "I don't look great, but to answer your question, I don't feel bad. I'm just tired of waiting. When you know something big is looming and you can't get to it, some days are anxious."

"I'm so sorry," Sarah Beth said, obviously upset.

"Hey, hey. It's okay. I'm going to be okay," Gina assured her, putting her arm around her shoulder.

Kids squealed and Shannon yelled from the kitchen for Brandy's help.

"Gina, I've got to tell you something," Sarah Beth said in an ominous tone. She took Gina's hand and pulled her over to an outdoor bench and sat down.

"I haven't been tested," Sarah Beth admitted.

"So? It's no big deal," Gina said.

"But it is! I can't give you my kidney, Gina, and I feel terrible," she said, tears in her eyes.

"It's okay. If you haven't been tested you might not match anyway," Gina explained.

"That's why I haven't been tested. If I match I'd have to turn you down."

A ball came rolling to their feet and Angel ran after it. She tossed it back to Travis and then turned back around to Gina and Sarah Beth.

"Is everything all right?" she asked, looking from Gina to Sarah Beth and back.

"Help me explain to Sarah Beth that it's okay she doesn't want to be tested as a kidney match," Gina said, feeling a bit thrown.

"It is okay," Angel said, kneeling in front of Sarah Beth. "It's a big decision and it's not for everyone."

"But you're one of my best friends," Sarah Beth said sadly.

"That doesn't have anything to do with us being friends," Gina said decisively.

"It sure doesn't," agreed Angel.

"Listen," Gina said, grabbing her hands. "I'm going to find my donor. It will happen. Afterwards is when I'm going to need you."

"After?" Sarah Beth sniffed.

"Yes! I'll need help," said Angel.

"You? I thought you helped her when she was sick last month," said Sarah Beth.

"I did, but this will be different. She'll need all her friends."

"I sure will. I love Angel, but you cook a lot better than she does," Gina said, looking from Angel to Sarah Beth.

"I never thought about that. You will need help while you recuperate. I've been so upset because I haven't been tested," Sarah Beth mumbled.

"Well stop it! I need you, Sarah Beth, for so much more than your kidney."

Gina pulled her into a hug and Angel stood up.

"I'm glad I can count on you after the transplant," Gina said to Sarah Beth.

"You can. I promise."

"Okay. Enough kidney talk for one day. Let's go play with these adorable kids," Gina said.

They started to join the kids and Angel pulled Gina back.

"Are you okay?"

"Yes. I'm just sorry she's been worried about that." She sighed. "And I'm so tired of these shitty kidneys."

Angel pulled her into a hug but didn't say anything.

Gina hugged her back, thankful she knew when words weren't needed.

* * *

After listening to Gina comfort an upset Sarah Beth, Angel had hugged Gina. Right then she decided she was getting tested. On Monday she'd talk to Travis and get it set up.

The rest of the afternoon passed with laughter and fun. While the kids napped, the adults caught up on their busy lives and made plans for next month. One of their New Year's resolutions was to get together at least once a month. So far they'd made it with Gina's New Year's dinner and in February they'd met at Shannon and Travis's for an afternoon. March was the Long Island weekend and now they were at Brandy and Dustin's for April.

"It's our turn for May," said Sarah Beth.

"I'm proud of us for making this happen so far," said Shannon.

"Let me look at my travel schedule and we'll text everyone," Michael said.

"Angel, you're one of us now since the kids have given their approval," Dustin said, grinning.

Angel laughed. "Good to know."

"Seriously, we're glad you've made Gina so happy," said Sarah Beth. "And you haven't let her run you off."

"What!" Gina exclaimed. "I'm trying to get her to stay. You'd better not run her off!"

"Why wouldn't she want to hang with us?" said Brandy. "We're awesome!"

Gina shook her head and looked at Angel apologetically.

Angel laughed. "Thanks for welcoming me." She looked around the room and knew that any of these people would help if she needed them. When she'd let Gina in her heart it had changed her life. She'd not only found love, but also gained a wonderful group of friends.

Later that night, they were back at Gina's apartment and lazily watching TV when Angel looked at her watch.

"Hey, want to go up on the roof?"

Gina looked over at her. "Because?"

"Because the stars are beautiful and I might have a little surprise for you," Angel said with a hopeful look on her face.

"A surprise! Let's go," Gina said, giggling.

They grabbed their coats. Even though it was April it was still chilly at night.

"Do you want to sit?" Gina asked.

"Yes," Angel said, walking to where they'd sat the first time they were there. "Hey, let's go to Montauk next Saturday," she suggested. "The weather is so much warmer. I think it'll be different."

"I'm sure it will and there will be more people, too."

"We can share." Angel grinned.

"You have a date," Gina said, kissing her on the cheek. "Is that my surprise?"

Angel looked at her watch again and then at the sky. "Nope. Here's your surprise. Do you see that star that's moving right there?" She pointed so that Gina could follow her finger and find the star.

"I see it!"

"It's not really a star. It's the International Space Station."

Gina looked at her in disbelief.

"I promise! I came across a site that will email you when it's going to be in the sky and viewable."

Gina looked back up and watched it move across the night sky. "There you go with promises again."

"I haven't broken one yet," she said, a smile in her voice.

"No, you haven't."

"Keep watching, it should disappear anytime."

Sure enough the light began to dim and then it was gone.

"That's amazing!" Gina said.

Angel chuckled. "It is. You know what's amazing to me?"

"What?" Gina said, her eyes shining.

"I'm amazed you've asked all your friends and people you don't know to be tested to be your donor, but you haven't asked me."

Gina studied Angel's face. She reached for her hands and held them in hers. "Because I don't want your kidney, Angel. I want your heart."

Angel looked at Gina and hoped she saw the love in her eyes. "Don't you know, you have my heart. You gently made your way through the scars, soothed and smoothed them. Then you embraced it, held it, adored it. And finally you wrapped it in love. You've had it for a while now."

"Oh Angel," Gina murmured.

Angel leaned in and kissed her tenderly.

"I can't ask, baby," Gina said breathlessly. "You've already given me all I need."

When Gina brought their lips together again Angel knew there wouldn't be any more talking. She knew their hearts matched and hoped the rest of them did too.

They went back downstairs and Gina gave Angel more love than she'd ever known. She loved her with her body, but also with her words. Angel had never shared that much passion and tenderness with anyone. Her heart had never been so full. She wasn't about to lose Gina to a disease or anything else.

26

"They said it may be a few days before I get my results because of some back up in the lab," Angel said, standing in Travis's doorway.

"Come on in, sit a minute."

Angel sat down and exhaled.

"I still can't get over that Gina wouldn't ask you to take the test. And I can't believe I didn't think about it either."

"You were too involved in finding as many people as possible to be tested," Angel said.

"I know, but it makes me wonder if I've missed some other people that were there New Year's Eve when it all started."

"I wish I could help you, but I didn't know many people then."

Travis stared at Angel. "I know you're hoping you match."

"More than anything."

Travis smiled. "Shannon and I were so disappointed when our results came back that we broke down in tears. Gina doesn't know that and doesn't need to," he added.

Angel nodded. She slapped her hands on her thighs. "You know what, it doesn't matter! It doesn't matter if she has to go on dialysis and we don't find a match. All that matters is she's still here with us and I get to love her."

"Those are nice words and a good attitude, but she deserves better. She deserves the chance to live a life without chronic disease. I know she'll still be on a lot of medication, but she'll feel good. She told me once that she can't remember what it was like to feel good and not be worried about sickness."

"I've got to be her match. I've just got to be."

"Does she know you were being tested?"

"No. I didn't tell her."

Travis nodded. "Okay. Fingers crossed and no matter what, we're here for the next step."

Angel nodded and got up and went to her office. She took a deep breath, closed her eyes and let it out slowly. Then she got back to work.

Two days later it was finally Friday and Angel couldn't wait for the day to be done.

"Hey," Travis said, walking into her office. "What are you and Gina doing this weekend?"

"We're going to Montauk tomorrow. I'll be glad to get out of the city even if it's just for a day."

Her phone began to ring before Travis could comment.

Angel answered it and listened. After a few moments she said, "Okay thank you. I'll await your call." Tears were flooding Angel's eyes when she ended the call.

"What's wrong? Angel, are you all right?" Travis sat forward, concerned.

"I'm a match," she said softly. "Travis, I'm a match!"

They both jumped up and hugged.

"Oh my God, Angel. Seriously!"

"Yes. They said I'm a match! I'm giving Gina my kidney!"

"You've got to call her."

"They said on the phone that her doctor was contacting her." Angel gasped. "Maybe they won't tell her who it is. I could tell her on the roof tonight or I can tell her tomorrow in Montauk." So many thoughts were running through her head, but most importantly, the knowledge that she was a match.

Travis excitedly started to say something when Angel's phone pinged.

"It's from Gina. She wants to know if I can get off early," Angel said, looking down at her phone. "She must know."

"Go!"

Angel quickly texted her back and said she was on the way. "You have to act surprised when she tells you."

"I will," Travis assured her.

She sat down in her chair and took a deep breath and then let it out. She put her face in her hands as tears ran down her cheeks.

Travis came over and put an arm around her. "I'm so happy for you both!"

Angel let out another deep breath. "They'll have more information for me Monday, but for now they wanted me to know I matched and would be an excellent donor for her."

"Halle-fucking-lujah!" Travis said, raising his arms to the heavens.

* * *

Gina couldn't wait for Angel to get here. She thought about a cute way to tell her, but knew her excitement would get the best of her. She heard the door open and close then ran to Angel.

She jumped into her arms and squeezed her tight.

"Are you all right?" Angel asked.

"I'm excited you could get off early with such short notice. I have a surprise for you," Gina said, her eyebrows raised. "Pack a bag, honey. Suzanne lent me her car so we can drive to Montauk and spend the night. Then we can stay as long as we like tomorrow and not worry about catching the train."

Gina was so excited that she mistook Angel's surprise and thought she was as happy about this little adventure as she was.

"Let me quickly pack a bag," Angel said, heading toward the

bedroom. She stopped and turned around. "Hey, I just realized this will be the first time we've spent the night at a hotel together."

"I know! That's why I'm excited," Gina said, beaming.

Angel grabbed a small bag she kept at Gina's. She packed in haste and began to smile.

"What are you smiling about?" Gina said playfully, walking in to get her bag.

Angel turned around and grabbed Gina. "I'm smiling because I get to spend the night away from the city with my beautiful girlfriend. Why are you smiling?"

"Because I'm taking my girl on a little trip. Can you imagine how those stars are going to look tonight from that beach?"

"They won't be any brighter than your eyes," Angel said.

Gina claimed Angel's lips, not being able to wait another second. After a few delicious moments she pulled back breathlessly. "We'd better go, those stars are waiting."

Angel leaned in for one more quick kiss before they grabbed their bags and left for Montauk.

The traffic was surprisingly light since they were able to leave before folks exited the city for the weekend.

"Why did Suzanne lend you her car?" Angel asked, watching the city whiz by her window.

"She felt bad that she wasn't a match so when I told her we were going to Montauk tomorrow she offered her car so we could go early and spend the night."

Angel looked over at her with affection covering her face. "She did that because you're such a good person, you know."

Gina glanced at her. "I love those kids and would do just about anything to make their troubled lives easier. She would too."

"Those kids are lucky to have you," Angel stated. Then she turned the radio up. "I love this song."

"Me, too!" Gina yelled.

"Lifestyle" by Jason Derulo blared through the speakers and they sang at the top of their voices and laughed. They stopped at a couple of little shops that interested them and then they made a list of places to try on the way back.

The little inn where Gina made reservations was quaint and an easy walk to the beach. They dropped their bags and walked among the little shops and places to eat.

Angel asked Gina to wait outside while she ran in one of the shops. While she waited, Gina looked in the windows of the shop next door and also down the way for a place to eat. It was getting dark and she hoped they'd be able to walk out to the beach and star gaze. She wondered what Angel was up to, but knew it would make her happy because Angel always made her happy.

She turned to see Angel walking toward her with a bag in her hand. Gina gave her a curious look, but Angel just said, "Ready to get something to eat?"

Gina played along. "Sure. There's a restaurant just down the way."

Once they were seated and had ordered Gina said, "Are you going to tell me what's in the bag?"

Angel narrowed her eyes. "Maybe I'll show you a little later. Can you be patient?"

Gina deadpanned. "Duh, I've been waiting for a kidney. Not always patiently, but for the most part. And let's see, I patiently waited for you to fall in love with me."

"Oh you did? I'm not sure that's how I remember it."

"Oh?" Gina asked.

"I remember having to tell you because I couldn't keep it in any longer," Angel said with a twinkle in her eye.

"You have that same look in your eyes tonight. What do you have to tell me, Angelica?" Gina said.

"Hmm, what does it mean when you use my entire name?"

"Truthfully, I love saying it. But you still have that look."

Angel smiled. "You'll see."

Gina stuck out her bottom lip in a pout. "Okay. I will patiently wait."

Their food came and they dove into it with eagerness, sharing between the two plates. After they paid they continued walking until the sidewalk gave way to the sand and rocks of the beach. As they approached the water they found a bench and sat.

When they looked up they could just see a few stars begin to twinkle.

Gina could feel Angel looking at her and glanced her way. "What?"

"You are so beautiful, Gina Gray."

Gina softly said, "Thank you."

Angel began to dig in the sack she carried from the gift shop. "I got you a little something."

She handed Gina a hoodie with a lighthouse imprint that said Montauk Point across it.

Gina held it up and smiled. "Thank you. I love it! When we're back home I can wear this and feel like I'm here with you." She smiled at Angel and noticed the bag wasn't empty. "What else do you have in there?"

She watched as Angel pulled out another hoodie.

"What do you think?" Angel said, holding it up so Gina could see.

Gina laughed with glee. "I love it. We match!"

When Angel didn't say anything, Gina looked up and saw tears in her eyes.

Concern covered Gina's face immediately. She dropped the hoodie in her lap and turned to Angel. "Baby, what's wrong?"

Angel smiled through her tears and grabbed Gina's hands. She took a deep breath. "I got tested. Our hoodies match, our hearts match, and our kidneys match."

"What?" Gina whispered, unbelieving. Her eyes wide with amazement.

"I couldn't stand it, babe. I got tested this week and got the results right before you texted me earlier today. I thought your doctor would have called you by now."

Gina sat in silence. "They did, but I missed the call. When I saw it they were gone for the weekend."

"Why don't you look happy? You heard what I said, right? We match. You can get the transplant."

Gina sighed. "I'm afraid, Angel. I don't want this to mess up our relationship," she said, shaking her head. "Good God, how much more can you give me? It's too much!" The fear was evident in her eyes.

"No, no, no. You'd do the same for me. I'll give you anything," Angel said, panic in her voice.

Gina looked at Angel and could see the anguish all over her face. "But what do I have to give to you?"

Angel tilted her head and her eyes widened. "Don't you realize? You've given me a life with purpose. You've got to let me do this." The tears were streaming down her face now. "For so long I've been empty and broken. My life was meaningless and then I met you. You filled me with love, but more importantly I can help you have a better life, a healthier life. That's worth everything, Gina! You have to let me do this!"

Tears filled Gina's eyes now. She pulled her hands from Angel's and cradled her face. "I can't believe this. You're my match." Then she began to laugh. "Of course you are!" She kissed Angel tenderly.

"You've given me a life, please…" Angel began, but didn't finish because Gina stopped her with a finger on her lips.

"You've given me a happy life, Angelica, and now you want to give me a healthier life," Gina said.

Angel grabbed Gina's hand and kissed her palm. "More than anything I want to give you my kidney."

"Does it come with any strings attached?" Gina said, trying to lighten the tension.

A small smile crept on Angel's face. "Maybe."

Gina grinned at her. "I'll tell you what, I may have some conditions before I'll take it, so you think about any you might have giving it." Then she winked. "Because right now, I want to do this," she said, kissing Angel passionately, wrapping her arms tightly around her shoulders.

When they slowly pulled apart, Gina sighed. "I had all these ideas how this would feel, but I still can't believe it's you."

"Do you want to call your dad or Shannon and share the good news?" Angel asked.

"Can I put my new hoodie on and gaze at these stars for a bit first? We can call her when we get back to our room and I'll call Dad in the morning."

"I'll put on my *matching* hoodie and join you."

Gina chuckled and after they had their matching hoodies on, Angel put her arm around her and they looked above. Gina leaned into Angel and felt protected, loved, and hopeful. She'd always felt that whatever happened she and Angel would find a way through it, but now it was as if their life had a new beginning.

"You know it's going to hurt," Gina said, staring at the stars.

"Yep."

"You'll probably want to call me names," Gina added.

"Nope."

"We'll see," Gina murmured.

Angel chuckled.

"Can you believe how much brighter these stars are?" Gina said, amazed.

"They should be to match your brightness."

Gina chuckled at Angel's word choice. "But they can't match your goodness. And don't try to dispute it."

Angel giggled, but didn't say anything.

They sat in silence for a while, soaking in the beautiful sky, content to simply be with one another.

Gina rested her head on Angel's shoulder. "I love you, Angel."

"Oh Gina, I love you too," she said, pulling her even closer.

"Thank you for the sweet way you told me you were my match. I'm sorry I made you cry." Gina sat up and brought her eyes to Angel's.

"I understand why you were apprehensive, but this way I'm hoping you'll keep me around."

Gina smiled. "You know that doesn't make any difference."

"I know, but it's a little insurance. Before you call Shannon I need to tell you that Travis was in my office when I got the call. He knows, but I don't think he'll tell her. He'll let you do that."

"Well, let's go find out," Gina said, hopping up and reaching for Angel's hand.

Once they were back at the room Gina grabbed her phone and made a FaceTime call to Shannon.

Shannon answered, looking at Gina, her brow furrowed. "Hey, where are you?"

"In Montauk. Suzanne gave me her car so we could come out and spend the night."

"How nice! So what's wrong? Why aren't you two doing the romantic things you do?"

"We've been stargazing and I had to show you something. Where's Travis?"

"I'm here," Travis said, appearing next to Shannon with a big grin on his face.

Gina stood next to Angel and extended her arm so Shannon could see them both. "Look at our hoodies!"

"Aren't you two cute! Matchy-matchy," Shannon said, laughing.

"That's right, Shan. Guess what else is matchy-matchy?" Gina said, her exuberance obvious.

Shannon looked at her, confused, while Travis beamed next to her.

"Help her out, Travie," Gina said, nodding her head.

"Let's see," he said, drawing it out. "Your kidneys!" he whooped.

Shannon's mouth flew open. She looked from Travis back to Gina and screamed. "No way!"

"Yes way!" Angel yelled back.

"Oh my God, oh my God, oh my God!" Shannon squealed. "How?"

Angel explained that she hadn't been tested and Gina didn't really want her to, but she did anyway. Shannon and Travis both had tears in their eyes as Gina replayed how Angel had told her.

"This may be the best news I've ever heard," Shannon said, her voice shaky.

Travis had his arm around her. "I'm so happy for you both! Go have fun, we'll celebrate with you Sunday."

"Wait!" Shannon yelled. "We'll take care of you after surgery, both of you! Now go have fun."

"Thanks! Bye, we love you," Gina said as she ended the call.

"I hadn't even thought about after the surgery," said Angel.

Gina began unzipping Angel's hoodie. "We'll figure all that out, but right now I want to start thanking you for everything you've given me."

27

Gina had never felt so alive. She could hear Angel's heart beating faster and faster as she kissed up and down her body. Angel's muscles visibly quivered where Gina's lips touched. This made Gina smile as her tongue slowly slid down her stomach to just above Angel's curly hairs. She could hear Angel's breath hitch and smell her intoxicating scent.

Loving Angel was more than a feeling or an emotion. It was an underlying current interlaced and woven inside her. Sometimes it hummed or fluttered; other times it made her tremble. At first she didn't know what was happening, but then she realized it was Angel's love. And now she woke up with it and it stayed with her always.

She could feel this love burning inside her and all she wanted to do was release it and let it flow into Angel. When Angel moaned it was like a sweet melody that surrounded them. Gina knew Angel wanted her, all of her.

So she kissed and tasted while she held Angel firmly. Angel was strong and when she writhed under Gina's touch it was powerful, sensual, and full of need. Gina didn't want to tease, but she did want to give Angel more pleasure than she'd ever known. With every moan and groan Gina stroked, kissed, nibbled, caressed, and pushed Angel closer to the precipice.

Gina felt Angel clamp down on her with her arms, legs, heart and her velvety center. With Angel tight around her, Gina gave her all she had and felt her explode into an all encompassing orgasm. It was so full and absolute that Gina felt it deep in her core as well.

Neither of them could speak. Nothing needed to be said. This was raw, pure love made, given, and exchanged. They held and occasionally caressed one another for several minutes.

Angel let out a deep breath. "You know those conditions for the kidney…"

"Mmm," Gina murmured.

"I think I'd give you all my organs if that's what you're going to do," she said, her voice softly playful.

Gina chuckled. "Just imagine what'll happen after I have your kidney."

"How could this possibly get any better?" Angel said incredulously.

"I don't know how, but I know it will," Gina said with certainty.

* * *

The next morning Angel felt Gina's arm tighten around her middle. She was still smiling from last night. Gina had not only given her the most intense orgasm she'd ever felt, but she'd delivered it with such love it brought tears to her eyes. How her heart kept from exploding was a miracle.

"Watch the sunrise with me, my Angel baby," Gina whispered in her ear.

Goosebumps appeared all over her body and a shiver ran through her. Good God she wasn't even awake and this woman could light her body on fire.

"Mmm," she mumbled, rolling over. "How are you awake?" she said, yawning.

"The manager said we get the best sunrise from our balcony." Gina nuzzled her neck and kissed her right below the ear.

Angel was definitely waking up now. Her whole body began to tingle. But when she reached to put her arm around Gina, she was gone.

"Come on. I promise you don't want to miss this," she said, jumping out of bed and putting on her hoodie and leggings. She went to the door to the balcony and opened the drapes.

It was beginning to lighten outside and wouldn't be long until the sun made its way above the horizon, which was the water right outside their balcony door. Angel could see Gina's profile and the expectation was easily visible on her face. This made her hop up and find her hoodie and pants to join her.

Gina gave her a pleased smile and opened the door. They both stepped out and leaned on the rail as the sky brightened. They didn't have to wait long for the first peeks of light to gently wash over the water and start to glisten.

In a matter of minutes the arc of the yellow orb inched above the water. The few clouds in the sky turned purple and orange above the yellow ball as it climbed out of the water. Yellow rays shot out and sparkled over the water.

Angel tore her eyes away to glance at Gina and seeing that sunrise reflected in her eyes was the most beautiful thing she'd ever witnessed. Her face was glowing with wonder and joy. Angel felt fortunate to share this moment with her and see the gratitude on her face. It was truly amazing.

She looked back to the sunrise and laced her fingers with Gina's and held tight. Something inside of her needed to touch Gina and hold her, to experience this together in the hush of the morning stillness.

"This is so beautiful," Gina said softly, still looking out over the water.

"It sure is," Angel echoed. "Thank you for getting me up."

Gina chuckled. "We can go back to bed. It's almost cleared the water."

"You have the best ideas," Angel said, kissing her cheek.

Gina giggled. "This morning feels a little different. I didn't realize what a load this kidney transplant put on me. But today it's lightened and I know it's because of you. You've taken part of it from me. I just hope it doesn't weigh you down, or weigh us down. That's one of my fears."

"I'm glad I could take it from you. Honestly, I feel lighter because now we know you can have the transplant. I'm not afraid, babe. It will be a little pain that won't last, but we will."

Gina tilted her head and stared into Angel's eyes. She smiled. "We've got this."

Angel smiled back. "We've got this." She had never been so sure of anything in her life.

She leaned in and brought her lips to Gina's. "Let me show you how much I love you." Then she pressed her lips to Gina's softly and traced her tongue along her bottom lip.

Gina pulled back, breathless. "Take me to bed."

Angel took one last look at the sunrise, smiled at Gina and led them inside. She had so much to show Gina and it started with that kiss.

* * *

Sometime later they did make it for a late breakfast. It was a glorious day full of sunshine and a gentle breeze. After they ate, they went back to the room so Gina could call her dad.

"He'll be so excited," Gina said, getting her phone.

Angel walked out on the balcony to give her some privacy.

She decided to FaceTime him because she wanted to show him the water. When the call connected she could see his furrowed brow. "Hi Daddy," she said, watching the smile grow on his face.

"How's my girl?"

Gina chuckled at her dad's familiar greeting. "I'm great, Dad. Look where I am." She flipped the view to show her dad the water. "There's

Angel, say hi," she said as Angel waved to him. She walked out onto the balcony for a better look.

"Hi Angel. How are you?"

"Hi Mr. Gray," Angel said, smiling. She had met Gina's dad several times now via phone. He was so nice and always asked about her.

"Papa, you'll never believe what happened," Gina said, her face glowing.

"Well, tell me!"

"I've got a match, Dad! I can have the transplant!" she said with tears in her eyes.

"Oh, sweetheart," he said, his voice thick with emotion.

"Don't cry Daddy, you know I cry when you cry," she said, sniffling. She handed the phone to Angel before the tears streamed down her cheeks.

Angel looked at Gina's dad and smiled. "It's okay." She put her arm around Gina so he could see them both. "I'll take good care of her."

He wiped his eyes. "I know you will. This is such a relief."

"Dad, there's more. You'll never guess who my donor is."

"I know that Shannon and Travis didn't match and I didn't think your other friends that I know did either, so I have no idea."

Gina pointed at Angel. "It's Angel!"

"What!" her dad exclaimed.

"I match! Nothing has made me happier than knowing I can give Gina a kidney."

"Oh Angel. Thank you so much," he said. "Sweetheart, you haven't forgotten your promise, have you?"

"No sir. I will come visit you before I have the surgery. But I haven't been to the doctor yet. It should be soon, so that means I'll be coming to visit before you know it. Maybe even next week."

"Angel, why don't you come with her so I can meet and thank you in person?"

Gina grinned at Angel. "I was going to ask you anyway. Would you like to go to Texas with me and meet my dad?"

She looked from Gina back to her dad. "I'd love to!"

"Great! Now you two go enjoy that pretty beach."

"You know if I'm at the beach I'm going to be eating seafood, so what do you want me to have for you, Dad?"

"Oh, let's see. Oysters! Have oysters for me."

Gina smiled. "Okay. I will. I'll call you when I know more, Dad. I love you!"

"I love you, too. Bye, Angel. Take care of my girl."

"I will," Angel said, grinning.

Gina blew her dad kisses and Angel waved as they disconnected the call.

"Wow, your dad…" Angel said, amazed.

"What?" Gina said, smiling.

"He's such a nice man and he's so nice to me."

"You say that nearly every time we talk to him."

"I know. It just amazes me. I understand why your kindness reached out to me. It's in your DNA."

"Well, let's be honest, that wasn't the only reason I was kind to you."

"Oh yeah?" Angel said, putting her hands on Gina's hips.

"Oh yeah," Gina said, her arms encircling Angel's neck. Then she kissed her so Angel had no doubt where her kindness came from.

* * *

They spent the morning on the beach and then went to the same lighthouse grill for lunch. There were more people in the area than when they'd visited before. They watched a couple of families come in as well as a few older couples. Angel watched Gina cautiously, not wanting a repeat of their earlier visit.

"I'm not going to run away from you," Gina said, catching Angel watching her again.

"What?" Angel tried to sound innocent.

Gina chuckled. "You know exactly what I'm talking about. The last time we were here I ran away from you on the beach. I told you I wouldn't do that again and I meant it."

"I know you did."

"It may be your turn to freak out; after all, you're losing a body part."

Angel shrugged nonchalantly. "I don't need it. You can have it." Then she winked.

Gina's low throaty laugh was Angel's favorite. If she could hear that every day her life would be made.

"Come on, let's see if we can find some trinkets to take to Shannon and Travis. We haven't been to the lighthouse yet," Gina said, wiggling her eyebrows up and down.

Angel gave her a slow, knowing grin. Her cheeks reddened, remembering pushing Gina up against the bathroom door. She exhaled visibly and shook her head. "Let's get something for your dad. I want to take him something," she said, nudging that memory back into her mind.

Gina turned to look at her. The love coming from Gina's eyes for that simple gesture made Angel's heart stop. That's it. All she needed was that look, that laugh, and Angel would be a happy woman.

They walked out of the cafe and Gina grabbed her hand. "I love you," she said softly as they walked to the shops.

"I love you, too." Angel answered, meaning it with all her heart.

They wandered into the shops and found little gifts for their friends and Gina's dad. She didn't forget Suzanne, who had generously lent them the car.

They went to the lighthouse and climbed to the top. They weren't alone up there this time, but were still able to enjoy the view. No quickies in the restroom, but sharing the memory as they walked by made them giggle. One more walk on the beach before they headed home because they had a couple of stops to make and explore.

By the time they got to Gina's apartment they were happily tired and content. Angel couldn't remember when she'd had such a good day.

She had thought of family, not necessarily her own, off and on all day. Gina was part of a family with her mom and dad, but Shannon and Travis and their other friends were family too. And then there was Suzanne and the kids at the youth center; that was another family. Angel realized that she was part of these families too and for a moment it scared her because she'd never been a part of anything like this before.

She had family now and it all started with Gina. The fear melted away because as long as she had Gina, she would be part of this family and accepted with all her weaknesses and flaws. And Gina knew she could lean on Angel with all her fears, doubts and worries and they would slay them together.

Angel couldn't believe she had a family, a real family. She'd tried to tell herself all those years that she didn't need anyone. But now she had Gina and a family and that was what she'd needed all along.

28

Sunday afternoon they went over to Shannon and Travis's and were surprised when Michael and Sarah Beth, along with Brandy and Dustin, dropped by.

"We have to celebrate and plan," Sarah Beth hugged Gina tight. "I'm gonna spoil you while you recover," she added softly, pulling away.

Then she went to Angel and hugged her too. "I'm going to spoil you too!"

"Gosh, it's crazy to think you were right here all along and didn't know you matched," said Dustin.

"I know," said Angel. "Thank goodness I didn't listen to her and got tested anyway."

"I get it," said Brandy. "That's a lot of pressure on a relationship, but I remember the first time we met you, Angel."

"What do you mean?" Gina asked.

"Yep, I remember it, too," said Sarah Beth. "We talked about it on the way home."

"What?" Gina said, impatiently.

"When we got here we didn't know you'd just met the night

before. We thought you'd been dating," said Brandy. "Angel was quiet when she was around us, which was expected."

Sarah Beth continued. "But we could see you in the kitchen. She was helping you get the food ready and there was a way you looked at one another."

"You shared a connection. It was obvious to us, but probably not the two of you because you were in the middle of it," Brandy explained.

"And since Angel was new we didn't harass her or you like we do now." Sarah Beth laughed.

"It's like when we were talking about love that weekend on Long Island. Sometimes it's easier for your friends to see it because you're too busy falling in love."

"Hmm, I knew we had a connection. I could feel it, but I didn't know where it would go," Gina said honestly. "I knew where I wanted it to go, but I had to be careful."

Angel gave her a small smile. "I didn't mean to be difficult, but somehow you got me to say yes when there's no way I would have before."

Gina chuckled and said softly in Angel's ear, "It was just one little yes."

"No fair. What are you whispering?" said Brandy.

"It all began when we decided to liven up our lives because we were boring. So I told Angel she had to practice saying yes, even if it was to something simple like getting coffee."

"So it all started with one little yes," Angel said, smiling affectionately at Gina.

"What was the yes?"

"It kind of started with me coming to Gina's New Year's Day. But really it was when Gina came to my office at the end of the day and convinced me to have dinner with her at a little diner that's halfway between our apartments. That was the little yes after you told me I needed to practice."

"And that one little yes became our favorite place to eat."

"That's so sweet," Sarah Beth said. "But we have planning to do."

"That's right," Shannon said after their little trip down memory lane. "Travis and I will take care of both of you here. We have an extra bedroom and you can stay there."

"What?" Gina said, looking from Shannon to Angel.

"Don't be that way. You're going to need help for a few days after you come home from the hospital. And who better to take care of you both than your best friends."

Neither Gina nor Angel said anything, but stared at one another and then at Shannon.

"You won't want to stay in your own apartments. You know you'll want to be together," said Travis, being realistic.

"I don't know," Gina said, looking at Angel. "It's going to hurt; she may be mad at me for a few days."

Angel scoffed. "As if."

"Okay, that's settled. You're staying here," said Shannon, ending the discussion.

"Next is meals," said Sarah Beth. "We're going to take turns bringing you meals here and when you go home."

"Yep and while Shannon and Travis are at work we're taking turns coming by and helping you get up and around because you know you're going to have to do that to get better."

"Wow, y'all are sounding kind of scary," Gina said hesitantly.

Angel smiled at Gina's Texas drawl making an appearance. "I think it sounds great. It'll be like a slumber party, with lots of slumber."

Gina looked over at Angel and wondered if she'd ever been to a slumber party growing up. Maybe they could find a way to make this fun after they got to feeling better. She made a mental note to talk to Shannon about that.

"Okay. That's a good plan," Sarah Beth announced. "Now let's celebrate. Our friend is giving our friend a kidney and she's going to get well!"

"Yep, you'll be connected for life," Michael said, grinning.

"Don't scare them like that," said Shannon.

"Scare them? It's wonderful when you find the person you share a connection with. I think you should celebrate it and hold onto it," Brandy said passionately. "Yes, lots of people get married and lots get divorced because they didn't connect. It's obvious you two connect and will for life."

Gina and Angel looked at one another as Brandy went on.

"I see it. I'm so lucky I found Dustin because he gets me. Shannon, what you and Travis have is special. I've seen it many times and I'm not that old. If you connect and get one another cherish it, nurture it, and don't let it go."

"Wow," Gina said, her eyes widening.

"It's how I feel. I spent several years with the wrong person and when I met Dustin we clicked immediately. I saw and felt the difference." Brandy paused to take a breath. "I see it in you two," she said, nodding at Shannon and Travis. "And I see it in you," she said, turning to Gina and Angel.

"She's not saying you should get married. Just honor it, celebrate it," Dustin said, putting his arm around his wife and smiling at her.

"Do you celebrate it?" asked Gina.

"We do. First, we celebrate with the kids and then we find time for ourselves. Mainly we don't lose sight of how we're connected; we stay mindful of it," Dustin said, shrugging like it was a natural thing.

"I love this family," Angel blurted out.

They all turned to her and smiled.

"You're part of it now. Don't doubt that," said Travis.

"That's right. Welcome to the fam," said Michael, coming over and bumping fists with her.

Angel sat next to Gina and grinned. Then she turned back to the group and her face fell serious. "You all know that I left my family as soon as I could get out of there, so I don't really know how to be part of one that shares and takes care of one another like you do. But I really want to try."

"Don't worry," Shannon said sweetly. "You've got the best example sitting right next to you."

Angel looked over and Gina winked at her.

"And the easy part is this," Travis said, holding up his arms. "We want you in our family." The others murmured in agreement.

"Thank you. I convinced myself I didn't need anyone or anything, but deep down I knew I was missing out. But not anymore. I needed family and now I've got one," Angel said, looking around the room.

"Speaking of family," Shannon began, "when are you going to see your dad?"

"I've got to call my doctor in the morning and find out what we do next. I think they'll schedule the transplant soon. So I may go next weekend."

"You're going for a visit before surgery?" asked Sarah Beth.

"Yes, he made me promise to visit before the surgery."

Brandy nodded. "I can understand that. He is such a good man."

"Yeah he is," echoed Travis.

"When I told him about the transplant he asked Angel to come to Texas with me," Gina shared. "He wants to meet her and thank her in person."

"I feel like I know him from our video and phone calls, but I'm a little nervous to meet him," Angel admitted.

"Don't be; he's the best. Oh and you'll get to meet my parents and Gina's cousins, too!" Shannon said excitedly.

"You will," Gina looked at Angel, thrilled.

Angel looked back at her, a bit overwhelmed.

"I recognize that look. You'll be fine. They'll love you because Gina loves you," Travis said.

"Yeah they will," said Brandy. "Don't sweat it."

Gina grabbed Angel's hand and squeezed.

"Okay," Angel said, letting out a big breath. "I'm trusting my family."

"I've got to go tell the kids at the youth center this week," said Gina, suddenly remembering. "They will be ecstatic!"

"Did you know they wanted to get tested?" Angel asked the group.

"I'm not surprised," said Shannon. "Those are some amazing kids."

"Have we covered everything?" asked Michael. "I know there's a cake hiding here somewhere and I want a piece."

Travis laughed. "I'll start cutting it."

"Oh, now I get it. You didn't come over to wish us luck. You just wanted cake," Angel said playfully.

"She fits in perfectly," Dustin said.

29

Gina and Angel walked up to the youth center hand in hand.

"I'm so glad I have good news to share with the rainbow warriors this evening," Gina said, squeezing Angel's hand.

"They will be so excited for you."

Gina bumped Angel's shoulder. "They'll be pretty pleased with you, too. Don't forget you're kind of the star of the show here."

Angel laughed. "I've never been the star of anything."

Gina gave her a sly look. "I doubt that, but you're definitely the star here." She opened the door and waited for Angel to go in first. She walked through, grinning.

Gina followed her and walked toward the back. "I'm looking for the rainbow warriors. Has anyone seen them?" she said loudly with a smile growing on her face.

"Really?" Dario deadpanned. He was sitting at a table with Maddie, Isaac, and Camila.

Maddie rolled her eyes and Isaac continued with the puzzle they were putting together.

Camila looked up, amused. "What do you need with the rainbow warriors?"

Gina narrowed her eyes and made eye contact with each one of them, not saying anything.

Dario couldn't stand it and said, "What!"

Gina relaxed her expression and then smiled. "I'd like you to meet someone."

They all saw Angel standing next to her, grinning.

"Duh, we all know Angel," Isaac said sarcastically.

"I'd like you to meet my kidney donor," Gina said, formally gesturing to Angel with her hand.

"No way!" exclaimed Isaac.

"What!" screamed Camila.

"Yes!" squealed Maddie, jumping up and down.

"Of course you are," Dario said, slapping hands with Angel and then fist bumping. "I can remember back when we worried you couldn't pull off an appropriate Valentine's date," he said, clasping his hands and holding them to his heart. He batted his eyes and fanned them miming fake tears. "I'm so proud."

They all laughed and congratulated Gina and Angel.

"Hey Gina, I wanted you to know that Maddie and I got permission from our parents to be tested when we turn eighteen," Camila said.

"So if something happens with this one," Maddie said, nodding toward Angel. "I'm sure one of us can be your backup."

Angel looked at Maddie, wide eyed.

"I'm just kidding. I'm sure your kidney will be fine, Angel," Maddie said, laughing.

"Wow, for a minute there I thought you were trying to get rid of me," said Angel. "You're not trying to get between me and my woman, are you, Maddie?"

"Seriously? You didn't just say that!" Maddie exclaimed.

The others hooted and laughed.

Maddie eyed Gina up and down. "Let me tell you something, Ms. Gina is out of both of our leagues."

"That's right," said Isaac.

"I couldn't agree with you more," agreed Angel, winking at Gina.

"Wow. I'm not sure what to say," said Gina, looking at all of them.

"You own that!" said Dario emphatically. "That's what you say!"

Gina laughed. "See why I love y'all so much!" She brought her hands to cover her mouth. "I can't believe you want to get tested. I'm so proud of you both."

"Did you hear that Texas talk?" Isaac said, grinning at Gina's accent.

"Sometimes it comes out," she said, shrugging.

They all looked at her with wide eyes then everyone laughed at her choice of words.

"When are you having the surgery?" Maddie asked, still laughing.

"Next week," Gina said.

"Come on, let's create some good mojo to wrap around you," said Dario. "You stand in the middle. Angel, you get in here, too."

Gina stood still and the others, including Angel, encircled her.

"Now, everyone put one hand on Gina and the other on the person next to you so we're all connected," explained Dario.

Gina could feel a hand on each shoulder, one on her back, and one on the back of her head. Angel held one of her hands. Dario and Camila were in front of her, Angel to one side, and Isaac and Maddie behind her.

"Okay, let's close our eyes," Dario said in a soothing voice. "Take a couple of deep breaths and let them out." He paused to let everyone breathe and the group visibly calmed.

"Let's draw power from the beyond, from one another, and from whatever we believe is true." He paused again for a moment. "Now, let your power and strength flow into Gina. We're chasing out all the sickness and leaving space for this new kidney to thrive."

Gina loved the idea that these brave kids wanted to do this. But now with Dario's words and feeling their hands on her body, she did feel something going through her. Angel squeezed her hand and then Gina felt an aura of calm begin to swirl around her like some kind of force field. It was the oddest, yet most pleasing sensation.

"Angel, I want you to hold her other hand and get in the center with her."

Angel did as she was told and she and Gina faced one another, holding hands. "Now we'll wrap you both in our rainbow warrior strength," Dario said as the four of them surrounded Gina and Angel with their arms.

It was a massive group hug with Gina and Angel at the center.

"Let's close our eyes one more time. Deep breath in," Dario said, inhaling. "And out," he said, blowing it out as the others followed. "Let's give Gina and Angel the strength we've amassed from being brave when we didn't want to be, speaking up when we were afraid, and courageously living our truth with the help of those that came before us."

The four young people held tight to one another and surrounded Gina and Angel with their power.

Gina could hear Angel's breath catch and she knew she felt it too. It was a force field of spirit, strength, and peace that these four created and wrapped around them.

After a few moments Dario said, "Open your eyes."

They all looked from one to another with smiles and wonder.

"That was incredible," Gina said softly.

"It was awesome," Angel said, as they came out of the circle.

Dario smiled. "We've done circles like that before when one of us is facing something hard and it seems to make it better. I hope it does for you, too."

"I know it will," Gina said, amazed.

"Will you give Suzanne the info for where you're going to have surgery?" asked Isaac.

"Yeah, maybe we can come wave to you. Do you know how long you'll be in the hospital?" asked Camila.

"Angel will be there three or four days. It depends on how my body does as to how long I'll be there."

"I'd say your body is going to accept that kidney just fine. It seems to like Angel." Maddie giggled. "A lot!"

Gina could feel her cheeks turning red and almost laughed when she looked at Angel. She'd only seen her blush a couple of times and she certainly was at this moment.

"Can we please put this puzzle together? I'm the one that's supposed to be supporting you and it's the other way around tonight," Gina said, walking over to the table and sitting down.

With these four brave teenagers, a group of wonderful friends, and her dad all supporting them in their own ways, Gina could feel success right around the corner. She could almost feel Angel's kidney nestled inside her, taking all the sickness away.

* * *

They went to Angel's after they finished at the youth center.

"Those kids are truly amazing," Gina said as she sat down on the couch.

"They really are. I can see why you like working with them so much," Angel said over her shoulder as she walked into the bedroom.

Gina looked up as Angel came walking back into the living room with her heart box. She smiled. "Whatcha got there?"

Angel grinned and sat down next to her. "You know, when we were at the doctor's office yesterday I noticed you were turning a coin over and over with your fingers."

"That wasn't just any coin. It was my Angel coin," Gina said, turning toward her and lovingly cupping her face with her hand. She planted a sweet kiss on her mouth then looked down at the box.

"Have you put a new want in there?" Gina inquired.

"I have," she said, opening the top of the box. There were several small pieces of paper inside.

"We're getting quite a collection," Gina said, leaning over and looking inside. "I have a few favorites, do you?"

Angel giggled. "I do. I wonder if our favs are the same?"

"I know one that is," Gina said, smirking.

Angel raised her eyebrows in question.

"I want to kiss you all over," Gina said seductively.

"That is a favorite," Angel said, leaning over and kissing her lips softly. "I know your favorite."

"Oh you do? What is it?"

"I want to wake up with you," Angel quoted.

Gina smiled and tilted her head. "That's my all time favorite."

"For now," Angel said. "I've added one you don't know about. I put it in right before I was tested." She reached in and gave the folded slip of paper to Gina.

"Okay," Gina said, unfolding the paper. "I want to be your match." Gina looked up with tears in her eyes.

"I thought we could use all the luck and good mojo, as the rainbow warriors call it, we could get. So I put it in there."

"Did you know?" Gina asked seriously.

"Know what?"

"You remember how you've told me more than once that you knew we would find my donor. You were certain about it. Did you have a feeling about this too?"

"No. If I'd had that feeling I would've been tested right after New Year's. Maybe I wished it into being."

"Wished it?"

"I can't think of anything I've ever wanted as much as I wanted to be your match," Angel said intensely, looking into Gina's whiskey brown eyes.

Gina could see the want in Angel's eyes and watched how it changed those greenish brown orbs into dark chocolate shimmering pools of lust and love. Gina knew that Angel was her match in more ways than just a kidney donor. She leaned closer and said, "I have a want that's only for you."

She pushed Angel down on the couch and they fulfilled several of those wants together.

30

Gina led Angel through the airport to their rental car. They got in and luckily traffic wasn't too bad that time of day. There always seemed to be road construction around DFW airport, but Gina navigated them to the interstate and they headed west.

Almost an hour later they were out of the city and driving along the highway dotted with small towns. Miles and miles of fences were on either side of the road where cattle and horses roamed.

"This doesn't look strange to you, does it?" asked Gina.

"No. I can tell those are wheat fields beginning to turn. They will be golden soon."

"That's right. I guess you had that in Arizona."

"Yeah, we had fields, but also desert. it's been a long time since I've been back there."

"I'm sorry. I didn't mean to bring up bad memories. Every time I come home I get swept back to childhood and growing up."

"That's understandable. I bet we did a lot of the same things growing up. What'd you do?"

"Let's see. The lake was the place to go. We have two lakes that are nearby and in the summer that's where we'd be. When we were kids we'd be at the ballpark watching or playing baseball games."

"We didn't have lakes, but we had baseball and there was a big park with a playground where we hung out."

"You'll see how small my town is. We went to church on Sundays and watched the Cowboys play football. The town isn't really gay friendly. They won't bother you as long as you're respectful about it. Needless to say, sneaking around was our super power back then."

"Exactly the same for me." Angel laughed. "Except I guess I wasn't as good at it since I got caught and didn't even know it."

"You needed Shannon. That girl was stealth!" Gina said, laughing.

"I'm not surprised."

"We'll go by my dad's first. There's only one assisted living center. He makes the best of it, but I know he'd rather be back home."

"Do you still have his house?"

"No. We sold it. I say 'we' because he wanted to keep it to entice me to move back home. But he knew that wasn't going to happen. We'll drive by it, so you can see where I grew up."

Angel smiled and looked over at Gina. She held out her hand so she could take it. "I'm really excited to meet your dad and cousins and see where you grew up. It has to be a special place because you lived here."

Gina kissed the back of her hand. "Oh please, that's too sappy for even me."

They both laughed.

When they drove into town Gina said, "Let's go by and get my dad. He'll want to drive around with us. He can tell you all about the history. He was born here, too."

"So you got to grow up with both sets of grandparents?"

"Yep. My dad's folks lived here, but my mom's were about five hours away in east Texas. They call it the piney woods. That is a whole other culture. When we would go visit, all the aunts, uncles, and cousins would come from the surrounding area to see my mom and of course her little girl."

"You must have felt really special."

"I didn't realize until I was in college. I thought they were just family get-togethers, but they were actually because mom came home. Here we are," Gina said, pulling into the parking lot of what looked like an apartment complex.

They came around the car and Gina took Angel's hand, leading them to the entrance.

"Don't be nervous. You already know Dad."

Angel took a deep breath. "I know, but still."

Gina smiled and shook her head.

They walked in and said hello to the desk attendant. Gina signed in and led them to her dad's. She knocked on the door and then opened it. "Knock, knock, is anyone home?"

"There's my girl," Hal Gray said, getting up out of his chair. He was eighty-two, but you couldn't tell by looking at him. His hair was brown sprinkled with gray and he had bright brown eyes, just like Gina's. He was taller than Gina and had a little belly. But his movements were agile and he was obviously thrilled to see Gina.

"Daddy!" Gina said, jumping into his arms for a big hug.

Angel could see the joy in his face and it made her smile. Surprisingly her heart lurched for a moment, knowing she'd never get a welcome like that from her father.

With an arm still around her dad, Gina reached for Angel. She took her hand, "Dad, you already know Angel, but she's even more wonderful in person."

Angel scoffed and looked at Gina. "Now who's being sappy." She turned to Hal and held out her hand, "it's really nice to meet you, sir."

He tilted his head exactly like Gina did sometimes. "I already know you." He held out his other arm and brought Angel in for a hug.

The pain in her heart was replaced with a surprising sense of belonging. She looked into Hal's eyes and could see genuine affection. "I'm going to try and call you Hal since you ask me to every time we talk."

"I appreciate that," Hal said, grinning at her with a twinkle in his eye. She'd seen that same look from Gina.

"I was about to drive Angel around town and go by the old house. I thought you'd like to go with us."

"Let's go."

He grabbed his cap and off they went.

* * *

The weekend had been packed with family and fun. Angel met all of Gina's family that lived nearby and also Shannon's parents. They ran into a couple of Gina's friends from high school that seemed really happy to see her and meet Angel.

They were all at Gina's cousin's house for a family lunch before they had to head back to the airport for their evening flight. Angel was out in the backyard playing catch with Gina's cousin Lana's two kids while Gina and Hal looked on from the patio. Lana was inside with her husband, Bill, getting lunch ready. Her Aunt Jane would be there soon to join them.

"You know your mom used to say, 'Our girl will be fine,'" he said, mimicking her mom's voice. "She said, 'She's got an angel looking out for her,'" he added, watching Angel throw the ball. "The more I've gotten to know Angel, I think she's who your mother was talking about," he said seriously, looking over at Gina.

Gina smiled and sighed. "She told me right before she died that she was sorry about my disease and hoped it would be taken care of before she had to go. She said that she'd heard a saying that tough times make us more able to appreciate the good. But she didn't agree with it," Gina said, chuckling. "She said good is good and we know it. She believed that the strength we built during tough times was useful all through our lives."

She turned to look at her dad and said earnestly, "I've built enough strength to handle this, Daddy." She didn't tell him how much she wished her mom was here, though.

He studied her for a moment. "Thunderation!" he exclaimed as tears pooled in his eyes. "I should be there with you when you have surgery."

Gina got out of her chair and went to him. She kneeled in front of his chair. "It's okay, Dad. Shannon and Travis are going to be on the phone with you the entire time. When they know something they will tell you immediately. I know you want to be there, but I'd rather you wait and come see me in the summer. I'll worry about you the whole time if you come now. This summer I'll be feeling so much better, there's no telling what we'll be able to do."

He smiled down at her, shaking his head. "I know you're going to be fine, but it's hard when you're the dad and your little girl is so far away."

Gina grinned. "I get that, Daddy."

Angel had caught the end of their conversation as she walked up.

"Hal, I'd love for you to go to Montauk with us this summer when you come visit. The views from that lighthouse are incredible," she said.

"Is that where you were when you called me last weekend?"

"Yes. I had oysters, just for you," Gina said, grateful Angel had guided the conversation to something happier.

"A lighthouse? Can you go up in it?" asked Marla.

"Yeah, you can," Gina answered.

"Maybe this year we can go with you, Uncle Hal," said Will.

"That would be fine with me," he said.

"I know what Mom will say," Will said, disheartened.

"We'll see," Marla said, mimicking her mother.

Gina chucked. "I'll talk to her. Maybe I can convince her."

"We could stay with Angel," Marla said excitedly.

Angel looked surprised, but pleased. "It's okay with me."

Bill came back out to check the burgers and hot dogs on the grill. "Who's hungry? These are done," he announced.

"I am!" they all said.

After lunch they loaded the car and got ready to go to the airport. They thanked everyone and took turns exchanging hugs.

On the way to take Hal back to his apartment Angel said, "Your family is awesome, babe. They even hugged me."

Hal turned to look at Angel in the back seat. "Did you stop and think that maybe they like you?" he said with a good-natured look on his face.

Angel looked down shyly.

"Angel, you have a kidney that my daughter needs and I'm grateful to you. But you're a good person and you like to have a good time. If you haven't noticed, that fits in perfectly with our family. So of course they'd want to hug you."

Gina locked eyes with her in the rearview mirror and smiled. "By the way, I kind of like you, too," she said, winking.

"You're going to make me blush," Angel said, chuckling. "But thank you both."

"Pull to the front door and let me out," Hal said. "I want to wave goodbye to you."

When they parked, Angel got out and walked around to hug Hal goodbye.

"I can't thank you enough, Angel," Hal said. "I know you'll take care of one another."

"We will," Angel said, smiling at him. She turned to Gina and could see tears in her eyes. "Why don't you let me drive?"

Gina nodded then went to her dad. They held one another for several moments. When they pulled back, tears were in their eyes.

"It's going to be all right," Hal told his daughter with confidence.

"It is," Gina said softly. "I love you, Daddy."

"I love you, too. Now go get that kidney and shine!"

"I will."

"That's my girl."

Gina got in the car and stuck her arm out the window, waving until they were out of sight.

She sat quietly and looked out the window, wiping tears from her cheeks. Angel simply reached over and held her hand.

Everything was going to be all right.

31

"Are you sure you don't want us to bring dinner over?" Shannon asked Gina while they FaceTimed.

"I'm sure. We got everything done today and now all we want to do is relax," Gina said. "I'm sorry you have to be there so early in the morning," she said apologetically.

"Don't you dare apologize," Shannon said, staring at her fiercely. "GG, this is what we've been dreaming about. It's finally here!"

Gina smiled and her eyes brightened. "I know! Can you believe it!"

"Where's Angel?" Shannon asked.

"Right here," Angel said, plopping down on the couch next to Gina.

"Hey kids," Travis said, coming into view next to Shannon.

"Now listen, Angel," Shannon said, pointing at her. "Don't you keep my girl up all night."

"Leave them alone," Travis said, bumping Shannon's shoulder.

"Yeah," Angel said, playfully. "We can stay up all night. When we get to the hospital they're going to put us to sleep anyway."

"Good point," Shannon said, laughing. "Okay then. You've got everything together and you're ready?"

"I swear I think you're more nervous than I am," said Gina.

"Two people you love aren't going under the knife tomorrow. Damn right I'm nervous!" she said, raising her voice.

Gina softened. "It's going to be fine. I'll be at your place complaining before you know it."

"Me too!" Angel echoed. "And Shannon, I love you, too," she said grinning.

Shannon let out a breath. "Call me if you need anything. We'll see you in the morning at six."

Gina nodded. "Love you both; see you then."

Travis waved. "Love you."

The call ended and Gina sat back on the couch.

"You okay?" Angel said, leaning back next to her.

"Yep. There's something I want to do," she said, getting up and holding out her hand to Angel. Angel took it and Gina led them to the bedroom. She stopped at the foot of the bed and turned to face Angel.

"Everyone thinks you're changing my life by giving me your kidney and that's true," Gina said, gazing at Angel's face. She took in every little nuance before resting her eyes on Angel's. "What they don't know is that you'd already changed my life. I've said this before; you showed me I can love with my whole heart and not be afraid. Believe me, I want this transplant to work, but I know if it doesn't I'll still have a beautiful life with you. You take the fear away, Angel," she said, holding her face in her hands. "It's still scary, but I'm not afraid as long as I have you."

"Oh Gina, I love you so," Angel said, her voice thick with emotion.

Gina found the hem of Angel's shirt and raised it over her head, their eyes locked. Angel did the same to Gina. They took the rest of their clothes off slowly, neither in a hurry.

Gina climbed on the bed and rested on her knees, once again holding out her hand to Angel. She joined her as they faced one another. Gina cupped Angel's face and gently ran her thumb over her bottom lip. Angel's hands rested on Gina's hips as she pulled her closer.

Gina stared at those luscious lips that she knew so well and couldn't wait any longer. She pressed her lips to Angel's and fire shot through her entire body. Her tongue traced where her thumb had just been and then slid into Angel's mouth with tenderness and passion.

She heard and felt Angel gasp and she pulled her closer. Gina could feel Angel's nipples harden as they pressed into her chest and then realized hers were doing the same. The kiss deepened and their tongues swirled around one another in their own sensual dance.

Gina eased a hand between them and slid it down Angel's taut body until she could feel those coarse curly hairs, wet and waiting. She ran a finger through Angel's wetness and she moaned into her mouth. Then she drew her hand up because she needed to taste Angel now.

She slowly licked her finger and could feel the heat from Angel's watching eyes. "This is the best taste in the whole wide world," she said in a breathless whisper.

She saw a flicker of a smile on Angel's lips as she reached down into her wetness once again. But this time Angel's hand followed hers. Angel ran her finger through Gina's folds briefly then pushed inside.

"Ahhh," Gina gasped, letting her eyes close and her head fall back. Angel instantly began devouring her neck.

Gina moaned and pushed two fingers inside Angel. This has to be the best feeling in the world: being inside the woman she loved while she was inside her. Surely this was heaven.

She opened her eyes and lowered her head to catch Angel's gaze. A throaty low groan slipped out as Angel's eyes bore into hers along with her fingers.

"Together," Gina whispered. "Let's do this together."

Angel responded by starting a rhythm that Gina matched. Their gaze never faltered. They were locked on one another in every way.

Gina pushed a little deeper and curled her fingers up, searching for Angel's favorite spot. And then she found the velvety goodness and her fingers were home. Angel did the same and Gina almost lost her breath.

Their groans were a melody to her ears. She could feel, hear, smell, and see the love they were creating. "Oh my Angel baby," she whispered, leaning in to connect their lips.

They both gasped and with one final moan together they exploded into orgasmic bliss. The waves kept coming as they held on to one another.

"That," Gina said, biting down on Angel's shoulder.

"Why are we just now doing that?" Angel asked, panting. Then she giggled and they fell down on the bed together.

"I love you," Gina said, trying to catch her breath.

"I could tell." Angel smiled.

Gina smiled back at her. "Just remember that through all the craziness tomorrow."

"I'll be clutching it tight so I can make it through."

"I wish I could be the first person you see when you wake up, but I'll probably still be out."

"I know. I wish that, too."

"I'll have my angel coin, though. I'm keeping it with me."

"I actually put a couple of wants in the heart box for us when we get better."

Gina assessed the look on Angel's face. "You're not going to tell me, are you?"

"Nope," she said, shaking her head. "But after this, I'm putting a new one in there."

Gina chuckled.

"Oh, I love that low laugh of yours. It does things deep in my soul." Angel moaned pleasantly.

Gina pulled the blanket over them and nuzzled into Angel. "We've got all night."

Angel moaned again and pulled Gina closer.

* * *

"Are you nervous?" Shannon said, rubbing Gina's back.

"Not really. I'm excited. And honestly, I'm ready to get it going," she said, sighing. She clutched Angel's hand and pulled it into her lap.

"I'm a little nervous," Angel admitted.

"You should be," Travis said, sitting next to her. "This is major surgery. I'd be worried about you if you weren't."

Angel squeezed Gina's hand. Gina looked over at her and winked. She could see Angel relax and that made her feel calm.

"I don't know how or why we were thrown into one another's lives, but I'm thankful," Gina said to Angel.

"We need each other. And as my wise girlfriend would say, we've got this," Angel grinned.

"We've got this," Gina agreed and nodded.

Shannon put her arm around Gina and reached across to pat Angel's shoulder. Travis did the same, putting his arm around Angel and patting Gina's shoulder.

"We've got this," they all said softly, looking at one another.

A nurse came and got them and showed them to the pre-op area. The beds were separated by curtains and he put them in adjacent spaces and left the curtain open.

"I know you're in this together, so we'll keep you close as long as we can," the nurse told them.

They started IV lines and took their vitals while the underlying smells of alcohol and cleaning products permeated their noses. There was paperwork to be signed and then the doctor walked in.

"Good morning," Dr. Olaya said, smiling at them both. "This is Dr. King who will be assisting me today. He'll take your kidney out, Angel, and then I'll transplant to you, Gina. I know we've been through this. Do either of you have any questions?"

Gina looked over at Angel and shook her head. Angel shrugged.

"Okay. It won't be long and we'll get started."

"Thanks, to both of you," Gina said.

"It's our pleasure. Really," Dr. King said with a kind smile.

"We'd better call your dad," Shannon said, taking her phone from her pocket. She pulled up Gina's dad and handed the phone to her.

"Hi Dad," Gina said, smiling.

"Hi. How are you?" he said, trying to sound cheery.

"I've got you on speaker," she said. "Everything is fine. They're about to get started. I just wanted to hear your voice and tell you that I love you."

"I love you too, sweetheart. Shannon, you'll keep me informed, right?"

"Yes, sir. Every time I get an update, I'll call."

"Thank you. And Angel?"

"I'm here," Angel said.

"Thank you again for everything. I'll never be able to repay you."

"You already have by bringing me Gina."

Gina looked at Angel and grinned at her sweet reply to her dad. Several nurses came in, ready to wheel them to surgery.

"We've got to go Daddy. I'll talk to you when I wake up. I love you."

"I love you!" he said.

Gina handed the phone to Shannon along with her angel coin she'd been holding all morning.

"Hold up," she said, pulling the sheet aside. She got out of bed and made sure her IV line would reach. Then she placed a kiss on Angel's lips. "I'll see you in a little while. I love you," she whispered.

"I love you too, babe," Angel replied around the lump in her throat. "I do."

Gina's smile lit up the room. "I know." She winked.

"Okay Angel, you're first," the nurse said and they wheeled her away. Gina could see her wave as they rounded the corner.

"She's got to be okay," Gina said with tears in her eyes.

Shannon grabbed her hand and leaned over. "Look at me," she said. When Gina's eyes were on hers she continued. "You and Angel have a lot of living to do. You hear me." Gina nodded and smiled. "That's my girl."

"Okay Gina, it's your turn," the nurse said.

Travis leaned down and kissed her cheek. "Don't worry, I'll be with Angel as soon as they let me."

Gina nodded.

"I love you, GG. See you soon."

"Call my dad."

"I promise," Shannon said as they wheeled her away.

* * *

Gina barely remembered them transferring her into the bed in her room before falling asleep. She tried to wake up because she wanted to see Angel, but the darkness took her down.

She didn't know how much later, but she eventually could hear Shannon's voice. Who was she talking to? And she could smell citrus. Where was that coming from?

"Yes, sir. As soon as she wakes up I'll have her call," Shannon said.

And then she remembered she was in the hospital. *It must be my dad*, Gina thought. She tried to open her eyes, but it was so bright.

"Hey GG," Shannon said softly, taking her hand.

She opened her eyes. "Hey Shan, how's Angel?" she said hoarsely.

"Right across the hall. She's doing fine and so are you. The doctor should be by anytime."

Gina nodded and closed her eyes. Angel was fine.

"They're going to get you up to walk soon."

Gina's eyes flew open. "Walk!" she said.

Shannon chuckled. "Yep. If you can wake up," she teased.

"I'm trying." She opened her eyes and took a deep breath.

A few minutes later Dr. Olaya came in. "Hey, how's my star patient?"

"Sleepy," Gina said.

Dr. Olaya smiled kindly. "Everything went great, Gina. Your levels are already coming down. The kidney is working."

This made Gina smile. "And Angel?" she asked.

"She's doing fine. Everything is just like it should be. I'll come by later this evening to check on you both."

"Thanks Dr. Olaya," Shannon said.

"Is Angel awake?"

"I'm not sure. Let me check." Shannon walked across the hall. When she returned Gina's eyes were closed.

Suddenly Gina woke up; she must have fallen asleep again. Then a nurse walked in. "Are you ready to get up and walk a little?"

Gina took a deep breath and grimaced. *I won't do that again*, she thought. "Can I walk across the hall to check on my girlfriend?"

"You sure can," the nurse said, pulling the sheet back.

Gina saw Shannon get up from the chair she was sitting in.

"Follow my instructions and it won't hurt too bad," the nurse said.

Gina did as she was told and first swung her legs off the bed then grabbed the nurse's hand. She pulled her to a seated position and let her sit there for a moment.

"Wow," Gina said.

"You okay?" asked Shannon.

"Yeah, it hurts a little and I feel so drained."

"It'll get better, especially if you get up and walk."

"Let's go," Gina said, anxious to see Angel even if it did hurt.

She took a few steps and couldn't believe how tired she felt. But she didn't care how much it hurt. She was determined to see Angel.

With the nurse on one side and Shannon on the other pushing her IV pole, she made it into the hall and across into Angel's room.

Travis hopped up from the chair he was sitting in. "Look at you!" he said, smiling.

"Hey Travie," Gina said with a weak smile. "How's my girl?"

"See for yourself."

Gina walked to the bed and saw Angel sleeping. She took her hand and bent over. She whispered in her ear, "Wake up beautiful, I need to see your eyes."

Angel's greenish brown eyes fluttered open. When she saw Gina hovering over her she smiled. "Baby," she said slowly, her voice dripping with affection.

"Why are you in this bed? I walked over here to see you."

Angel shook her head. "I can't do it. It hurts, baby."

Gina smiled compassionately. "I know, but the sooner you get up the better it will be."

"Okay. I'll try. The nurse is supposed to come back later."

"That's my Angel. I don't want to leave, but I've got to go lie back down. Give me a kiss," Gina said leaning over her.

Angel tried to raise up, but grimaced. It was a brief kiss but made them both feel better.

Gina walked back to her room and eased into bed. She called her dad and went back to sleep.

32

Gina couldn't believe how much better she felt already. Yes, she was very sore from the surgery, but she could feel a difference. She looked over at Angel as she reclined on Shannon and Travis's couch. The hospital had released them together and for that she was grateful. Angel was having a harder time recovering than Gina. Her incision was healing, but she had pain and not much energy.

"I can't believe it," Angel said to Gina, pouting.

"Honey, you're doing great," Gina encouraged.

Angel scoffed. "If I'm doing great then why am I not up walking around as much as you are?"

Gina chuckled. "It's like this, babe. I've got a kidney that's doing what it's supposed to be doing. That's given me a shot of life! They took one of yours out, so you have to give it time. I'm sure the love that came along with your kidney had a lot to do with it," she said, rubbing Angel's legs where they rested in her lap.

"I read somewhere that oftentimes it's harder on the donor than the recipient in a kidney transplant," Travis said, bringing them each a drink.

"Besides, you didn't react well to the anesthesia. That takes time to get over too," added Shannon. "Sit back and enjoy being waited on for a change."

"Exactly," Travis said. "There's no way you could've known that. Now that you do, if you ever have surgery again, the anesthesiologist can adjust what they give you so you won't be sick afterwards."

Angel sighed. "Thanks for being so nice to me. I'll stop pouting and whining. I promise."

Gina laughed. "Darlin' you pout all you want. It's kind of cute."

"So what now?" Travis said, beaming a smile at Gina. "It's like you've been waiting most of your life for this. What's next?"

Gina sat back gingerly and smiled. "I thought it would feel like a brand new life and in some ways it does. But my new life started New Year's Eve," she said, looking over at Angel.

"I feel the same way. I can't imagine my sad lonely life now."

"Well," Travis said. "I remember when you first started and you rarely smiled. Now, you're grinning all the time and it looks wonderful on you."

Angel smiled shyly.

"And you," Shannon said, nodding at Gina. "You were afraid to feel anything for anyone else. I'm surprised you still loved Travis and me."

"I know," Gina said apologetically.

"I couldn't get you to see what you were doing. I guess you needed an angel to intervene," she said, laughing.

"I sure did," Gina said, laughing with her.

"You didn't answer my question. What's next?" Travis asked again.

"Well, we're going to Montauk this summer," Gina said, smiling at Angel.

"You two really like that place," Shannon commented.

"We do, but we want to see it in all the seasons. So far we've been in winter and spring, and it changes."

"Can we go with you?" asked Travis. "That sounds fun."

"You sure can," answered Angel. "We may have to go more than once because we want to take Gina's dad when he comes to visit."

"And the cousins want to come with him this time," added Gina.

"Do you mean Lana?" asked Shannon. "That will be a hoot if she comes."

"Yes. Can you imagine turning her loose on New York City?" Gina chuckled.

"Then what?" asked Travis.

"I'll tell you something I want to do and it's in the want box," Angel allowed.

Gina looked over at her with raised eyebrows.

"Not all of them have to do with sex," Angel laughed.

"I know that," Gina quipped, her cheeks becoming red.

Shannon giggled. "We may have to get us one of those boxes, Trav."

"I want to sit at Battery Park and look out at the Statue and the water and eat a knish with the woman that has my kidney, my heart, my..." Angel said, listing each on her fingers as she laughed.

"Your what?" Gina said, slapping her on the leg. "Keep going!"

"My love, my devotion. Do I need to go on?"

"That's good for now." Gina laughed. "Smiles and laughter look good on you."

"They feel good, too. Maybe I just needed to get out of the hospital," Angel said, beginning to sit up. She groaned and eased back down. "Maybe not."

They all laughed.

Several days later Gina and Angel relocated to Angel's apartment.

"It's been ten days and finally I have a little energy," Angel said, walking into the living area with the heart box.

"You know, you took care of me when I was so sick. It's my turn," Gina said.

"You've been taking care of me. I can't tell you had surgery!" exclaimed Angel.

Gina shook her head. "Maybe tomorrow we can go down to the park and soak up some sun."

"That sounds good to me," said Angel.

"Whatcha got there?" Gina asked playfully as Angel slowly sat down next to her with the box.

"A box full of joy."

Gina smiled. "You're right. That box is full of joy."

"I thought you might want to look at the other one I added," Angel said, handing Gina the box.

She took the top off and noticed how some of the slips of paper showed wear from being opened several times. Happy memories floated through her head, remembering unfurling these little notes of joy.

"The two on top are the newest," Angel told her.

She unfolded the first. "This is the one you told me about at Shannon's." She looked over at Angel. "Maybe you'll feel like going to Battery Park in a few days."

"I think so. I really do feel better."

"Good. I'm sorry you had such a hard time doing a kindness for me," Gina said, gently placing her hand on Angel's cheek.

"It's worth every little pain. I'd do it again in a heartbeat," she said, taking Gina's hand and kissing her palm. "Open the other one," she said, indicating the box.

"Okay." She opened the other slip of paper and read aloud. "'I want to be your New Year's Eve date this year. Will you join me, please?'" Gina looked at Angel and furrowed her brow. "New Year's Eve? It's six months away."

Angel nodded, but didn't say anything.

"I would love to join you for New Year's Eve. I can't imagine it topping our first one though, can you?"

"Is that a little yes?"

Gina laughed at the reference. "I never had problems saying yes. That was all you."

"I'd like you to know that in just the few months I've practiced saying yes that now when you ask me to do something, my first thought is yes."

"I have noticed. How long did that take?"

"Hmm," Angel murmured, looking up in thought. "I think after we went to the diner that first time, my first thought was yes from then on." She looked at Gina. "I couldn't let you know that though."

Gina laughed. "The way I remember it is that after that you were the one doing all the asking. I didn't have to."

Angel grinned. "I think you may be right. How about that!" She slowly moved to face Gina without grimacing in pain. "All it takes is one little yes. I can still hear you saying that to me."

"I'm so glad you said yes," Gina said, her eyes full of adoration.

They leaned toward one another and their lips met in a gentle, sweet kiss. Angel ran her hand through Gina's hair and rested it on her neck. She kept her close and deepened the kiss. Gina gently rested her palms on Angel's chest and could feel her heart beating. She fisted her shirt and held on, not wanting to pull on Angel and cause her pain. Then she let her mind go and sank into this kiss they'd both been wanting for days.

It was wet and hot and they both moaned, enjoying the physical intimacy they'd missed while recovering. They pulled away just far enough to see into one another's eyes.

"I missed you," Gina whispered.

"I missed you, too," replied Angel. With a mischievous grin she said, "Let's do that again."

Gina smiled and pressed her lips to Angel's and let their tongues work their magic. She snaked her hand around Angel's shoulder and held her closer. These were the most magnificent lips and she could go on kissing them all night.

When they pulled back to breathe Angel said, "Now I really feel better."

"I know," Gina said, easing back against the couch. "Those kisses are what I needed."

"There's another want in the box," Angel said.

"There is? I thought we'd opened all the others," Gina said, reaching for the box.

Inside she saw a little green slip of paper she recognized from the notepad each of them had in their hospital rooms.

"Did you make this one in the hospital?"

Angel nodded. "The first night after Shannon and Travis had gone home and I walked to your room."

"I remember. I was so proud of you because I could see on your face how much you didn't want to be doing it."

Angel laughed. "I really didn't."

Gina opened the folded piece of paper and read it. She looked up at Angel with surprise all over her face. "You want to live with me?"

"Why are you so surprised? We practically spend every night together now." She grabbed both of Gina's hands in her own. "When I walked out of your hospital room that night it hurt more than having my kidney taken out. I don't want to spend another night away from you. Let's move in together."

Gina tilted her head. "But I thought you liked your space and that's why you stayed at your place a couple of nights a week."

"I thought you'd get tired of me, so that's why I let you have time to yourself," said Angel truthfully. "I didn't want to leave and when you're here I don't want you to leave."

"You said whenever you thought of moving in with someone, that's when you messed it up."

"That's because they weren't you. We're in this together. We're not going to mess this up. If we do then we'll fix it together." Angel's face softened and she added before Gina could speak, "One little yes."

Gina's eyes shone with love. "I want to live with you, too. I couldn't figure out how to ask you without scaring you, so I've waited."

"Then it's a yes?" asked Angel.

"Yes." Gina grinned.

"Yes!" shouted Angel, punching the sky. Then she doubled over in pain.

They both laughed.

33

Angel had been planning this night for months. She wanted it to be special, but more than that she was trying to come up with the words to express just what Gina meant to her and how much she loved her.

After they'd both recovered from the transplant they started looking for an apartment together. First, they thought about moving into Angel's place, but decided to find a place to make their own. They split time at both their apartments just like before, but they were always together.

When they couldn't find exactly what they wanted, an apartment opened up in Shannon and Travis's building. Neither thought they would like it, but when they walked in Angel immediately felt at home. She hadn't felt like that since the first night she'd stayed at Gina's.

When Gina looked at her, Angel knew she felt it too. Shannon and Travis couldn't have been happier to have them living a couple of floors above them.

They'd moved in three months ago and Angel couldn't believe how much fun she'd had decorating it with Gina. She'd never really cared much what her places looked like before, but with

Gina everything mattered, everything was more fun and had meaning.

This was what she wanted to tell her. Gina had made her life matter.

She took a deep breath and slowly let it out. She hoped the words would make sense tonight because for Angel this was the most important night of her life.

* * *

Gina sat with the Rainbow Warriors at a table in the Youth Center. Angel was meeting her here when she finished work. She'd told Gina to come ready for their date because it started from here.

"I like your hair longer like that," Camila said. "You look very pretty. Big date, huh?"

Gina smiled shyly. "It is. Angel asked me six months ago for this New Year's date and I know she's up to something."

Dario grinned. "She'd better be. I can't believe it was almost a year ago that I doubted her on that Valentine's date. She pulled it off and I'm sure she will again."

"She asked you six months ago? Was she afraid you'd be busy?" Maddie laughed.

"No. It was right after we got home from the kidney transplant. We'd both been thinking about how our year had changed up to that point and she wanted to be sure we were together tonight."

"That's sweet," said Isaac.

"Why are we talking about me? We're supposed to be setting goals for each one of you since the New Year starts tomorrow."

"Our goal is to graduate," said Isaac.

"That's a good one. What else?"

"I want to go to college so I'm asking you to help me find more money. I've got some scholarships, but I need more," said Dario.

Gina smiled. "I'd love to help!" she said, clapping her hands.

"I want to get another job, so I can save enough to get away from my homophobic parents," Camila said. "I have a chance at a place with three other friends I know from school. I just have to make enough money."

"Okay. We can help you look for a job."

Angel walked in and they all looked over at her.

Dario whistled. "Damn, Angel! You're looking good!"

The others whooped and commented while Gina looked Angel up and down. *My God this woman was beautiful.* Her heart started beating faster and her mouth was dry. This felt like such an important night. She remembered the same feeling on Valentine's Day and again when they moved into their apartment together.

She thought back to all the moments they'd had together and the memories they'd made. All the trips to Montauk. The special ones included that sunrise from the inn when she knew Angel was her match. And then when her dad and cousins came in July. The look on her dad's face would be forever etched into her memory bank as they sat on that very same bench and watched the sun glisten on the water. Her cousins played in the water with Angel and all she could hear was laughter. What a day!

Gina realized Angel was talking to her and said, "Sorry baby, you look beautiful."

Angel grinned. "That's what I just said. You look beautiful."

The kids giggled.

"Aw, look at you two. All love and smiles. Where are the kisses?" Dario asked.

"Right here," Angel said, walking over to Gina and kissing her softly on the mouth.

"If you guys aren't the cutest!" Maddie squealed.

"Did you set good goals for the year?" Angel asked the group.

"We did," said Camila. "Now what do you have planned for tonight, Angel?"

Angel smiled at Gina. "Not much. Did you know that Gina and I met one year ago tonight on New Year's Eve?" Angel asked, looking at the kids.

"No way!" said Isaac. "How did we not know that?"

"I did. You must have forgotten," said Dario. "I'm not even worried. I know you have this night all lined up. Right?"

Angel nodded once. "Right."

Gina chuckled at the exchange.

"You'd better watch out. My girl Gina knows what's up. She's full of surprises," said Camila.

Gina nodded and winked at Camila.

"Okay, it's time for you to go. We have things to do," said Maddie.

"Okay, okay. Happy New Year, y'all. I'll see you next week," Gina said, reaching for Angel's hand.

"Happy New Year," Angel said. She gave the group a thumb's up without Gina noticing and they all nodded.

Out front Angel had a car waiting. She opened the door for Gina and they slid into the back seat. Angel gave him the address and Gina looked at her curiously.

"I thought you said we weren't going back home," said Gina.

"I love how you call it home now. Did you know before we moved in there I don't remember ever hearing you call your apartment home?"

Gina chuckled. "I didn't. I know you thought it felt like a home, but it didn't to me until you came along." Gina grabbed her hand and held it in her lap.

The driver pulled up to their apartment building and they got out of the car.

"Do you mind if we walk for a bit?" asked Angel

"You know I love walking with you, especially when you hold my hand," Gina said, batting her eyelashes.

Angel grinned, grabbed her hand and swung it as they walked along the sidewalk. "I love you."

"I love you, too," Gina said, bumping shoulders. "Now what do you have planned for us?"

"You'll see. For now let's just walk and remember. What a year."

"Best year ever," said Gina.

"Best year ever. I love that! Let's try to make this next one ever better."

"What do you have in mind?"

"Hmm, should we pick a new place to visit every season?" suggested Angel.

"That's a thought. I do love Montauk, but it would be fun to do that somewhere else. Any ideas?"

"Maybe Maine? I hear it's beautiful. Is that too far?"

"I don't know. We can look when we get home."

"Best part of the year? You go first," Angel said.

"Oh, that's hard. How about Montauk with my dad, cousins, and Shannon and Travis."

"Good choice. That was a wonderful day."

"Your turn," Gina said.

"I'm going with the bench where we drank hot chocolate a year ago," she said, looking over at Gina.

"Really?"

"Oh look, here it is. Let's sit and I'll tell you why," Angel said, imitating a game show host.

Gina's smile couldn't get any bigger. "Would you look at that. We just happen to be here."

Angel wiggled her eyebrows as they sat down.

"No drinks this time. Hot chocolate or wine?"

"Not this time," Angel said.

"So why is this bench the best part of the year?"

"If you'll remember we toasted to not being afraid because at that time we both were."

"I do remember that," Gina said.

"That night, on this bench, you looked inside me and saw something that mattered."

"Oh baby, you do matter," Gina said, earnestly.

"I know that now. But back then, my heart was so mangled and somehow, someway, you got in."

Gina smiled as she put her arm through Angel's and squeezed her tight.

"You got in and that night I felt something. It wasn't bad; it was good. I hadn't felt anything good in so long. I think that's when I started falling in love with you."

"Really?" Gina smiled, looking into her eyes.

"I remember thinking, how can this woman that I've just met make me feel something good? There is something special about her."

"And then you thought, who is this crazy woman talking about black eyed peas and luck?" Gina said, laughing.

"I didn't think that at all. I thought, why does this woman care if I have luck this year?" Angel laughed. "But as the year went on I watched you spread kindness. When you were down and I know you were at times, you were still kind. And most of all, you were kind to me."

"I could see your pain, just as you saw mine," Gina said.

"And what did you do? You scratched and crawled into my heart and smoothed the scars, then you filled it with love and gave me hope."

"You make me sound so wonderful, but I wanted your heart. I wanted it to love me," Gina said, tears stinging her eyes.

Angel tilted her head. "I do love you. You gave me hope that I could have the kind of life other happy people have. I never dreamed that could happen to me. But then I fell in love with you and that gave me a new life with a family."

"I believe we both started a new life right here on this bench one year ago," said Gina.

"I do, too." Angel reached in her pocket and slid down on one knee in front of Gina.

Gina's hand covered her mouth as her eyes grew wide.

Angel held her other hand and looked into her eyes. "One little yes made all the difference in my life. So Gina Gray, now that we have these new lives, will you spend yours with me? Can I have one more yes? Will you marry me?"

Tears pooled in Gina's eyes. She swallowed and said plainly, "Yes. Yes. Yes. You have all my yeses!" Then she grabbed Angel's face and leaned over and kissed her. This kiss was full of joy, happiness, and promise.

Then Gina heard clapping and whooping and cheers. She looked at Angel who was smiling with tears in her eyes too, and then looked to where a crowd had formed.

She saw familiar faces. There was Shannon and Travis, along with Brandy and Dustin, Sarah Beth and Michael. Then she heard and saw the familiar cheers of the Rainbow Warriors, Dario, Camila, Maddie, and Isaac.

"She said yes!" Angel yelled to them and to the heavens.

People around them began to join in the applause and cheers. Angel took Gina in her arms and held her close. Gina embraced her just as tight. Everyone circled around and congratulated them.

"I can't believe you're all here!" Gina exclaimed.

"It's not every day you get to see your best friend proposed to," Shannon said, grinning.

"I thought we were going to your party?" Gina said, confused.

"We are. We're going to be a little late to our own party," said Travis. "But this was worth it," he said and hugged Gina.

"And you guys never said a thing," Gina said, pointing to the warriors.

They laughed and Gina could see the love in their eyes.

"Come on. We've got an engagement to celebrate," Michael said.

They hailed a cab and the six friends jumped in.

"We'll be there in a little while," Angel yelled after them.

"Nicely done, Angel. I couldn't hear what you were saying, but I could see the love in Gina's eyes," said Dario.

"Congrats. Let's go; let them celebrate," Camila said, leading them in the other direction.

Isaac and Maddie waved. "See you next week!"

Angel turned to Gina. "In all the excitement, I didn't give you this." She reached for Gina's ring finger on her left hand and slid the ring on.

Gina looked at it and gasped. "Where did you get this? It's my grandmother's ring."

"I got it from your dad. He said you had to have it when he gave me his blessing to ask you."

"You talked to my dad?"

"I know I'm not the most traditional person, but I wanted him to know that I love you and hoped you'd spend your life with me."

"What did he say?"

"Welcome to the family," Angel said with tears in her eyes.

"Oh baby," Gina said, kissing Angel softly. "Can we go home before we go to the party? There's something I want us to do."

Angel nodded.

They caught a cab and Angel watched Gina admire the ring on the ride back to their apartment. Once inside Gina led them into the kitchen. She lit a couple of candles and took out her phone. Music began to play and Angel tilted her head curiously.

"Could I have this dance?" Gina asked.

Angel walked into her arms.

"We are going to start our own traditions, but this is one we can borrow from my parents. Dancing in the kitchen always made them happy."

"Is that 'Marry Me' by Train?" asked Angel, recognizing the song.

"You weren't the only one that had ideas about tonight," Gina said, swaying in Angel's arms.

Angel gave her a curious look and narrowed her eyes.

"I was ready to ask, but you beat me to it."

Angel threw her head back and laughed. "Camila said you were full of surprises."

Gina lifted her eyebrows and shrugged as a grin spread across her face. She reached for the heart box that was on the table. Deliberately, she took the top off and held it for Angel to look inside. There was only one slip of paper.

Angel looked at the paper then at Gina, who nodded. She unfolded it and read, "'I want you to marry me.'"

Gina tilted her head. "All it takes is one little yes."

FIVE YEARS LATER

Gina looked out over the water from her towel on the beach. Laughter echoed in the background. Four years ago she and Angel had stood right here and promised to spend their lives together. They'd done the sickness part and were still enjoying the good health part of the vow.

Her dad walked her to a beaming Angel that day. She could still see the memory in her mind like it was yesterday. All their family was there. Angel liked to call their friends, as well as Gina's cousins, family. It also included the Rainbow Warriors who were living busy lives of their own. Angel said it was like having favorite relatives that you didn't get to see very often, but they kept in touch via text and FaceTime regularly.

A squeal of laughter made Gina smile and giggle. She didn't think there was a better sound in the world. She waved to the swimmers just when her phone's ringtone began to play.

"Hi Daddy," she said, happy to see his face on the screen.

"How's my girl?" he said as usual.

"Happy. Let me show you why." She flipped the view around so he could see the water.

His laughter joined that of the others. "Aren't they having a good time!"

"They are. I think Angel's having the most fun of all." Gina watched her wife with such love in her heart. Everyday she fell more in love when she didn't see how it could be possible.

"What are they doing?" he asked.

"They're looking for shells. You missed it earlier when they were teaching Angel how to swim," she giggled.

"Let me guess, Willa was telling Angel what to do while Hallie showed her."

"That's pretty close. Mostly they were all three laughing."

"I still can't believe you named them after your mom and me," Hal said.

"Angel insisted. She didn't realize before we were married how much traditions meant to her. So she is always starting a new one for our family while incorporating family from the past."

"But naming your kids after your wife's parents is something."

"She wanted to name our kids after family and she thinks you and mom are the best part of it. Well, outside of me and the kids," Gina explained.

"Is someone else with them?" he asked.

"That's Dario and his boyfriend, Max. You remember him from the youth center, don't you?"

"Yes. I remember him from your wedding. He was the life of the party."

"He still is." Gina laughed.

"I'm looking forward to your visit."

"It won't be long now. Two more weeks and chaos will descend upon you," Gina teased.

"I'll be ready. Jane, Lana, and the kids have been talking about it for weeks. The whole family can't wait to see you."

This made Gina remember all those years ago when her mother's family would gather when she came to visit. Her heart swelled with love, but she sometimes had a moment of sadness when she thought of Angel's family and what they were missing. It didn't matter because Angel had a huge family now that loved her and showed it.

"Go have fun, sweetheart. Kiss those babies for me," Hal said, ready to end the call.

"I will, Daddy. I love you."

"Love you, too."

"Come on, let's show Mommy," Angel said, leading their three-year-old twins toward her.

After they'd been married a year, Gina had noticed how motherhood was tugging at Angel. They didn't think it would ever be a reality for them and then an opportunity dropped in their laps.

Camila's cousin had given birth to twins three years ago and wasn't able to raise them. Gina and Angel were the first people she thought of to adopt and raise them. The idea was frightening and exciting at the same time.

She remembered after Camila told them the situation, they sat on their couch holding hands and talked about the first night they met. They remembered sitting on that bench and toasting with hot chocolate to a new year of being unafraid, to taking chances.

She could see how much Angel wanted this, so she got up and went into the bedroom. A few minutes later she came back with the heart-shaped box. She sat down next to Angel and took the top off the box. Inside was one folded piece of paper.

She unfurled it and it read, 'I want to have babies with you.'

Angel smiled, wrapped her arms around Gina and held her close. This was possibly the best *yes* of their lives. At least so far.

"Look Mommy," Hallie cooed, holding out her hand with four tiny shells in it.

"Ohhhh," Gina exclaimed. "They're beautiful. Look there's one for Momma, one for Sister, one for you, and one for me."

Hallie looked at her with the most expressive clear, greenish brown eyes she'd ever seen. They looked so much like Angel's, even though they didn't share DNA.

Willa toddled up, holding out her hand. "See!" she demanded.

"I do. Aren't they beautiful?" Gina said, looking into dark brown eyes. If Hallie's eyes resembled Angel's, then Willa's looked like Gina's.

"Just like their mommy," Angel said, sitting down on the towel next to her.

"And their momma," Gina said, leaning in for a kiss.

Dario and Max were splashing and playing in the water and then looked over at the girls.

"Come on, babies. Let's swim!" Dario waved them over.

"Not baby," said Willa while Hallie took off running toward Dario.

"I know. You're a big girl. Do you want to swim with Max?" asked Gina patiently.

The smile that lit Willa's face was bright as the sun. She nodded one time and took off after her sister.

Angel and Gina laughed.

"That one is going to keep us on our toes," Gina said, exhaling a deep breath.

"Yeah she is," Angel chuckled. "Have I thanked you lately for wanting me?"

Gina laughed. "Wanting you? That's a new one."

"Our lives together have been based on wants and you started it when you gave me that heart box."

"Hmm, I guess you could look at it that way."

"Do you remember the first want you put in the box?" Angel asked.

"I can remember the first two wants in the box because they went together. The first was mine and it said, 'I want to get naked with you.' And yours said, 'I want to kiss you all over.'"

"Well, Dario and Max asked if they could keep the twins with them in the guest house tonight."

"Are you kidding?" said Gina.

"Nope. Dario thinks I've been neglecting my wonderful wife and should take her on one of my special dates."

"Oh he does?"

"I swear that kid has no faith in me," said Angel.

The rest of the family, as Angel called it, would be here tomorrow.

They had rented a house with five bedrooms and a guest house on Montauk to bring in summer. Shannon and Travis would be there in the morning. Brandy and Dustin along with Sarah Beth and Michael had rented a van for the trip. Liam, Izzy, and Chloe couldn't wait to play with the twins. Camila and her girlfriend Aubrey were spending the day with them. Unfortunately, Isaac and Maddie couldn't join them this time.

"We'd have the house to ourselves. I think we should take them up on their offer, but I have a request," said Gina.

"What's that?"

"Can we skip to the end of the date because you always get that part just right," Gina said, wiggling her eyebrows.

Angel raised her own eyebrows and gently pushed Gina down on the towel. She hovered over her and Gina could see and feel the love in her eyes. They stayed like this for a moment while Gina put her arms around Angel's neck.

"I need you to kiss me," she said softly.

Angel didn't hesitate and pressed their lips together. This was a soft, tender kiss full of love. Their tongues met for a languid taste of what was to come later that night.

"Is everything all right up there?" Dario shouted teasingly.

They pulled back just enough to look in one another's eyes and smile.

Together they softly said, "Yes."

ACKNOWLEDGMENTS

First and foremost I want to thank, my readers, for taking a chance on me and reading my books. None of this would be possible without you. And thanks to those of you that have reviewed my books. Your kind words are appreciated, but reviews enable other readers to discover my books.

If I hadn't found TB Markinson and Clare Lydon's podcast, Lesbians Who Write, I wouldn't have the courage to write. Their suggestions and insight made me think I could do this.

I am so lucky to be part of the most amazing writer's group. They encourage, listen, promote, suggest and make my life better. The DJ's have become dear friends and I look forward to talking to them everyday.

My family and friends have encouraged me every step of the way. They believed I could do this long before I did and I'm especially thankful they continue to listen when I go on and on and on.

If you would like to help others and become a donor contact the National Kidney Foundation at their website or 855-NKF-CARES.

ABOUT THE AUTHOR

Small town Texas girl that grew up believing she could do anything. Her mother loved to read and romance novels were a favorite that she passed on to her daughter. She found lesfic novels and her world changed. She not only fell in love with the genre, but wanted to write her own stories. You can find her books on Amazon and on her website at jameymoodyauthor.com.

You can email her at jameymoodyauthor@gmail.com

A review would be appreciated and helps independent authors.

Printed in Great Britain
by Amazon